# RA-D8

The Halloween Hypothesis

## STEVIE ALEXANDER

Edited by
**ALICIA MILLER ENNIS**

First paperback edition September 2021

Edited by: Alicia Miller Ennis

Cover Art by: Ian Bailon

ISBN: 978-1-7370104-0-1

Published by Princen Press

www.steviealexander.com

 Created with Vellum

# CONTENTS

# 1

## HALLOWEEN 1986

It was an unseasonably warm October in Grayson Ridge, a small town in Central Texas. The leaves had grown tired of waiting on the cooler weather and instead took their cue from the shorter days. They started turning bright red, orange and yellow, falling off the trees and skittering around the pavement. Nearly every house on Loganberry Lane was decorated for Halloween – paper ghosts and witches hung from front doors, jack-o-lanterns littered porches and bowls full of candy were waiting inside to be handed out to little trick or treaters.

Six blocks away at Ambrose Elementary School, the bell rang. A minute later, the cafeteria began to swarm with fifth- and sixth-grade students rushing in to grab their favorite tables. Excitement bubbled in the air while everyone settled at their respective tables to compare notes on their Halloween costumes for the evening.

At a table in the back, left corner of the room, a small group of sixth-grade friends congregated under the watchful gaze of their school mascot, a giant roadrunner painted on the back wall. They immediately got down to business.

"Okay," said Robby Swain as he plopped down his bright blue lunchbox with a flying DeLorean emblazoned on the front. He shoved his brown hair off of his forehead and sat on the bench. "We have the ultimate trifecta. It's Friday, it's Halloween, and we get to have a party at my house after we go around. Since this is probably the last year that we can trick or treat before we're too old, we have to maximize our haul," he declared as he took out his ham sandwich, a baggie filled with Doritos and a Capri Sun.

"My mom told me this morning that she's freaked out by those people saying there are razor blades and needles in the Halloween candy. So I won't be allowed outside of our neighborhood," lamented Marcus Daniels, averting his chocolate-brown eyes to avoid making eye contact with his friends. He was afraid they would cut him out of the night's festivities.

"Yeah, mine too," chimed in Joel Jacobson, not worried at all. He and Robby had trick or treated together since they were in strollers and not even an asteroid could keep them from going together their final year.

"My mom's new boyfriend works at the hospital, and he told her we can get our candy X-rayed after we're done trick or treating," said Robby with a flick of his hand. A wave of relief swept across Marcus's face. "But even if we go a little outside of our neighborhood, that's not a ton of candy. We need to be creative!"

"I heard last year some of the kids over in River Falls traded costumes and went out for a second round. Do you think your mom would let us do that, Robby?" asked Javier Alanis, as he scrounged around his lunchbox looking for a dessert. Giving up, he popped open a Jolt Cola, the one concession his mom made to his sweet tooth when she packed his lunch that morning.

"How did they get away with it? Won't people remember them?" asked Robby.

"What if we use our costumes from last year for the second trip?" Marcus suggested.

"Mine definitely won't fit," said Javier. Highlighting his point, he pulled his T-shirt down where it had ridden up exposing a little of his back. He was the tallest of his friends by a few inches since experiencing a growth spurt over the summer. "Why don't we just swap some parts of each of our costumes to come up with new characters?"

Marcus shook his head and noted, "Sorry, dude, my costume is entirely homemade from stuff my dad had at work, and once I'm in it, that's pretty much it. I could maybe swap out the helmet...I don't know."

The boys chewed in silence for a while as they plotted to make this the best Halloween ever.

"I mean...we've all lived in this neighborhood since we were babies. People will know who we are unless we cover our faces really well," said Joel. "My Luke Skywalker costume has a plastic mask that covers my whole face, and no one will know who is under it. Luke is probably still popular this year, we could take turns going around in that, and it will just be another *Star Wars* character looking for a Snickers. Or we could cut some holes in sheets and go as ghosts."

"I don't want to share a mask," Robby said, immediately dismissing Joel's suggestion. "We need to all go together." He thought for a moment, his blue eyes scrunched up in concentration trying to solve the puzzle. Then he turned to Javier, "What are you coming as?"

"Oh man, you know that's a secret!" Javier's soft brown eyes twinkled, and his dimples became more pronounced when he displayed his mischievous smile. "You're going to die laughing when you see it though."

"Come on dude, we need to plan, you have to tell us!" begged Robby.

"You'll see in a few hours. It'll be worth the wait. Let me just say that you'll never guess what it is, even if I gave you all the time in the world."

Javier was spared further harassment when Robby's younger sister, Nicki, approached the table with two of her friends. Nicki could almost pass as Robby's twin with brown hair that settled just past her shoulders, the same piercing blue eyes and a dusting of barely noticeable freckles across her nose. Although she was a year and a half younger, they were only one grade apart since Robby was one of the older kids in sixth grade and Nicki was on the younger end in fifth.

"Hey guys, are you ready for tonight?" asked Nicki as she

adjusted the armful of brightly colored jelly bracelets she wore, the impressive number of which was only interrupted by not one, not two, but three Swatch watches.

"Almost, we're still working out a few details," confirmed Robby, slightly annoyed at the interruption.

"Okay, well mom told Jazz and Dom's parents to bring them over by 5 o'clock, and we'll order pizza before heading out," said Nicki.

"Marcus and I are walking home with you guys, but Javier wants to make an entrance," Joel said, rolling his eyes and shaking his head, his blonde bangs drifting back and forth across his forehead.

"Please, man, it will all be totally worth it!" defended Javier, who by this point in his highly caffeinated beverage was beating out a raucous drum solo on the cafeteria table with his fingers.

Nicki recognized the beat and sang the lyrics to "Danger Zone" from *Top Gun*. Javier smiled at her and kept tapping as Nicki turned back to Robby. "Cool, I'm so excited Halloween is on a Friday this year! It's totally rad that we can eat candy and watch movies all night afterward," declared Nicki.

"Less rad that I have to share it with my sister and her little friends," teased Robby.

"Whatever, I already asked mom to stop by Blockbuster and get *Goonies* and *Back to the Future* on her way home. You're welcome for having such a cool sis," Nicki said with an extra helping of sass. She flipped her hair dramatically and turned around to sit with her friends at a nearby table.

•

"We're watching *Back to the Future* first!" hollered Robby. Nicki turned around and gave him a little smile. They gave each other a hard time, especially in front of their friends, but the siblings were close.

---

At the girls' table, Nicki, Jasmine Drake and Dominique Ross unpacked their lunchboxes while chatting.

"Have you ever noticed that Robby is starting to get kind of cute," asked Dominique, as she popped a chip in her mouth and smiled devilishly at Nicki, green eyes sparkling.

"Hey Jazz, did you hear something? I could swear I heard someone talking, but my brain refuses to process what they said," Nicki stared down Dominique, who laughed. Jasmine looked over at Robby thoughtfully while she dipped a carrot in ranch dressing. "He's not a troll," she said slowly. Then more quickly, "But don't worry Nicki, I would never go with your brother. Now, Zachary Perkins on the other hand..." she said as she waggled her eyebrows at the other girls.

"Ewww, Zachary Perkins who plays football and acts like he's the coolest guy in the school?" asked Nicki looking around for him. "Gag me with a spoon. He is most definitely not your type."

"I didn't say he was my type. I just think he's cute!"

"Hey, Dom, did you meet the new girl yet? I think she's in your class," asked Nicki, trying to change the subject.

"Yeah, she's quiet, but she seems pretty smart," replied

Dominique. "I feel bad for her starting school in the middle of the year. Is she the one who moved in next door to you?"

"Yep, the movers were there last weekend, but I haven't seen her or anyone else around the house. My mom said it's just her and her mom. I guess her parents got a divorce," shared Nicki with a grimace.

"Oh, that sucks. If we see her, we should offer to let her trick or treat with us," suggested Jasmine, who was always the first to lend a hand to a cause. "She can't miss Friday night trick or treating!"

"Yeah, definitely. The more the merrier. And maybe she could spend the night, too? That way the boys don't outnumber us," Nicki added with a wink. "What's her name?"

"It's Rani."

"Ronny, like my uncle?" Nicki raised her eyebrows.

"No, R-A-N-I. I think her parents are from India, but she seems like she's from around here. At least she sounds *like a southerner*," Dominique exaggerated her drawl. "I'll ask her when we get back to class."

"Great, so...I can't wait for you guys to see my costume!" shrieked Nicki, clapping her hands excitedly.

"Yeah, you said you're making it? Why didn't you just buy the Jem costume they have at Kmart?" enquired Dominique. "It would be so much easier."

"Meh, I don't know. It's just so boring. I don't want a mask with plastic hair when I can have a wild pink wig. And I found those cute Jem earrings at the mall a few months ago, you wouldn't be able to see those behind the mask. So my mom helped me dye a blonde wig and we bought a pink and purple dress at that shop in the mall by the ice skating rink. It's going to be a million times better than the plastic version. What about you guys, do you have everything ready?"

"Oh yeah, so get this," Jasmine jumped in. "You know how I'm going to be a fortune-teller? My mom found this old crystal ball of my grandma's in the attic that I'm going to bring with me."

"So you're just going to carry around a ball with your trick-or-treat bag?" asked Dominique as she gave Nicki a side glance. "Won't that be annoying?"

"But it's so authentic! I don't care. I'll make it work," said Jasmine. She fluffed up her nearly waist-length permed brown hair and then used her hands to help describe her homemade costume. "I also have some of her old scarves and I found the perfect necklace at a thrift shop that looks like little coins on a thin gold chain. My mom is going to do my makeup before I come over."

"Cool. What about you, Dom, did you decide between Princess Leia and a cheerleader?" asked Nicki.

Dominique took several moments to deliver a heavy sigh. "My mom went to the store yesterday and all they had left in my size was Annie. I mean, I love the movie, but why would I want to cover up my hair with that scrappy wig?" she said as she ran her fingers through her long, glossy black hair.

"Annie is sassy like you. I think it's a good fit," laughed Nicki. "And besides, now I'll have someone to sing with me. You can't go out as Annie and not sing!"

"Says who? My singing would make every dog in the neighborhood howl like crazy. I'll leave the singing to you! And next year, I'm buying my costume over the summer."

Nicki serenaded her friends, using a celery stick as a microphone, singing "Cruel Summer" by Bananarama.

---

The boys wrapped up their lunch and made plans to meet on the steps right outside the front door after school. Javier chugged the last of his Jolt Cola, then quickly shoved all of his lunch trash in his box and raced to catch up. He did a sideways skip to try to face the other boys while they walked.

"Okay, so 5 o'clock, I come over, we scarf down pizza super fast so we can get going for round one. We'll head back to your house, figure out something for our costumes and then go for round two," recounted Javier.

"Yep, then we go get our candy X-rayed at the hospital so we don't have to worry about razors or whatever," confirmed Robby, stopping since he was at the door to his classroom.

"*Then,* we eat obnoxious amounts of candy while watching Marty McFly flirt with his mom," added Marcus with a sly grin at Javier.

"Hey, lay off Marty, he didn't flirt with her, she was into him because she didn't know!" defended Javier. And the boys navigated their way to the last few classes of the day, the only thing that stood between them and an epic Halloween night.

## 2

# ALL DRESSED UP

After what seemed like an eternity to both the fidgety students and their exasperated teachers, the last bell of the day finally rang. Robby, Joel and Marcus quickly located each other on the front steps of the school before most students had even finished gathering their lunch boxes, jackets and backpacks.

"We should just go, Javi is going to his house first anyway," insisted Joel as he ran his thumb across the Gremlins button on his backpack.

"Actually, can we stop by my house on our way to Robby's?" asked Marcus. "I want to drop off my school stuff and see if you guys could help me take my costumes and sleeping bag over to Robby's. My parents were going to bring it all later, but I can't wait for them to get home from work."

"Yeah, no problem," Robby agreed. "Oh, there's Javier. Let's go!"

The boys quickly wove their way through the buzz of students still exiting the school and practically jogged back to Loganberry Lane.

"It's still kind of hot, I'm going to get so sweaty in my costume," said Marcus, glaring at the oppressive Texas sun.

"Nah, man, it's always cool at night. Don't *sweat* it," Javier laughed at his own joke, the others did not. He shrugged it off and asked, "So, do we know what we're doing for round two?"

"I was thinking about that in science class," Marcus said as he hitched his backpack further up his scrawny shoulders. "I'm going to borrow my brother's high school football jersey. I'll already have the helmet from the robot costume, I'll just take the foil and the screen off of it."

"No offense, Marcus, but your brother's jersey will come down at least to your knees," Joel said glancing sideways at his friend, treading carefully as Marcus was sensitive about his size compared to his athletically built older sibling.

"Well, that's the part I was thinking about," Marcus said, too busy strategizing to take offense. "If I leave my robot arms and chest part underneath, I'll be bigger, which will make the jersey fit better."

"Hmm, that could work," nodded Joel pondering this approach. "I'm probably just going to keep my Luke costume on. No one will be able to tell. Maybe I'll change pants or shoes or something since those stick out under the costume."

"I'm going to look at our closet full of old costumes and figure something out," said Robby unconcerned.

"Great! So, we've got our costumes, but we haven't mapped out our route," Marcus informed his friends.

"Why do we need to map out our route?" asked Robby, glancing over his shoulder at his friend as he spoke.

"Well, if your mom is taking us to the hospital, we'll have to be back by a certain time. And I don't want to miss out on the good houses. So while I was in art class today, I started a list of all the houses that we really need to get to early. Of course, our friends' houses, but top priority needs to be Old Man Johnson, he gives out the full-size candy bars."

"Oh yeah, we definitely need to go there first," Javier nodded fervently, bouncing his dark curly hair up and down.

"Slow down, man!" admonished Marcus with a quiet chuckle at his friend's exuberance. "Maybe not first, but we'll definitely start by heading in that direction."

"Sounds good," Robby agreed. "I just have one question."

"What's that?" Marcus asked.

"How is it that you spend all of your time planning for tonight, and you still have the best grades in the whole class?"

Marcus smiled and said, "Just naturally gifted, I guess."

"Okay guys," said Javier turning toward his street, which was perpendicular to the street all three other boys lived on, "I will be over at 5 o'clock exactly. Will you ask your mom to order me pepperoni and a Coke? The old Coke, not that nasty New Coke." He shuddered as he said this.

The other boys gave Javier a thumbs up and turned the opposite way toward Loganberry Lane.

"This is going to be the best night ever!" Javier yelled after his friends.

---

Robby, Joel and Marcus were sitting in the middle of the Swain's living room floor surrounded by elements of costumes past when Nicki unlocked their heavy front door and walked in. She was humming out loud to "West End Girls" by Pet Shop Boys, which was playing on her Walkman.

Her steps faltered as she took in the giant disaster. The Swain living room was a relatively open space with a book-shelf and a TV against one wall, a couch on the adjacent wall and a loveseat and fireplace on the third wall. Only a couple of bean bags, a small round side table and a coffee table in between the couch and loveseat interrupted the expanse of shaggy brown carpet. But very little of it was currently visible because Robby, his friends and their mess of costumes, sleeping bags and backpacks were covering nearly every available inch.

Nicki tried to process what she was seeing while automatically reaching down to pet her dog. Completely unfazed by the chaos in the living room, the black-and-white Australian Shepherd nuzzled Nicki's hand.

"Um...what are you guys doing?" she asked slowly, taking her headphones off and wrapping the cord around the Walkman. "You only got home like a minute before me, how did you already make such a mess?"

"We're trying to figure out what our second round of costumes can be," said Joel, not looking up from the Rambo mask he was holding. Turning to Robby he said, "Maybe you can keep your karate uniform on and use this mask to hide your face for round two?"

Not letting them off the hook so easily, Nicki asked, "What round two?"

Finally, Joel looked at her and said, "It's our last year to trick or treat. Next year we'll be in junior high, and no one there goes out. So we want to do a victory lap, but we don't want anyone to think we're just trying to get double the candy, so we need to disguise ourselves."

"But you *are* trying to get double the candy," she clarified as she put her backpack on the coffee table with a soft thunk.

"Hey kiddo, it's about the *experience*," said Robby pompously. "You wouldn't understand."

"Robby, give me a break, you're a year older than me," she said with an exaggerated eye roll.

"Technically, two," he was quick to correct.

"*Technically*, one and a half. But everyone knows fifth-grade girls are more mature than sixth-grade boys, so it evens out. We're practically twins."

"Whatever," he said, dismissing her.

Her eyes roved over the pile. As she started to move toward the kitchen, she noticed her Wonder Woman costume from the previous year. "Oh wow, I forgot about my costume from last year. I should ask Dominique if she wants to borrow Wonder Woman so she doesn't have to go as Annie. It will match her hair better anyway," she said with a soft giggle. "Don't put that one awa-...wait, what am I saying, you never put anything away." And with those parting words, she skip-stepped into the kitchen to grab a snack.

———

A few minutes before 5 o'clock, Sharon Swain swept into her house with a full paper grocery bag, a stack of VHS tapes – each with the blue Blockbuster logo marching down the side – and her work bag, all of which she set on the dining room table. She kicked off her shoes by the coat closet, simultaneously pulled her hair back into a ponytail holder that she had on her wrist and summoned the children to the kitchen with three rapid handclaps.

"Okay kiddies, we have some serious trick or treating to do, so I'm going to need a quick answer to this question: what toppings am I ordering for the pizzas?"

"Pepperoni!"

"Plain cheese!"

"I don't care," the children shouted over one another.

"Okay, so we have eight kids...," Sharon calculated.

"Eight?" asked Nicki. "Me and two friends plus Robby and three nerds is only seven."

"Ah, well in the rush to unload and get the pizza started, I neglected to mention that I ran into the new neighbors as I was getting out of the car and invited the daughter, Rani, to join us."

"Fantastic! The girls and I were talking about that at school today. As long as she's not dressed as Jem...," Nicki's voice trailed off as this new thought occurred to her.

"Honestly, honey, I have no idea, I didn't ask," Sharon said as she grabbed the phone book to look up the number for Big Jack's Pizza Shack. "Back to my point though, I think I'll get four pizzas since there are eight kids, plus me, and then Dale might stop by later."

Just then the doorbell rang, and Nicki bounced out of her seat, raced to the door and opened it to find Jasmine holding a crystal ball in one hand and a plastic orange pumpkin to collect candy in the other.

Jasmine was already fully costumed in a beautiful, flowing turquoise blue dress with gold detail and layered colorful scarves. Nestled amongst the scarves was the necklace she had described at lunch, and it was indeed perfect, as was her smoky eye shadow, deep red lips and the thin gold chain that she had draped around her forehead.

Nicki started to shut the door but halted when she saw Dominique's mom's car roll to a stop in front of their house. Dominique was still in her GUESS jeans and a hot pink top that sat slightly askew off one shoulder. Once they were all inside, the girls congregated in the kitchen where Sharon immediately waved them out since she was on the phone ordering pizza.

"Oh wow, Jazz, let me see your crystal ball!" exclaimed Nicki, leading the girls down the hall to her room.

"Pleeeeeeease be careful. It was my Baba's, and she

brought it all the way from Russia. It was one of the few things she was able to bring when they came to the United States. She actually got it from *her* grandma."

Nicki examined it closely, noting the variations in color in the glass as she held it up and rubbed at a scratch near the bottom. The ball itself was mostly clear with a few bluish wisps barely visible, and it was set onto a blue-and-white polished stone base that Jasmine said was moonstone. "You're right, this is super authentic. Your costume is perfect! Oh, and speaking of costumes, Dom, I have my Wonder Woman costume from last year if you want to try it on?"

Issuing one of her trademark woe-is-me sighs, Dominique said, "I can't, my mom was so excited she found a costume that wasn't just a plastic mask and a smock, I don't want her to find out and have her feelings hurt."

"Awww, look, you're sweet after all," teased Nicki.

"Grody to the max, Nick. Loving my mom doesn't make me sweet, it makes me not a jerk," she said and then stuck out her tongue.

Sharon stepped into the room and announced that pizza would be arriving in twenty minutes. As if on cue, the doorbell rang, causing everyone to look around quizzically since it was impossible for the pizza to have arrived yet. Then Nicki's face dawned with realization and she shouted, "Rani!" and ran to open the door to usher in her new neighbor. Rani seemed alarmed by the number of people and the bouncing dog gathered around the door and took a timid step back, but

Jasmine grabbed her arm and gently pulled her into the center of the hurricane.

"Rani, it's so great you could come along!" she exclaimed. "Do you know anyone besides Dominique? I know you're in the same class. Or should I introduce everyone?"

"Um...I've met Dominique, but that's it."

"Okay, well I'm Jasmine. Nicki, Dominique and I have been friends since kindergarten. This is Nicki, she and her brother Robby live here," she said and pointed at the siblings as she gave their names. "The blonde kid over there is Joel. He and Robby are basically Siamese twins – you will rarely see one without the other." Joel gave a little wave to Rani.

"Marcus over here is our smart guy. If you ever need help with math or science, Marcus is your man," she pointed her open palm at Marcus, who nodded shyly as he blushed through his dark mocha cheeks. "Javier isn't here yet, but he's basically the class clown..." she continued telling Rani all about the gang.

---

Meanwhile, Sharon stepped out onto the front porch to share details with Rani's mom, Dr. Alisha Gabri.

"Don't worry about Rani," Sharon said with a genuine smile to her new neighbor. "She's in great hands. We have pizza coming, and then the kids will go trick or treating. My two, Robby and Nicki, are aware of which houses they're allowed to go to. But even knowing all of the neighbors, many of the parents are worried that someone could have tampered with the candy before it was bought, so we're going to the hospital to have it X-rayed before I let them eat any. Is Rani going to be able to join the kids for the sleepover?"

Dr. Gabri shrugged her shoulders uncertainly and flipped her thick French braid behind her shoulder. "Rani's dad and I recently divorced, so we're kind of new to being on our own. Are you sure it's not too many kids? She can come home after they're done trick or treating," she said nervously fidgeting her fingers together.

"Nonsense!" Sharon gently declared with a smile and a little wave of her hand. "It's tradition to sort the candy afterward and then tell scary stories. You're welcome to come check on her if you'd like, but this is a great chance for her to bond with her classmates if you don't mind..." Sharon trailed off realizing mid-sentence that Rani's mom might not want to be alone so soon after moving to a new house.

But Dr. Gabri considered quickly and conceded that Rani needed to make some friends in her new neighborhood.

"Fabulous! We'll take special care of her and we're right here if you need anything. You've moved into a great neighborhood." Sharon gave her a comforting squeeze on the arm, took Rani's costume bag that Alisha handed her and returned to the melee inside.

Jasmine was just finishing her introduction of the boys when Sharon stepped back in.

"So where is Javier? It's not like him to be late when there's pizza," she asked her son.

"Beats me," he said. "Probably putting some finishing touch on his costume. We'll save him a piece of pepperoni."

"Speak for yourself! He better hurry up," teased Marcus.

"And I saved the best for last," Jasmine was saying to Rani. "This furry little beast is Shmoofy Wooferson Swain." Jasmine rubbed Shmoofy on his ears and kissed him on top of the head.

"Shmoofy?" Rani repeated the name with a smile.

"Yeah," jumped in Nicki. "I named him when I was, like, three. Now we just call him Shmoof or Muff or Muffin."

Rani seemed comforted by the presence of the dog and sat on the floor to rub his belly, inadvertently releasing little tufts of fur that floated around in the late afternoon sun streaming through the windows.

"Nick, can you please get the plates out? Robby, you're in charge of drinks, so go grab some of the plastic cups and fill them with ice," delegated Sharon.

At that moment, the doorbell rang and Joel jumped up to answer. Waiting with four steaming hot pizzas, a bottle of Coke and a bottle of Mountain Dew, was a teenager only a few years older than the boys, in a bright green-and-purple delivery uniform. As Sharon finished paying for their dinner, she saw Javier walking up the sidewalk with his finger to his lips in a shushing gesture. Sharon gave him a small, discreet nod and held the door open for Javier to jump in and surprise his friends.

"So guys, can you guess what I am?" he grinned doing a full 360 to show off his jeans, orangy-red puffy vest and, inexplicably, a set of black wings attached to the back of his vest.

"Um...well it's Marty from *Back to the Future*, but..." trailed off Marcus, his brows knitted together in confusion.

"It's Marty," Javier said gesturing from his shoulders to his feet, "Mc*Fly*!" he finished with a huge grin, turning around and pointing his thumbs at the wings. "Get it?"

There was a pause while everyone took a moment to assess whether this was funny or dumb, and then there was a round of nods and general acceptance.

"Good job, buddy, you'll definitely be the only one," said Sharon. "Alright, these pizzas are hot and ready to eat, so let's head to the kitchen!"

---

In record time, pizza was consumed, drinks were finished, and those who weren't already in their costumes started getting dressed.

"Whoa, Marcus, your robot costume is so bad!" exclaimed Joel, checking out the flexible aluminum duct piping that comprised the arms, the papier-mâché body with red-and-yellow lights built in, the white gloves, silver parachute pants and a football helmet wrapped in aluminum foil with mesh across the face to create a realistic-looking robot head.

"Thanks!" he exclaimed with pride. "My dad and I came up with it together using things he had in his workshop. Pays to be the son of an electrician and the brother of a high school football player! Look, the lights even turn on," he demonstrated by flipping a switch that was hidden under the neckline. "By the way, I like your lightsaber, Mr. Skywalker."

Joel made the appropriate zhoom zhoom sounds as he waved it around.

Just then, Robby appeared from his room dressed in a white karate gi, black belt and signature Daniel Larusso *Karate Kid* headband. He bowed to his friends and came up in a fighting stance, two fists protecting his face and his right foot in front of his left. "Who's ready to go kick some butt and take some candy?" Robby shouted, overhyped from the Mountain Dew and the thought of Halloween shenanigans.

"Aren't we supposed to wait for the girls?" asked Marcus.

Robby flopped his arms down by his sides and looked around, "Where are they?"

"They're in Nicki's room getting ready," chipped in Joel.

"Nicki! Time to go!" shouted Robby.

"Hey kiddo, let's dial it back just a bit, alright?" scolded Sharon with a lift of her eyebrows. "You know the houses that are okay to hit, right? I'm serious about not going outside of those this year."

"Yeah, mom, we got it. Don't worry!"

"Oh, and I need a picture!" Sharon said as she ran to her room to grab the Polaroid from her closet.

Right as she re-entered the living room, the girls walked

out, Nicki dressed as Jem; Jasmine in her fortune teller costume; Dominique with her knee-length red dress and tight curly, red wig (which was indeed somewhat scrappy); and finally Rani in a She-Ra Princess of Power standard costume with a plastic mask, smock and plastic sword to finish off the look.

"Everybody gather by the front door and say 'Halloween' for me!" commanded Sharon.

The kids squished together and gave a loud, "Halloween!" Sharon hit the bright red button just as Shmoofy ran into the picture and jumped on Robby, punching him in the stomach and doubling him over.

"Oh, Muffin! I only have one more picture on this cartridge. One more try guys," begged Sharon. This time she got her picture and dismissed the children.

"Come on, let's go!" ordered Robby.

"See you soon, don't forget that we are *not* eating any of the candy until it's checked out. No cheating!" Sharon reminded the kids. She slipped on a headband with fluffy, black kitty ears: her nod to a costume for handing out candy.

And the children set off for what would be a Halloween that none of them would ever forget.

# 3

# MOSTLY TREATS

"The boys are going this way so we can get to the house with the full-size candy bars before they run out," said Robby turning to the right at the end of their sidewalk.

"Well I hate to cramp your style, Mr. Ninja, but so are the girls," retorted Nicki.

"Suit yourself," said Robby shrugging.

The kids formed a loose group and started marching up and down sidewalks, ringing doorbells and chanting the required "trick or treat" as each door opened, while holding out their bags for the expected goodies.

Most of the kids they passed had the obligatory plastic mask and smock easily found in stores across America, so the homemade costumes within the group drew a lot of interest. Javier giddily explained his costume to anyone who inquired. More than one neighbor asked Marcus about his intricate homemade robot costume, and Jasmine jokingly provided made-up fortunes for a few friends they passed on the streets.

Following Marcus's instructions, the kids wound their way along Loganberry Lane, down Forest Hollow where Javier lived, then cut up a couple of blocks to knock on the doors of Jasmine's approved neighbors. Dominique lived a little too far away, so the crew headed back to the Swain household, their bags bulging with quite an impressive haul.

On the walk back, Jasmine looked up at the sky and took in a deep breath. "What a great night! Oh look!" she pointed to the horizon. "The moon looks really rad. When it's just a little sliver like that, my Baba calls it a 'koshachiy glaz,' which means 'cat eye.'"

"Your grandma sounds fun," said Rani with a little twitch of her lips behind her mask. She had been quite apprehensive about starting a new school, even more so about trick or treating with strangers, but this group of friends made her feel like it wasn't such a bad thing after all.

———

Sharon was sitting on her couch with her feet curled under her reading a mystery novel when Shmoofy's head popped up to stare at the door. His head cocked to one side, one ear flopped down and the other standing straight up. Moments later, Sharon heard the thunder of feet on her front porch. She set down her book on the little round table next to the couch and took off her glasses to place them on top. Before she could get up to hand out candy to the next round of guests, her kids and their friends burst through the door.

"Mom, check it out, people are giving out awesome candy this year!" cheered Robby as he led his friends inside.

"That's great! I assume you still have your second round before we can head to the hospital?" she asked.

"Yeah, we have to get changed first, though."

"Okay, but the system they have set up for trick or treaters closes in a little over an hour, and we need at least ten minutes to load up and drive there, so you guys have to get a move on," Sharon cautioned.

The girls filed back to Nicki's room while the boys worked quickly to get changed.

"Mrs. S, I got so many compliments on my costume," said Javier with a look of delight on his face. "It's a bummer I can't keep it on for our second round."

"What did you bring for the victory lap?" Sharon asked him as she helped Marcus pull his orange-and-blue Willow Creek High School football jersey over his robot costume. She gently yanked down the short sleeves as far as they would go to cover the piping from the robot arms and smoothed the cheetah mascot on each shoulder. Luckily, Marcus was much shorter than his brother and the sleeves came past his elbows even with the robot gear underneath. Sharon scrunched up the flexible piping and tucked it under the sleeves as best she could. Marcus layered his forearms with sweatbands to minimize the effect of bulky biceps suddenly turning into scrawny limbs.

"I'm going to be a ghost. My mom got new sheets over the summer, so I'm using the old ones. The pillowcase is to collect candy, and I cut eyes in the sheet for my costume. It's not as exciting, but it's a classic, and no one will see me," Javier said as he pulled off the McFly puffy vest and wings.

"That works! And Robby, what did you decide?" Sharon asked, finishing up with Marcus and turning to her son.

"I'm just going to use the mask part of my Superman costume from a couple of years ago and leave on my gi. As long as I cover my face, it's no big deal, and the hair looks more like the Karate Kid than mine does anyway. Hey mom, can we take Muffin out with that cow costume you made him last year? It will hide the second round even more because people will be mostly paying attention to him. I have the costume here with all the other stuff I dug out of the closet."

"Sure, honey. Just hurry, I need you back here in half an hour. And that's a real half hour, not a Robby half hour."

"I know, mom," assured Robby in a slightly put-out voice.

"Riiiight," she shook her head. "Marcus…"

"I got it, Mrs. S. Half an hour!" Marcus assured her.

Robby slid a cape with cow spots on it out from under the pile of old costumes, tied it around Shmoofy's neck and smoothed it out so it laid straight along his back. Then he grabbed the leash and attempted to attach it to Shmoofy's collar as the dog wriggled around with excitement, thrilled to be a part of everything. Once the dog was situated, Robby led the boys back outside into the night wearing his Karate Kid costume and a Superman mask. Joel fell in line behind him with darker pants and the same Luke Skywalker costume he had worn on the previous trip. Javier tripped along behind them until he got his ghost sheet situated over his plain shirt and jeans. Marcus brought up the rear as a football player for the Willow Creek High School cheetahs, strutting around looking much more buff than usual thanks to the robot costume that still hid underneath.

An inky black night had fully settled over the neighborhood while they were getting changed, so they started their trek with just a waning crescent moon and a few street lamps to guide them to each lit porch.

Robby was right: as they made their second lap around the neighborhood, Shmoofy was the star of the show. Everyone wanted to pet him as they proclaimed him the cutest cow in town. No one looked at the boys closely enough to realize they had already seen them less than an hour before.

"I'm still saying I'd rather fly than be invisible," Javier told his friends as they walked away from the house with the full-size candy bars for the second time. "I could go anywhere I wanted, I wouldn't have to wait for a driver's license, and besides, how fun would it be to zoom around and do tricks?"

"But if you're invisible, you could be a famous international spy," pointed out Joel. "And for now, it would be cool to hear what girls have to say about us."

"Yeah, but if you fly, you could run around and be a

superhero saving people from burning buildings and stuff," argued Javier.

Marcus shook his head, "No one said you also get superpowers or enhanced strength."

Joel wondered aloud, "So if you're invisible, are your clothes invisible? Or do you have to run around naked if you want to spy on someone?"

Marcus answered, "Your clothes are invisible, but nothing you pick up or carry is. So you can't just walk out of a bank with a lot of money."

"What if I WEAR the money?" challenged Javier.

"That's why I hate this conversation. It's always so ridiculous," said Marcus rolling his eyes and turning back toward Robby's house. He glanced at his watch and then picked up his pace. "Come on, we're late!"

---

Forty-three minutes after they started their second round, Robby and the boys lugged their candy collection back into the Swain house where Sharon and the girls were ready to head to the hospital. Marcus whispered a quiet "sorry" to Sharon as he rushed in the front door. After each of the kids had dumped their respective baskets of candy into Javier's large pillowcase, they all piled into Sharon's minivan, a few of the girls squished in the back behind the last row of seating to get everyone in.

At 8:57 p.m., Sharon navigated the mini-van into a parking

space at the hospital and everyone jumped out as she hurried them along, reminding the kids that the X-ray tech was leaving in three minutes.

The automatic doors slid open, and Sharon hustled to the front desk to speak to a short, plump woman with thick, black glasses and a name tag that said "Donna." Her face was hard to read. She had pleasant features, sparkling brown eyes and bowed lips that curved up so she always looked like she was about to smile, but the hard lines around her eyes indicated that she didn't suffer any foolishness when it came to her job. As the group noisily approached her, she looked away from her computer and moved her glasses to nestle them in the auburn bun piled on her head. Nicki admired the collection of rings she had on several fingers across both hands.

"We're here to have candy X-rayed, can you please point me in the right direction?" Sharon asked the hospital employee, slightly out of breath. "My name is Sharon Swain, I'm a friend of Dale Watts." She hoped mentioning the name of one of the woman's co-workers would buy her a little grace.

"Yes, let me check to see if they're still running, one moment," and she spun her chair around then walked through a door out of sight.

Five minutes ticked slowly by as the girls griped at the boys for taking so long on their precious round two. Finally, the woman popped her head back through the door and said, "Follow me."

As they walked down the hallway, she told Sharon, "It's lucky you're a friend of Dale's. Chad is the lab tech, and he had already turned off the machine since no one had been by for a few minutes and it's practically 9 o'clock. He's getting it restarted now."

She held open the door to a room with a long, flat table. The kids filed in with Nicki giving Robby an I-told-you-so glare as she squeezed past him. Over the table hovered a monstrosity of equipment: wires covered in tubing, handles to maneuver it to the correct position and metal casing around what appeared to be some very outdated machinery. "People Are People" by Depeche Mode crackled out of a clock radio perched on the desk next to the X-ray machine.

A tall, scrawny young man with feathered, sandy brown hair was wearing a white lab coat and leaning backward across the table looking underneath the machine above his head. He stood back up, smacked it with a wrench and uttered a little curse under his breath.

"Um...excuse me?" said Sharon uncertainly.

"Oh!" exclaimed Chad whipping around to see a roomful of children in costumes. The machine startled everyone as it chose that moment to make a loud thud noise and whirr to life. "Sorry, I'm just getting this hunk of junk fired back up. Here, you can place your candy right there."

Javier shuffled forward and put the pillowcase full of candy on the table. He hovered near the machine trying to read the labels on it.

Chad, who was clearly miffed to still be working, stepped around him, quickly shifted the bag around a little, positioned the machine right over it and hit a few buttons.

Mumbling under his breath for a couple of minutes, he typed on a beige computer that occupied one corner of his desk, and then turned back around when he caught a hint of a smoky smell. As he approached the machine to determine where the smell was coming from, it started to emit green sparks from the plate under the candy. Everyone jumped back out of range of the sparks, then the machine powered itself down.

Chad, beyond irritated by that point, stuck his jaw out and his nostrils flared. He smacked the machine on the side again with the wrench he had left laying nearby when Sharon and her entourage had arrived. The lights in the room flickered, but then the machine came back on. Everyone stood staring at it, holding their breaths a little, but it appeared that it was going to behave. Chad hit the sequence of buttons that made it start again, this time staring at it as though he could make it work by sheer force of will. Then he turned to pick up the X-ray sheet where he saw an image of the bag contents. While the candy all seemed fine, there was a strange blank orb in the middle, so he walked back to the bag, opened it up and took out a crystal ball.

"Is this one of yours?" he asked, holding it out carelessly.

"Oh! That's mine," said Jasmine as she rushed forward to take it with both hands. "I had it in my trick-or-treat bucket and must have dumped it into the pillowcase without thinking about it," she stammered, ashamed that she had forgotten about her prized crystal ball. She examined it closely, but there didn't seem to be any damage to the ball or the moonstone base.

This time, Chad took the time to shuffle the candy around more so that it was flat. Since it was late and he was hungry, he palmed a couple of the smaller candy bars and slid them in the pocket of his lab coat before he took a second X-ray.

"What are these markings?" Javier asked, still staring intently at the machine.

Chad looked over to see what Javier was referring to and said, "Who knows, it's all in Russian."

"How does it work?" Javier inquired.

"How does Russian work?" Chad asked, barely paying attention around his other project on the computer.

"How does the machine see into the bag and the candy?"

"It's just a beam that passes through whatever is on the table. Some things absorb and others reflect, so we get an image," he said, still not looking at the children. He didn't mention that he should have taken the candy out of the bag for better results. He just wanted to get on with his evening.

"So is the white part the stuff that absorbs or reflects?"

"Look kid, I'm trying to wrap this up so I can get to a Halloween party, can you give me just a second to get your reading so we can all get out of here?" Chad said over his shoulder as he grabbed the second X-ray.

After placing it on the lightbox and glancing at it again for a few moments, he said, "All's clear, you can take back your candy now."

Javier grabbed the bag, Sharon thanked Chad and then

ushered her crew out the door with a flurry of "thank yous" and Chad flipped the machine back off. It made a weird grinding noise.

"You useless piece of junk," he said glaring at it while he unwrapped one of the pilfered candy bars and popped it in his mouth. Savoring the creamy caramel and crunching on the peanuts as he gathered his wallet, keys and a beaker that would complete his costume, he shut down the computer and turned off the radio, then flipped the light switch and exited the room.

# 4

## TAKING STOCK

The Swain household went from dark and quiet – the only movement was Shmoofy wandering over to his bowl to sniff around for any food he might have missed and taking a couple of lazy licks from his water dish – to barely controlled chaos in a matter of seconds as Sharon and the children streamed back in. Javier unceremoniously dumped the candy right in the middle of the living room floor and, with the pillowcase still in his hands and held triumphantly over his head, announced that the sorting was ready to begin.

All of the kids sat down, barely taking time to move their costumes. Joel, Robby and Rani shifted their masks on top of their heads. Javier pulled his ghost sheet off of his face and draped it around his neck. Marcus finally gave up trying to keep his robot arms tucked under the football jersey and let them flop down to his wrists. He set his football helmet on the floor and stood up.

"We need a system!" insisted Marcus. But it was too late, both the boys and the girls were already starting piles.

"We need to separate by candy type – chocolate, fruity sweet and fruity sour," said Nicki already grabbing all of the chocolate that she could find.

"No, that's barely sorting, we should sort by name: Snickers, Milky Way, like that," clarified Joel.

"Guys, leave it to the master," said Marcus, standing in the middle of the room with his arms out to stop the haphazard activity. "I already planned this. We can start with what Nicki said and sort into three groups: chocolate, sweet, sour. But then we need sub-groups. Kind of like in science how we have Kingdom, Phylum, Class, Ord..er..," he trailed off as the other kids looked at him incredulously. "Okay, well still, it's the best way. So once we have our three main categories, we'll break them down into more specifics depending on what we have. Cool?"

"I'm not sure 'cool' is the word you were looking for," quipped Dominique with a smirk she shared with Nicki. "But it works."

For the next several minutes, near silence was restored as everyone studiously passed candy back and forth for the appropriate piles. As soon as the last piece was dropped into its pile, Robby threw his hands in the air and yelled, "Now we eat it all!"

Sharon was quick to step in, "Kiddos, it is after 10 o'clock, I don't think it's a great idea to eat it *all*. How about you start with one from each pile per kid and see how you feel. I don't need rainbow barf clogging my toilets."

The boys cackled at the idea of rainbow barf but reluctantly agreed to her plan.

Everyone dived in and started pulling off Snickers wrappers, dumping piles of Skittles into their hands and peeling off the box tops of grape and strawberry Nerds. Javier slipped a nibble of his Chick-O-Stick to the dog and pet his head affectionately. Once everyone had consumed at least a piece or two of candy, Nicki turned down the lights and declared it Scary Story Time.

"Has everyone heard the story about the killer with the hook for a hand?" she asked in a spooky voice.

"Oh yeah, and his hook gets caught in the handle of the car door where the teenagers are making out in the backseat?" said Javier, unaware of the murderous look Nicki gave him for spoiling the ending because he was busy unwrapping his third Baby Ruth.

"Javi! You can't just give away the ending. Maybe not everyone had heard it!" she flopped her hands in her lap as she admonished him.

"Oops, sorry," he said around a mouthful of nougat, although he was obviously way more interested in violating the sugar restrictions his mom had imposed on him than issuing a real apology.

"Fine," Nicki sighed. "What about the woman alone in her apartment with her dog? JAVI, DO NOT SAY A WORD," she whipped her head back in his direction and gave him a hard stare.

"What?" he said defensively, finally looking up at her, "I don't know that one!"

"Great! Okay, so..." and she went about telling the story of a man who would sneak into the apartments of single women and attack them in their showers. Her heroine lived alone but had a dog who would sleep beside her bed and lick her hand when she had bad dreams. That night, she was too tired to take a shower and went straight to bed. When she got to the reveal where the intruder had written in red lipstick on the bathroom mirror "Humans can lick too," everyone, including the boys, screamed and laughed at each other. Javier howled and rolled on the floor amidst the candy wrappers and boxes.

Shmoofy, who had been poking around at the empty wrappers, stuck his head under the coffee table and came out with something in his mouth.

"Whatcha got there Shmoof?" asked Dominique. "Oh! It's the Lasso of Truth from that Wonder Woman costume," she said and extracted it from Shmoofy's mouth. She wrapped it up in a circle and placed it in her lap. "You probably shouldn't play with that." Dominique grabbed another piece of candy and ate it while Shmoofy tried to play tug-of-war with the lasso. "Seriously!" said Dominique laughing. "That's not a toy!" She wound it up again and put it under her criss-crossed legs.

Just then, the doorbell rang and Shmoofy took off to guard his family from whatever evil might lurk behind the door. Nicki opened it to find her mom's boyfriend Dale and his son, Kevin, who was still dressed in the uniform from his job at a local fast-food restaurant. Typically his uniform consisted of a red bandana to cover his hair, black pants and a long-sleeve white shirt with a black vest, which was supposedly reminiscent of a pirate. But in honor of Halloween, Black Beard's Fish Tavern added an eye patch and a paper three-point hat. Kevin had ditched the hat in the car but strutted into the Swain home still sporting the eye patch and bandana covering his dark brown hair.

"Mom's in the kitchen," Nicki told Dale, who waved at the kids as he made a beeline to see Sharon.

Kevin stayed in the room with the kids and pointed at Marcus's football jersey. "Hey, that looks familiar. Where did you get it?"

Marcus looked down at his brother's jersey and said, "It's my brother's. He's on the varsity team at the high school."

"Yeah, so am I, who is your brother?" Kevin followed up while surveying the piles of candy.

"Adrian Daniels," Marcus replied.

"Oh wow! He's really good. We've played together all four years in high school. Small world." Marcus just shrugged as he inspected a box of Nerds and a bag of Skittles, plotting his next conquest. He didn't know anything about high school football and wasn't looking to get into a big conversation about it.

Kevin picked up on his indifference and instead

commented on the piles of sorted candy. "So looks like you had a pretty solid haul tonight."

"Yep!" agreed Javier. "We already ate all the full-size candy bars. It was even more impressive before."

"Ah, well then you won't miss it if I skim off a little Halloween tax," said Kevin, bending down to swipe a few chocolate bars and a bag of Skittles. "That's what kids have to pay their elders who spent the night working." He unwrapped a Snickers and took a bite. The kids just shrugged, they were already in a sugar coma. Not getting any pushback, Kevin wandered into the kitchen with his dad and Sharon while the kids returned to their scary stories.

After a few more anecdotes, Sharon entered the room. "Kids, it's after midnight and officially November 1st. I need you to clean up this room, then clean up yourselves and get to bed."

"But we still have to watch a movie!" protested Robby.

"Sorry guys, maybe tomorrow morning over breakfast," she said firmly.

Robby started to run out of the room, and Sharon stopped him with a straight arm blocking his way. "I believe I said 'clean up *this* room.' I've already picked up your costume mess and your pizza mess. This one is on you, buddy."

With more grumbling than was truly necessary, the kids started cleaning the living room while Sharon walked Dale and Kevin out. When the front area was reasonably tidied, the kids split up, boys to Robby's bedroom and bathroom, and the girls to Nicki's.

Sharon led Shmoofy to the back door and bent down to remove the cow cape. "Why are you still wearing this, Muffin? I guess it's been a chaotic night." She let Shmoofy out for a final trip to the yard. Once he was back in, she took a last look around, checking that doors were locked, and then headed to her room to get some sleep so she could get up early and pick up donuts for breakfast.

Back in Nicki's room, Rani was slowly walking around, taking in everything. The decorations were an odd mismatch of little girl and wannabe teenager. The top third of the bed in the far corner was covered with a variety of pillows and stuffed animals. She picked up a Teddy Ruxpin doll and examined it before placing it back on the duvet. Across from the bed sat a desk that held a collection of half-used fingernail polish bottles, a tangle of bracelets and hair ties, a ballerina music box, a stack of celebrity magazines and a mirror that was lined with pictures cut out from past issues of the same periodicals. Next to the door was a shelf that held an eclectic mix of Dr. Seuss and Sweet Valley High as well as the new Babysitters Club book. The two walls at the head and side of the bed were practically wallpapered with posters of Poison, Billy Idol, Bon Jovi and other popular bands.

"So you really like rock music, huh?" Rani asked Nicki.

"I really love a lot of music! I listen to some of the stuff that my mom listens to like Jimi Hendrix and Led Zeppelin.

When I study, I listen to musical soundtracks. Right now I'm just really into glam rock," she explained as she sang the chorus from "You Give Love a Bad Name," and pointed to Jon Bon Jovi on her wall as she belted it out with gusto.

"Oh yeah, Nicki basically knows every lyric to every rock song out. You will hear her sing *a lot* if you keep hanging out with her," said Dominique who was already in her PJs, lying on her stomach on the floor with her feet in the air while she flipped through one of Nicki's *Teen Beat* magazines.

"So, Rani...what do you think of Ambrose Elementary so far, is it like your old school?" asked Jasmine as she brushed her long hair and looked at Rani through the mirror above Nicki's desk.

"I mean, I've only been there for a few days, but it seems fine," she shrugged. "Most of the classes are about as easy as the ones at my old school. I was kind of hoping they'd have a more advanced science program."

"You like science?" asked Dominique, looking up at her from the floor. "Marcus is the only person I know who actually *likes* science."

"Yeah, my mom is a doctor and my dad is an engineer, so they've always told me how things work, and I just find it interesting. But at both of my schools, it seems like they only teach stuff that my mom or dad told me about years ago."

"And, your parents aren't together?" asked Nicki quietly.

"No." Rani paused, not sure how much to share with her new friends. "They had been fighting a lot for a long time, so I wasn't really surprised. We actually lived in the next town over, only about fifteen minutes away. My dad wanted to move to California because there are more jobs for him out there. But my mom already has a practice that's going pretty well here in Grayson Ridge. That seems to be what started it, but they just fight about everything now. As much as I hate being the kid of divorced parents, it's actually kind of a relief, you know?"

"I don't really know, I'm sorry," said Nicki. "My parents were so in love for as long as I can remember. Like in a gross way for a kid, always holding hands or kissing in the kitchen while they made dinner together. My dad passed away when I was seven, he had cancer. My mom is kind of dating that guy Dale now, but it's still new, so they don't really fight."

"Oh wow, Nicki, I'm so sorry, I didn't know. When I didn't meet your dad, I thought maybe your parents were divorced too," Rani rushed to apologize.

"It's okay. I mean...it's not. I hate it, but you couldn't know, so please don't apologize."

"Well ladies, I hate to be the first to drop out, but I'm desperately tired," yawned Dominique as she unzipped her sleeping bag enough to get in and then pulled the zipper back up to her chin. "Do not, I repeat DO NOT, stick my hand in warm water when I fall asleep."

"Haha! No promises!" said Nicki as she grabbed a few pillows from the closet for her friends. Once all three were tucked into their sleeping bags, Nicki turned off the light and crawled into her bed, wishing everyone sweet dreams.

# 5

# HERE'S THE TRICK

Saturday morning felt like it arrived very early. Sharon sneaked out of the house and came home with two boxes full of assorted donuts. She set the waxy, white boxes on the table next to a stack of napkins and left the kids a note directing them to the milk and orange juice in the fridge. Then she returned to her room to get some more rest.

A little after 9 that morning, several of the children were awakened by what sounded distinctly like a cow mooing. Robby rubbed his eyes and sat up a little, straining his ears when he heard it again. It could not have sounded more like a cow was mooing outside his door.

He got up and stepped around Javier's empty sleeping bag to open the bedroom door and found Shmoofy wagging his tail just outside of it.

"Hey Muffin, did you hear that noise too?" Robby asked, still in a sleepy haze. "Is Javier out here goofing around?"

Shmoofy looked right at him with his light brown eyes, opened his mouth and mooed. Robby's eyes popped opened wide, and that's when he noticed that some of the spots on Shmoofy's back looked noticeably different than he remembered. More black than gray and more like a couple of large spots than the smattering of dots that typically decorated his fur.

Robby ran back into his room to wake up his friends and tripped over what looked like an empty sleeping bag, but felt very much like an occupied one. He caught himself on his mattress and looked around to find Javier sitting up from his sleeping bag.

"What's going on?" asked Joel, still laying on his stomach with his eyes closed and his face smooshed into his pillow.

"Um...I honestly don't know," said Robby, completely perplexed. "I am awake, right?"

"What do you mean, of course you're awake," said Marcus. But then he looked down at his arms, which still had the texture and movement of skin, but his normally chocolate complexion was a shimmering silver. "I think...?"

Javier was staring at Robby. "Dude, what's going on with your hair?"

"My hair?" asked Robby, crossing the hall to his bathroom and staring at his black hair with a perfect curl smack in the center of his forehead.

He walked back to his room and pinched his own arm. "Okay, well I felt that, but I must still be asleep. In the past minute I've seen Muffin moo, Javier disappear and reappear and whatever this is," he said pointing at his own head.

"Agh!" Marcus yelled rubbing furiously at his arms.

"Marcus! What is wrong with your arms? What is happening?" said Robby spinning around in confusion.

At that moment, Nicki walked into Robby's room to find out what all the noise was about.

"Hey, my friends are sleeping, can you keep it down?" she loudly whispered, but then took in the sights of Robby's room and was left speechless. "What did you guys do last night?"

"Are you girls all normal?" Marcus asked, trying to figure out if this was just a boy issue.

"I think so," said Nicki, but she was clearly uncertain. "I'll go check."

She came back a moment later and said, "The girls are still asleep, and Jazz looks normal. But I could swear Dom took off her wig last night and her hair is still red and curly. And Rani has long, blonde hair, *actual* hair, not the mask. And it looks like she has on bright red lipstick. What is happening? We need to go get mom."

"No, wait! Let's wake up the other girls first. We need to know more about what we're dealing with before we bother Mrs. S," countered Marcus.

"Okay," said Nicki uncomfortably. "You guys wait here, I don't want them to freak out when they wake up to a gaggle of boys in my room."

Nicki ran back down the hall, but then slowed when she got to the door. She peeked in to make sure everyone was still asleep, but Jasmine was sitting up and rubbing Shmoofy's ears. She smiled at Nicki when Shmoofy opened his mouth and mooed at Jasmine. Both girls looked at each other, wide-eyed with alarm. Then Jasmine let out a small squeal and pointed at Nicki.

"What?" shrieked Nicki as she looked down at herself, not seeing anything different until some pink hair fell from behind her shoulders and into her view.

The noise woke the other two, and soon all four girls were clamoring for a spot in front of the mirror to see what had happened to them overnight after taking in the effects of Nicki, Dominique and Rani's hair.

The sound of their freaked-out voices brought the boys down the hall and into the doorway of Nicki's room.

"Well, I think we can safely say this is not just a boy thing," said Marcus holding his arms out for the girls to see.

The noise had finally reached a level that crossed to Sharon's side of the house. She came shuffling through the living room to the hallway leading to the kids' bedrooms and asked if everyone was ready for donuts. When she saw Robby's hair, she stopped and her jaw dropped as Marcus turned around to show her his arms. "What on earth did you kids do after you were supposed to go to bed last night?"

"Mom, we didn't do anything," Robby said emphatically. "We just woke up like this."

Sharon stared around at each face in turn, searching for the one that would reveal this was all a prank. Then, Shmoofy mooed, and Sharon stood there completely dumbfounded, not sure which incomprehensible fact to try to make sense of first.

"Okay, everyone in the living room, now. I have so very many questions," she declared and turned on her heel to lead the way.

———

Once everyone was settled, some with donuts, others too scared to eat, Sharon said, "So start at the beginning."

Robby began, "Well, I heard something mooing and it woke me up. I mean, it was Muffin, but I didn't know that then." He proceeded to outline his morning up to the point where Sharon joined the fray.

Sharon turned to Marcus, "And your arms, have you tried washing them?"

"I rubbed at them and then used soap and water. But the chemical makeup seems to be more metallic than cellular," he said. "I've analyzed and prioritized several other methodologies for trying to clean them, but if I'm correct, and the very makeup of my cell structure has changed, no amount of cleaning product will have any impact whatsoever."

"Um, Marcus, you're being weird, even for you," pointed out Dominique. "No offense."

"None taken, I've already determined that my thought processes have also undergone some sort of transformation since last night," he added. "I would like to start breaking down the issue by outlining what has happened to each of us. Mrs. S, do you have a pen and paper?"

Sharon stood up to go get the requested items and returned a moment later with a yellow, lined notepad and two blue ballpoint pens, which she handed to Marcus.

He took the items from Sharon and immediately started drawing a grid with each person's name in the squares down the side of the page.

"So here are the things we know: Robby has dark hair."

"Yeah, and I can't get this stupid curl to stay off my forehead," he said through clenched teeth while trying to press the curl on top of his head and holding it with his hand for a few seconds. The moment he let go, it sprang right back to the center of his forehead.

"Got it, stubborn curl," Marcus said as he made a note. "What else, Robby?"

"What do you mean, 'what else?' That's not annoying enough?"

Marcus let his gaze quickly assess the parts of Robby that he could see and then asked, "Well, have you checked the rest of your body? Is anything else discolored like my arms or your hair?"

"Yeah, or can you fly?" quipped Javier.

"Why would I be able to fly?" asked Robby with more than a hint of annoyance in his voice.

"Well, you have the Superman hair from your mask, maybe you got other powers," Javier said shrugging.

"You know, for the purpose of information gathering, it's not a bad thing to check out," Marcus said to Robby.

So Robby climbed up to stand on the arm of the couch, bent his knees and then jumped off. To Javier's extreme disappointment, he landed unceremoniously in a heap on the floor.

"Well, I guess you were only wearing the mask and not the cape," Javier said shrugging.

"Great," came Robby's reply, dripping with sarcasm as he stood up and brushed dog fur off his pajama pants.

"No flight," said Marcus as he wrote it in Robby's square on the grid.

"What about X-ray vision?" threw in Joel.

Robby held out his hand and stared at it as hard as he could. "Ouch! That burned," he said rubbing his palm.

"Well, that makes sense, Superman has both X-ray vision and heat vision. Maybe you just need to learn how to control it," said Joel.

Sharon, who along with the girls had been silently watching the exchange so far, was shaking her head. "Let's hope we can fix this before we even need to learn how to control it. It would be great if we had a solution or it wears off before your parents come to pick you up. It looks like Nicki's hair has gone back to normal, so maybe this is temporary?"

Nicki hadn't noticed her hair, she picked up a strand and examined the brown color she saw every day when she looked in the mirror. "Well that's good news," she said with hope in her voice. "I should take off the earrings so they don't activate again." But after several attempts by both Nicki and her mother, it was clear the earrings' backs were fused to the post with no way to remove them from her ears without ripping the lobes. "Great," she said huffily.

Too focused on analyzing their 'symptoms,' Marcus ignored Nicki's comment and turned to his right, "Okay, so Javier, what do we know about you? Besides the fact that Robby swears you disappeared this morning."

"He did! I thought he was already up and in the bathroom or something because his sleeping bag was waded up and it looked empty. Then I tripped over it and when I turned back around, he was inside of it just waking up."

"So Javi, buddy, did you do anything that you remember to turn invisible or return to, um...full visibility?" Sharon asked uncertainly. She was still having trouble addressing the issue as a real problem when it seemed so far away from anything she could explain.

"Nope, I didn't even realize it happened."

"Can you try to do it now?" asked Marcus, his pen poised above the notepad to record anything interesting.

"How?" asked Javier looking around at his friends.

"Hmmm, maybe close your eyes since you were asleep when it happened and think really hard about turning invisible," suggested Marcus.

"Okay, but dang it, why couldn't this have happened while I still had on my McFly wings? I'm the one who said I wanted to fly!" Javier proceeded to squeeze his eyes shut as tight as he could, held his breath and clenched his jaw. Every muscle in his body was rigid as he tried with all his might to concentrate on being invisible.

"Well, you aren't invisible, but you do look like you're pooping," said Robby.

A short guffaw escaped from Dominique's lips. This drew a dirty look from Jasmine. "What? He's not wrong," she said.

Marcus, who was still reviewing the situation as a computer or robot might, suggested closing his eyes and relaxing to further mimic sleep. So Javier took a deep breath, closed his eyes and exhaled slowly. By the end of the breath, he wasn't fully invisible, but he had taken on an unmistakable ghostly presence.

At that point, anyone who thought the rest of the kids were pulling the most thorough prank of all time had to concede that something very strange was happening.

---

"I think we should call someone," said Sharon.

"Mom, it's not like they have a Yellow Pages ad for people who accidentally turned into their Halloween costumes," said Nicki.

A sob escaped from Rani, and Jasmine reached out to hold her hand. "It's going to be okay, we'll figure this out!"

"That's easy for you to say, you look completely normal!" said Dominique, angrily flipping her tight red curls with the back of her fingers.

"Can we call my mom?" Rani asked Sharon in a small voice. "She's a doctor."

"That's right! Yes, let's do that," said Sharon jumping from her spot on the couch and reaching for the phone. "I'm sorry, I should have thought of that sooner. This is all just so...unexpected," she finished feebly.

A few minutes later, there was a knock on the front door. Sharon went to let in Alisha, who took one look at her daughter with her bright blue eyes, long blonde hair and flaming red lips and stood rooted to the spot with her jaw hanging open. She recovered quickly when she saw the fear flash in her daughter's eyes and calmly said, "Could someone please catch me up?"

So once again, the story was told from the beginning, this time with the added information that they'd collected during their discovery session in the living room.

"But not everyone was 'infected?'" asked Alisha, holding the back of her hand to Rani's forehead and noting that she didn't have a fever.

"Not that we can tell. But we have noticed that some people have a few new skills that weren't immediately obvious," Marcus answered.

"And everything seems to be somehow tied to the Halloween costumes you were wearing?" Alisha asked.

"Correct," confirmed Marcus. "And it's clearly specific to what people were wearing at the end of the night. For example, Robby doesn't have all of Superman's powers, but we think he might have his X-ray or heat vision since he was wearing the mask. Also, some of these things are not constant. They come and go, like Javier's invisibility and Nicki's Jem persona."

"So what about any accessories you had?" Alisha turned to look at Rani. "Like your sword?"

"I don't know, it's in Nicki's bedroom," Rani responded.

"Hang on, I have my lightsaber right here," said Joel. He found it where it had been discarded the night before and picked it up. As soon as his fingers wrapped around the hilt, what used to be a flimsy plastic toy that glowed in the dark after being held next to a bright light now crackled to life in a brilliant blue shimmer in Joel's hands.

"Whoa," came a chorus from almost everyone in the room. After staring for a few long seconds, Marcus scribbled this new information on the notepad.

"Let's go ahead and put that away before anyone gets hurt," cautioned Sharon. "I already have a lot to explain to your parents."

"Yeah, so if I may ask the obvious, how did this happen?" asked Alisha, turning back to Sharon.

"We've been trying to piece that together. The kids went as one big group on their first trip around the neighborhood. The boys went alone for a victory lap since they think they'll be too old next year. We all went to the hospital, and then we all came back here. Since it affects both the boys and the girls, it had to have happened either on the first round of trick or treating, at the hospital, or once we were back here."

"But Shmoofy was mooing, so it can't be the first round or

the hospital," remembered Nicki.

"So it looks like there is at least one of you who might not have been affected?" Alisha looked at Jasmine.

"Well, we haven't tested Jasmine yet. She was a fortune-teller, so she didn't have a mask or wig or anything," Rani told her mom. "But what about your crystal ball? Have you tried it?"

"Nope," said Jasmine, hopping up off of her spot on the floor. "Let me go grab it."

"Don't forget, you were wearing those kitty ears, mom. Do you feel weird?" Nicki asked while they waited for Jasmine.

"Nope, one-hundred percent normal," she shrugged but examined her hands and arms to be sure there were no signs of cat fur.

Jasmine came back from Nicki's room a minute later with the crystal ball and sat down on the floor again. She held it in front of her and asked it, "Crystal ball, can you tell me anything about our future?"

It was quiet for a moment and then Jasmine gasped.

"What is it Jazz?" asked Nicki as she nervously chewed on her thumbnail.

"I just saw us sitting here and then in the ball, the door-bell rang and it was Mr. Watts. Is he coming over?" Jasmine asked Sharon.

"We hadn't made plans for today," responded Sharon.

But at that exact moment, the doorbell rang. With everyone watching her closely, Sharon opened the door and found Dale standing on her front porch.

# 6

## MORE THAN A SUGAR HANGOVER

"Hey babe, I just stopped by on my way to the hospital to make sure you survived the night. It seemed a little overwhelming when Kevin and I left last night," Dale said as he stepped into the entryway and gave Sharon a quick peck on the cheek.

It took a moment, but he caught the tension in the room and looked around at the faces all gaping at him.

"Um...I can go if this isn't a good time," he said searching Sharon's eyes for some assurance that everything was okay.

"Actually, can you stay for a minute?" she asked. Then she turned to Alisha and introduced the two adults. "Dale and I have been dating for about a month. He's an administrator at the hospital. Dale, this is Dr. Alisha Gabri, she's a general practitioner with her own practice downtown."

"Oh yes, I've seen your name as the referring doctor on forms at the hospital before. Your patients really seem to like you," he said as he leaned over the coffee table to shake her hand. "So what's with the somber mood? Is everyone sick from a sugar hangover?"

But then he really started to look around and noticed a few things that seemed quite odd. While he had only met Dominique once or twice at the Swain house, he knew she was prone to running her fingers through her silky, dark hair. So why did she have on a curly, red wig with her pajamas when trick or treating ended many hours ago? And why did Marcus have silver arms that reflected light in a way that no paint or makeup should?

"So you haven't been to the hospital yet? Or heard about anything unusual this morning?" Sharon asked anxiously.

"No, I actually called and told them I'd be a little late because Kevin was having a problem with his eye when he woke up. Super irritated to the point where he can't open it. I'm going to have to leave early to take him to his doctor and have it checked out. Why, what's up?"

Sharon didn't really know where to start. She was afraid anything she said would sound foolish or hysterical.

But Marcus, deep in his analytical state had no such qualms. "We woke up this morning with parts of our costume seemingly woven into our DNA. For example, I can't get rid of the silver on my arms. Several people have taken on the hair from their wig or mask," he said pointing at Robby, Dominique and Rani in turn. "And some other stuff we're still figuring out." For some reason, he was reluctant to share information about Javier's invisibility or Jasmine's seemingly accurate crystal ball.

Dale sat in silence for a moment, looking around the room taking in more details.

"And before you ask, we have no idea what caused this," said Nicki.

"Right, but if you could check at the hospital to see if anyone has come in with unexplainable symptoms, that would help us try to figure it out," Sharon pleaded. "I know it's against policy to share medical information about another patient, but would you be allowed to at least let us know if there are more?"

Dale gave a quick glance to Alisha to gauge her reaction. Frankly, he wasn't as cautious as he should be about that type of privacy issue and had been known to entertain his beer-drinking buddies with a story or two of some quirky patient symptom or another. But he knew she was likely much more conservative as a doctor with a private practice.

She seemed to read his mind and said, "I don't think it would hurt to just mention if there were other cases that appear to match this situation. We wouldn't ask for names or any other personal information."

"Of course, I'm happy to help any way I can," he said as he stood up to go.

"Thanks, Dale, I really appreciate it," Sharon hugged him and walked him to the door.

As soon as the latch clicked, everyone turned to Jasmine and asked her what else she could see in the crystal ball.

"Does it say how to get rid of this," asked Dominique hopefully as she pulled at one of her curls.

Jasmine sat cross-legged on the floor, both palms cupping the ball from underneath and holding it in front of her face.

"It shows Javier getting up and going down the hall," she said. "I think he's going to the bathroom."

Javier's eyes widened in alarm. "I was just thinking that I really needed to go."

"And it shows Mrs. Swain bringing the box of donuts from the kitchen and setting them on the coffee table in here," Jasmine read the next image.

Sharon gave a small smile and said, "I was feeling that itch to wake up from this nightmare and be a good hostess. I guess I'll go ahead and do that now."

Both Sharon and Javier stood up to take care of their respective needs.

"So, I guess the question is: does it tell you anything that's more than twelve seconds in the future?" asked Robby, who had been uncharacteristically quiet for a while.

"I can't really tell it what I want to see. I just gaze at it, and it shows me things. But let me try."

Jasmine studiously stared at the orb while the others kept their eyes glued to her for a couple of minutes before her arms got tired and she let it fall to her lap.

"Nope, it was empty. I guess because none of us are doing anything for it to show."

Sharon, who was back with the donuts, squared her shoulders and said to the room, "Well, I think we have to accept that I need to call your parents and let them know what's going on. I'll invite them here so we can all get through this together." The group nodded solemnly as they realized there was no quick fix to their problem. As she nodded, Nicki's earrings flashed and her hair once again turned a bright bubblegum pink.

---

Sharon called each of the parents and assured them that their children were safe, but that there had been an issue if they could please come over right away. They all showed up within a few minutes of each other and the story was told yet again. After the initial shock wore off, and the parents had all hugged their children and tried to convince them they would find a solution, everyone sat down to figure out what to do next. Only Dominique's father had yelled at Sharon before her mother pointed out that they weren't even sure what had happened or if it was Sharon's fault at all. Marcus gave his rundown of what they knew so far.

"Do we have to go to school on Monday? Or church tomorrow?" asked a teary Dominique when he finished.

"That's a great question. I think we need more information first. For example, is this contagious," said Alisha. Everyone looked around nervously as they hadn't given it any consideration before.

"I don't think it is," said Marcus, and all eyes turned expectantly in his direction. "My main reason for thinking this is Mrs. S had been around us last night and all this morning and she's fine, despite the fact that she was wearing a sort of costume last night."

"What costume were you wearing?" asked Sonia Drake, Jasmine's mother.

"Just a headband with cat ears on it," replied Sharon.

"So why didn't you turn into a cat or whatever?" asked Gregory Daniels, Marcus's father.

"Yeah, what did you do that we didn't?" said Robby with his brow furrowed studying his mom.

"Or more probably, it's what we did that she didn't," corrected Marcus. "Did you eat any of the candy or pizza?"

"I had a piece of each, but I'm sort of on a diet, so it was just the one."

"What kind?" Marcus persisted.

"I had a piece of the pepperoni. And the candy was one from the bucket that I was handing out. I think it was a Milky Way," said Sharon trying to remember more details.

"So you didn't eat any of the candy that we had X-rayed," said Marcus, tapping the blue pen against his cheek.

"Do you think it had something to do with the X-ray machine?" asked Robby, lifting his eyebrows as he considered the possibility.

"I mean, it was really old and had all that Russian writing on it," Javier recalled. "And it made some pretty gnarly noises when that lab guy was trying to get it to turn back on when we first got there."

"Right, and then it did that thing with all the sparks," chipped in Joel.

"Green sparks," emphasized Nicki. "I don't know that I've ever seen green sparks before."

"Sharon, I think we need to hear back from Dale and then ask him about that machine," Alisha said.

"I totally agree," Sharon nodded to the increasingly distressed faces around her living room.

---

At the hospital, Dale walked through the sliding front doors. He slipped his keys into his pocket, shifted his sunglasses to the top of his head and stopped to talk to the receptionist on duty. "Hey Marsha, any strange cases come in this morning?"

She paused typing on her computer and looked up at him quizzically. "No, why?"

"You know, last night was Halloween, which usually brings out the crazies," said Dale, trying to sound light-hearted as he leaned on the desk to watch her face.

"Oh, of course," she said, as she give her head a few quick shakes and finally focused on their conversation. "No, it's been pretty quiet this morning," she told him. "And Donna didn't mention anything when we switched shifts."

"Awesome, glad to hear it. Have a great day!" he knocked

his knuckles on the desk twice, smiled one last time and then used his badge to access the hallway behind her desk.

He was on the way to his office when he felt a presence lurking behind him. Dale looked over his right shoulder and saw something slip away, quickly followed by the sound of a door closing softly. More curious than concerned, he knocked on the door and then entered. Inside he found Chad Stevens standing near the door with the lights out. But even with just the sunshine peeking in from behind the closed blinds and the glow from the computer monitor, Dale could tell that something was off with Chad. He flipped on the light and noticed that Chad's normally sandy brown, feathered hair was streaked with gray and fluffed out away from his head, reminiscent of Albert Einstein.

"Hey Chad, crazy party last night?" Dale asked with a hint of a conspiratorial smile as he leaned on the door frame.

"No Dale, I promise. I went to a party that some of my old college friends were having, but they had already been drinking and it just wasn't fun for me. I was tired from working all day and then working that extra shift for the candy X-rays, so I went home and watched a movie. I fell asleep on the couch and when I woke up..." he opened his palm to indicate his hair, unable to finish the sentence.

"That's not a wig, then?" Dale asked hopefully, he shifted from his casual stance and crossed his arms over his chest, already putting two and two together and realizing there was a connection to Sharon's problem.

"No, and no amount of brushing will make it calm down. It's like it has a mind of its own," Chad was almost whining.

"Okay, I need you to stay in here for a minute while I make a call," Dale said, resuming his mission to get to his office phone.

"What? Where are you going, who are you telling?" Chad sounded panicked. He rushed up behind Dale and stopped just inside the doorway where no one else could see him.

"Someone who I think can help," said Dale. Chad watched him enter his office on the other side of the hall. Chad closed and locked the door to his own room and sat down in the chair, his hands flopping uselessly in his lap, shoulders slumped. He stared at the computer screen but didn't really see anything.

———

Dale sat down in his office chair, took the sunglasses off his head to place them on his desk and rubbed his eyes while leaning back in the chair. Then he leaned forward and drummed his fingers anxiously on the desk while he stared at the phone. He wanted to call Sharon, but he strongly suspected that technically this was his fault. After all, he had bought some faulty equipment from that sketchy salesman. If both Chad and Sharon's kids had been affected, there was a chance it was from the shoddy, old Russian X-ray machine. In his defense, Grayson Ridge was a small town and the hospital didn't have the funding that the big city hospitals received, so when the man with the thick Slavic accent approached him about buying his considerably cheaper machinery, it seemed like a no-brainer.

He was quite enamored with Sharon and didn't want to upset her. She was beautiful, smart and funny, and they liked the same kind of food and movies. It didn't hurt that her husband left her a nice house and a substantial insurance settlement when he passed away, so she was pretty set financially. He finally worked up his courage and reached for the phone. Before he managed to touch the receiver, it rang and he yanked his hand back as though it had been burned. Taking a deep breath, he picked up the phone and answered, "Dale Watts."

"Dale, it's Sharon. I'm sorry to bother you at work, but I think we figured something out. Did you hear if there were any other odd cases?"

"Nope, I checked when I got here and Marsha at the front desk didn't have anything to report. She or Donna would have seen it if anything unusual came through," Dale replied. "What did you figure out?"

Sharon paused, not wanting to sound accusatory. "Well, we think there's a chance that the X-rayed candy somehow infected the kids. I can explain how we narrowed it down, but is there any chance that's what happened?"

Dale paused, not wanting to admit the source of the issue or Chad's appearance until he could think this through. "I suppose it's possible, but then wouldn't other kids who came in last night have the same problem?"

"Alisha went home to make some calls to her doctor colleagues to see if anyone else has seen something. The kids are watching the news in case someone has reported it there. But so far...nothing," she said hopelessly. A small sob escaped her lips.

"Hey, hey, it's okay, we're going to figure this out," Dale assured her.

They finished their conversation, and Dale went back across the hall to Chad's room.

"Hey Chad, is there any chance that you ate some of the candy that was X-rayed last night?" he tried to sound casual.

"Um...maybe just a piece or two, why?" he asked, not able to look Dale in the face.

"Do you remember who you took it from?"

Chad looked at Dale, trying to gauge how much trouble he was in. Finally, he sighed and said, "When that friend of yours came in late, I was starving, so I swiped a Snickers from their bag and ate it on my way to the party. But hey, I had already shut down the machine and was ready to go when they got here. I had to start it back up and it took forever. Please don't fire me."

Dale looked thoughtful for a moment then asked, "And what did you dress up as for your party?"

Chad, looking confused at this line of questioning said, "I just left on my lab coat and took a beaker to go as a mad scientist." Dale nodded, lost in thought and then silently walked out the door, leaving Chad standing in the middle of the room looking desperate and perplexed.

Chad finally collected himself and turned around to sit at his computer to get some work done when he noticed a bump in the pocket of his lab coat. Reaching in, he pulled out the other candy bar that he had taken from the group of kids the previous night. He started to call for Dale, but stopped himself and slowly slid it into his pocket.

Back at the Swain house, parents and children alike looked at Sharon expectantly as she hung up the phone and turned to the group.

"What did he say? Has anyone else come in with issues?" asked Sonia Drake with such anxious excitement that she practically bounced out of her seat.

"Nothing. No one has reported anything. And Dale isn't so sure that it's the X-ray machine since we're the only ones who appear to be affected," she looked solemnly around the room as she delivered the update.

Javier's dad, Antonio Alanis, snorted, "I'm sure a hospital administrator doesn't want to admit that his hospital equipment could have caused any sort of issues with our children."

"Yeah," agreed Marcus confidently, "that doesn't mean anything. Two other reasons: one, not everyone has a contact at the hospital. And unless they had some sort of pain or illness, they might not rush straight there. We're better off asking Dr. Gabri's friends if anyone came into their offices this morning. And two, everyone else might have had a totally normal experience with the X-ray machine. We had all those problems with the power and the sparks. Our situation could be just different enough that it triggered this reaction."

Alisha returned from her house and tentatively knocked on the Swain's front door, then let herself in. She just shook her head in response to the others' questioning looks about whether or not the doctors in her network had heard of anything unusual that could possibly be related.

The group talked for a while longer with Marcus documenting everything of significance on the yellow, lined paper. Eventually, the kids drifted away to Robby's room while the adults stayed in the living room to talk about their options.

In Robby's room, Rani and Dominique squished in next to each other on an oversized, navy blue bean bag chair. Jasmine hadn't yet noticed any real 'symptoms' other than her ability to actually use her crystal ball as a future-telling device, albeit not the distant future. And, for the moment at least, Nicki had no visible signs of their adventure. So Rani and Dominique found comfort in each other's company as they both had new physical attributes that weren't ones they would have chosen for themselves.

Robby, who was typically oblivious of their distress, bounced around his room and confided in the rest, "I know the adults are all freaked out, but I'm dying to find out if I have any superpowers. I want to know if I have super-hearing or super-breath! Or maybe I'm like a black belt in karate. I need more space to see if I can do some bad kicks!" he said looking around his packed room.

"Robby, can't you see that not everyone is as excited as you are?" Nicki brought him back to earth with a sharp scold. "Besides, what are you going to do with super-breath? We live in the middle of nothing, you can't make a hurricane here."

"Hey, super-breath can put out fires and freeze things too. Maybe I could blow my super-breath at the sky and make a snow day!" he said hopefully.

"I don't remember Superman making snow," said Joel doubtfully. "But, do you know what Superman does have? A Fortress of Solitude," he looked around the room for someone else to catch on to what he was thinking.

"And..." Nicki prompted, clearly not seeing it, but realizing that he had a point he wanted to make.

"Well, I was just thinking," Joel helped them along, "this is some messed up stuff. We have no idea how kids at school are going to react. Or the teachers, if you really think about it. It would be nice for the eight of us to have like a secret lair if we need it to just be us."

Marcus jumped in, "Joel, you are brilliant! We can also use it as our place to figure out what happened and how to fix it. Or if we just need a place to not be the weirdos."

"I thought you would be used to that," said Dominique, but with only a fraction of the sassy tone she usually used when delivering a zing to one of Robby's friends.

Marcus almost snapped back but saw that her heart wasn't in it, and she still radiated sadness, so he went back to the topic at hand. "Where can we make our Fortress?"

Joel already had an answer, "Remember that old storm

shelter in my backyard? We used to play in it all the time when we were little. I think we've used it once as an actual tornado shelter. But it's still there, and we could use that."

"Where do you live?" asked Rani. "I'm not allowed to go too far from my house unless my mom knows where I'm going to be."

"Don't worry," said Nicki, "Joel lives three houses down, four from you, on the opposite side of the street."

"That should work," Rani said, as she twisted up her waist-length blonde hair and pushed it to her back.

"Maybe we should meet there after school Monday so we can all support each other if any of us have a hard day," suggested Jasmine, looking at the beanbag where one of her oldest friends and her newest friend sat huddled together.

"I still cannot believe I have to go to school Monday looking like Little Orphan Annie," Dominique shook her head in disgust.

Nicki sang the first few words of "Tomorrow" from Annie.

"Can it!" Dominique shut her friend down before she could even finish the first line with a fierceness in her eyes that quieted Nicki immediately.

"Well, are we going to meet at Joel's Monday after school?" Marcus tried to confirm the plans.

"The boys will," said Robby.

Nicki locked eyes with Dominique who glared for several seconds before giving an almost imperceptible nod. "We'll be there too," said Nicki softly.

Sharon knocked on the door, poked her head in and

announced that the parents were getting ready to go before softly closing the door and giving them a minute to say goodbye to each other.

"Actually, I don't think I can wait until Monday to see you guys again," said Dominique once the kids were alone again. "Can we meet there tomorrow?"

"Sure!" said Joel excitedly. He was used to all of the action taking place at Robby's house these days and was thrilled to share his underground bunker. "After breakfast?"

Everyone confirmed and then filed out of Robby's room to find their parents, return to their homes and have their own private conversations about what had happened.

## 7

## X-RAY VISIONS

Sunday morning was still cool and crisp, but with a hint of the warmer day to come that floated in on the breeze. Robby, Nicki and all of their friends were crammed into the 6-foot by 8-foot steel storm shelter in Joel's backyard. Given that it hadn't been used in the past few years, it was a little musty, but a perfect hideaway for privacy.

"Man, this place seemed a lot bigger when we first started hanging out here," said Javier, looking around and hugging his arms as close to himself as possible so he didn't accidentally touch one of the girls. He was still uncomfortable in his body after his summer growth spurt, and it showed in the way he tried to fold in on himself.

"Well, we were much smaller and there were only four of us," said Marcus matter-of-factly.

"If we decorate it a little, I think it will be rad!" Nicki exclaimed. "I can't believe I forgot this was back here." She looked around the small space that held two long benches running the length of either side and imagined it with a few posters and maybe some pillows or beanbags. "I'll bring a few things we can put on the walls the next time we get together."

"Cool, thanks. So, what did all your parents say last night?" asked Joel. "Mine refused to talk about it in front of me." He was desperate for some sort of update since his parents grew tight-lipped every time he walked into the room.

"My mom hasn't seen me disappear yet, so she's still really weirded out about the whole thing and doesn't know what to think," said Javier. "She's in some serious denial. My dad is ready to sue the hospital."

"We'd have to prove it was their equipment first, which I don't think we've successfully managed yet," Marcus stated the obvious.

Dominique, who didn't have her usual confident posture, pulled on one of her curls and said, "My parents fought half the night. My dad is super angry, but my mom just keeps saying that doesn't help anything, and we need to figure out a way to fix it. She also pointed out that he was the one who wanted the candy X-rayed in the first place after he saw some news report. But since there isn't an obvious way to come up with a solution or even prove that it was the hospital's X-ray machine, they just keep going in circles."

"Speaking of angry dads," Nicki said looking nervously at Rani, "what did yours say?"

Rani just shook her head slowly back and forth staring at the jumble of feet on the floor.

"That bad?" asked Jasmine, reaching across the bunker and putting a reassuring hand on Rani's arm.

"He blamed my mom for everything. Said if she would have just moved to California, I'd be fine and now instead my whole life is ruined so he wants to get custody before she can do any more damage," she told her new friends. "Do you guys feel like our lives are ruined?"

"Yes!" said Dominique emphatically, her voice echoing in the metal room.

"Not really," Marcus replied at the same time.

The rest looked uncomfortable and shrugged or shuffled their feet in the small space. Silence filled the air for a few moments until Robby turned to Marcus and asked, "Did you think of anything else important to add to the list we were making at my house yesterday? Anything helpful?"

"The more I think about what led up to it and what we've heard since, I think it's obvious it had something to do with the X-rayed candy and the costumes we were wearing when we ate it. But what I'm still trying to figure out is why it's just us. No one else has reported anything to the hospital, doctors, police or local news stations," he said ticking off on his fingers what they had already researched.

"Technically other than Dale, we haven't reported it to anyone either," pointed out Jasmine.

"True," said Marcus nodding. "I guess we'll find out when we go to school tomorrow if there are others."

"Ugh, I don't want to go to school like this!" Dominique

wailed, her face contorted with despair. "I'm going to try to get my mom to let me stay home until we figure this out."

"But Dom," said Nicki choosing her words carefully, "we don't know how long that might be. You can't miss too much school or you'll be held back, and I need my best friends with me in sixth grade!"

"At least your hair looks normal sometimes," Dominique said bitterly to Nicki. "And you," she said to Jasmine, her voice dripping with accusation, "your hair is as beautiful as ever! If I had just made a stupid decision and been a cheer-leader or Princess Leia, I wouldn't even care about all of this."

"Dom," started Nicki cautiously.

"No, I don't want you to tell me it's okay, or that I look fine. It's NOT okay, and I most definitely do not look fine! I look beyond ridiculous, and I didn't even get cool powers like the rest of you. This just sucks," she said with tears streaming down her face.

"That's the truth, it does suck that you don't have powers," said Marcus. "Wait...powers, truth," he was muttering now, his eyes shifting back and forth as though he were reading his thoughts from a screen that no one else could see. "Dominique, you were playing with Shmoofy with that Lasso of Truth when we were eating candy. Do you think it would work for you?"

Dominique tried to slow her breathing and wiped at her eyes, embarrassed that she had lost her cool while surrounded so closely by all the other faces staring at her with concern. "I don't know, I'm not even sure where it is."

"Perhaps we should go to Robby's and find it, then get back to that list. Has anyone else figured out what other powers they might have?" Marcus inquired.

"I totally tried to use The Force in my room last night," Joel admitted, "but so far only the lightsaber does anything for me."

"That makes sense, that's how it was for Luke at first, too," Marcus pointed out. "Maybe you have to practice to get it." Joel brightened at this thought and resolved to rewatch *Star Wars* and practice using The Force that night.

"Who else?" Marcus looked around the bunker. "I haven't found anything that wasn't already obvious. Silver arms and legs and robotic analytical skills."

"But you were wearing the football uniform when you ate the candy," said Jasmine, furrowing her brow trying to figure out what powers that might involve.

"Yeah, but I had the silver parachute pants and aluminum tubing on still. You do bring up a good point though. Am I now an awesome football player?" he asked grinning.

"Now *that* would be a transformation," Javier laughed. No one had ever used the word "athletic" to describe Marcus. "Or maybe you'll start getting spots like a cheetah since the jersey had cheetahs on the sleeves."

Marcus's head whipped up as he stared wide-eyed and open-mouthed at Javier.

"What?" asked Javier, nervous from the intensity of Marcus's gaze.

Marcus chewed on his thought for a moment and then

revealed, "Last night when I was going to bed, my legs cramped up. It was like an eleven on a scale of one to ten. I wonder if we're still undergoing the transformation, and maybe I *can* run super-fast."

"There's only one way to find out," Robby said, putting his hand on the door handle of the shelter. He opened it and sprang out before anyone else had a chance to say anything.

A little more slowly, everyone else exited the bunker, squinting in the bright sun and walking out to the street in front of Joel's house. Marcus bent down in a runner's sprint and told Robby to tell him when to start. Nicki looked at the second hand of one of her Swatches to count the time.

"Ready, get set, go!" shouted Robby.

Marcus stood up, leaned forward and took off. In less than two seconds, he had run past twelve houses to the end of the street. He stopped and looked back at his friends, not even breathing heavily. Two seconds later, he was back among the pack. "How fast was that?" he asked Nicki.

She raised her eyebrows and shrugged her shoulders. "Um...I don't really know. I didn't even have time to look back at the watch before you got to the end of the street. If I had to guess, I'd say like three seconds tops."

Marcus grinned, enjoying his newfound skill. He tipped his head to the left and then to the right as though he were cracking his neck, even though it didn't make a sound. "I can't wait to show my brother. Definitely something for the list," he tried to sound casual but failed miserably. Dominique just rolled her eyes as they all set off for Robby and Nicki's house to look for the Lasso of Truth and get the notepad to log the latest bit of information.

---

Chad was in his small second-floor apartment perched on the edge of his brown-and-beige hand-me-down couch, leaning forward and stabbing his thumbs aggressively into his Nintendo controller. He absentmindedly guided his character over platforms and gaps, collecting coins and mushrooms, while replaying the conversation with Dale in his head. Something just didn't make sense, but he couldn't quite put his finger on it.

Finally, he flung the controller down on the couch, walked to his refrigerator, popped the top on a Dr Pepper and headed into his bedroom.

The previous night, he had started to map out what he knew and what he thought he knew on a whiteboard that adorned the wall. Prior to that, the board still held the equations from a physics class that he had taken in college a couple of years ago. It had required several tries, more than a few damp paper towels and some elbow grease to get the old markings to come off, but now he had bullet points about the time, date and settings on the X-ray machine and the type of candy that he ate scrawled on the board in his barely legible handwriting. He had also taped the Snickers wrapper next to his notes in case it became useful at some point. The second, uneaten candy bar was hiding in the back of a drawer full of folded T-shirts. He reread the list for what must have been the twentieth time with frustration. There just weren't enough details to draw any reasonably scientific conclusions.

Pacing around the apartment, he tried to figure out what else he could add to the meager details that he had so far. He flung himself onto the couch, giving up and returning to his game. Sighing, he immediately got back up because the game was frozen. He took out the cartridge, blew on the part that inserted into the console and put it back. Voila! The game restarted. But only a few seconds in, he realized where a wealth of new information likely resided. The kids! Why else would Dale have asked about the candy and his costume?

Something must have happened to them, and Dale knew it because he was friends with the mom. But how could Chad find out? He hadn't trusted Dale before, even less so now that he'd been so cagey with his questions. Chad would have to try to find the kids after school tomorrow. He wasn't sure where they lived, but there was only one elementary school near the hospital so he'd need to camp out there until he saw them leave. Luckily, since he had worked on Saturday, he had Monday off. Smiling broadly at his epiphany and subsequent plan, he tapped the black arrows and red buttons on his controller with far less force.

---

"Soooo," said Nicki in a singsong voice, "who are you going to use it on?"

Dominique stood in the Swain's living room holding the Lasso of Truth. She looked from person to person, trying to figure out who would be most likely to have a deep, dark secret. Finally, her eyes settled on Javier.

"Javi," she said with a slow smile. It was the first genuine smile anyone had seen from her since Friday night, but it still caused everyone to feel a bit unsettled due to the mischievous gleam in her eyes.

"Me?" he asked with legitimate surprise. "Go ahead, I'm an open book."

"Okay," she said, lacing the lasso through her fingers. "Who do you have a crush on?"

His face turned red and he looked sideways at Joel before shifting his eyes immediately to the ground and mumbling, "No one."

"Really?" she said with unveiled disbelief and she whipped the lasso from her fingers and around Javier's stomach. "Let's try again, who do you have a crush on?"

Javier looked at her with pleading eyes, but his mouth reacted on its own and said, "Nicki."

"Dude!" Robby stepped toward his friend with his palms facing up and out to his side.

"I would never do anything about it, you're one of my best friends!" said Javier miserably. "No one besides Joel was ever supposed to know."

Nicki was staring at Javier. She'd known him as long as she could remember and had never thought of him as anything other than one of her brother's goofy friends. The silence dragged on longer than anyone could stand. Finally, Marcus said, "We need to get the notepad and mark this down. I think it's pretty clear the lasso works."

Dominique gave Nicki a satisfied little smirk. She loved her friend, but she was pretty irritated that Nicki and Jasmine had come out comparatively so well with this whole debacle.

Joel looked sympathetically at Javier, who was so red he was almost purple and barely breathing. He searched for a way to change the subject while Marcus went off to get the notepad. "Hey, what about your sword, Rani? Wasn't She-Ra able to do almost anything with it? I can't believe we haven't been testing it this whole time."

Rani excused herself to run back to her house so she could grab the sword and returned a minute later. She ran her finger over the golden hilt and the turquoise stone embedded in it. "I haven't actually seen the cartoon much. What do you think I should try first?" she asked Joel.

"Well," he said thinking out loud, "first of all, you should know that it's called the Sword of Protection. That blue jewel is the key to all of its powers, so make sure it doesn't fall out. As far as what she could do with her sword, she could turn it into all kinds of other objects. Like a shield or a rope, and one time it was still a sword, but on fire. A flaming blade," his eyes were glistening as he said this in an awed tone. "Even without the sword, She-Ra is supposed to have super-strength and speed. And she can even talk to some animals. If you can do half of that, you have the best powers of all of us."

Rani looked at the sword with renewed interest. So far, all

she had considered was how she didn't think her new blue eyes and blonde hair matched her darker skin. And how her bright red lips always made it seem like she was about to go somewhere fancy, which also didn't jive with her fifth-grade casual look. In general, Rani wasn't the kind of girl who liked to stand out. But the sword could make this whole situation a lot more interesting.

"Try something!" said Robby, never the most patient of the group.

Rani lifted the sword and stared intently at it as she focused all of her energy on picturing a shield. She closed her eyes and continued to focus while taking a deep, slow breath. Suddenly her eyes flew open as the weight in her hands shifted and she was now looking at a silver-and-blue shield.

"That's so cool!" declared Robby. "Do something else!"

For the next few minutes, Rani converted the sword into various items, both weapons and everyday objects that Joel remembered from the cartoon. The more she practiced, the quicker she became at the transformations. Marcus was jotting it all down on the notepad and eventually had to start another page just for Rani.

"What about the non-sword stuff. Do you have super speed or strength?" inquired Joel.

"Hey, we should go outside and have Marcus and Rani race!" said Javier, finally finding his voice again.

"Brilliant!" said Robby, "Let's go!"

The kids made their way back outside where Rani and

Marcus positioned themselves behind a seam in the concrete. Once again, Robby did the honors. "Ready, get set, go!"

Both children flashed out of sight so quickly that it took a moment for everyone to realize that they had already reached the end of the street and were rounding the corner. Before anyone could ask where they were going, Rani and Marcus both stopped short right where they had started, having been around the block in just a handful of seconds, Marcus only a step or two ahead of Rani.

"Dang you guys, you should be in the Olympics," marveled Javier.

While everyone was gushing about super-speed, Sharon popped her head out of the front door. "Robby, Nicki, I need you to wrap it up and come inside. Dale and Kevin are bringing over some dinner in a bit."

"Okay mom, we'll be there soon," Nicki confirmed. "Well guys, I guess this is it," she said turning back to her friends. "The next time we see each other, it will be at school." Everyone nodded, serious again after the rush of the race.

Jasmine said, "It's going to be okay. We'll be there for each other. We'll sit together at lunch, talk at recess and just tell everyone all the cool stuff. Focus on the positive, you know?"

"We actually haven't talked about how much we're going to tell other people," pointed out Marcus. "Are we sure we want to tell them everything? Once you say it, you can't take it back. I mean, they'll obviously see the physical changes. But do we want to let others know about the crystal ball, the sword, the lightsaber?"

Silence again as they all pondered the consequences of sharing their newfound powers.

"I don't know that I want to tell people about the crystal ball," said Jasmine after careful consideration. "I feel like that's the kind of thing people would want to take advantage of or even try to steal."

"Okay, fair enough, no one tells anyone who doesn't already know about the crystal ball," Marcus nodded.

"I don't really care if people know about the lightsaber," said Joel. In his imagination, people knowing about his lightsaber would elevate his cool status. "But I probably won't mention The Force until I figure out if I can actually use it or people will just think I'm lying."

Rani hesitated, but then said, "I'm with Jasmine, I'm not ready to share with the rest of the school any of my stuff – the sword or the super-speed. I'm still the new kid. I don't really need any extra attention when I can barely find the bathrooms by myself."

"Sounds good, so everyone is agreed on how we approach tomorrow?" Marcus asked the group. He received a round of nods after which everyone headed toward their own homes while Dominique, Robby and Nicki went into the Swain house to wait for Dominique's mom to pick her up.

---

"What was that all about?" Nicki spun around to face Dominique as soon as they were inside and out of earshot.

"What?" Dominique tried to sound innocent, almost succeeding, but not quite.

"You know what, Dom, don't play dumb. Why did you do that to Javi? And how did you even know?" Nicki was still on the verge of yelling.

"Oh, come on, it's been obvious to everyone for a while now," said Dominique flippantly.

"Speak for yourself," said Robby. "I had no idea."

"Well, now you know," said Dominique.

"Look," Nicki tried to calm down and reason with her friend, "I know you hate this more than anyone. I don't blame you. But you can't go around lashing out at the rest of us. Javi is a nice guy and you purposefully embarrassed him in front of all of us."

Dominique had the good grace to look somewhat ashamed. "I know, he *is* a nice guy. He should have just done his ghost thing and disappeared."

Robby snorted, "Yeah, I'd rather be invisible than fire engine red."

"Wait...," Nicki started thinking out loud. "Do we know what makes him disappear? He did it on command that one time. He had to relax, right?"

"Yeah, so what?" asked Robby as he flopped down on the couch. The girls followed him from the entryway into the living room and found seats as well.

"So, I'm thinking that in our notes, we should include what it takes to activate. We sort of know Javi's, it seems like Rani just has to concentrate on her sword or running. Hers actually seems like the easiest to control. Other than my Jem stuff, the visual part of everybody's doesn't seem to go away. And I don't know what activates my Jem stuff."

"The earrings," Robby stated the obvious.

"Yeah, duh. But why? Is there any reason they activate when they do?"

"Hmmm," Dominique thought out loud. "The first time was when you heard Shmoofy moo."

"And the second time was when mom said we were going to call everyone's parents," contributed Robby. "I remember because I was thinking well at least only a couple of us will look weird when they get here, so maybe we could hide until they were warned, and just then your hair changed."

The three of them sat thinking, but not coming up with any commonality between the two situations other than that everything about the day had been crazy.

"We'll have to keep thinking about mine, but we should definitely write down what we figured out about the others," said Nicki.

They heard a honk out front, and Dominique jumped up to go get in her mom's car. "Well, I guess I'll see you guys at school tomorrow," she said with a half-hearted wave.

Nicki nodded with a grim look on her face and shut the door behind her friend.

Later Sunday evening, Nicki opened the same door to let Dale and his son Kevin come in. Kevin was holding two giant bags of what smelled like still hot fried food and wearing an eye patch.

"Hey Kev, did you come straight from work tonight?" Sharon asked, nodding at his eye patch as she took the bags from his hands and moved them to the dining room table.

"Yeah, but the eye patch is a more permanent thing," he said as he shoved his hands in his pockets. "I mean, not permanent, but not just for work. I have some infection that my regular doctor can't figure out, so I have to wear this in case it's contagious. It's not my work eye patch, it's one the doctor gave me. My dad is going to call an ophthalmologist tomorrow to see when I can get an appointment."

"I'm so sorry," said Sharon who was setting paper plates and cups around the table.

"I personally think it looks cool," said Robby, who had just walked into the room. "It was the most pirate-y part of your costume anyway."

"It's not a costume," Kevin said as he ruffled Robby's Superman hair, causing Robby to swat his hand away. "It's a uniform. Working men wear uniforms."

"Okay, *man,*" said Robby sarcastically.

"Robby, please tell your sister it's time for dinner," said Sharon as she dumped fried fish, fried shrimp, popcorn shrimp, French fries and hush puppies onto a large platter that she set in the middle of the table. "Kevin, thanks for bringing dinner. As you know, this weekend has been more than I can handle, and I really appreciate not having to cook."

"Of course, Miss Sharon. Thanks for letting my dad and me eat with you guys. It gets boring with just the two of us."

"So now I'm boring?" said Dale with mock hurt in his voice. Kevin gave him a look that clearly said Dale didn't want to know the answer to that question. Everyone laughed as Nicki walked in with Shmoofy trailing at her heels.

"Hey, look it's Rug Muppet!" exclaimed Kevin, giving Shmoofy a rub on the head.

"It's Muffin," said Robby testily.

"Sorry, look it's Rug Muffin!"

Shmoofy turned his head so Kevin would scratch under his chin. When Kevin stopped petting him, Shmoofy looked at him and issued a soft "moo," causing Kevin's eyebrows to fly up his forehead.

"That's a crazy trick you taught your dog," Kevin said. Robby and Nicki looked at each other and Nicki gave a slight shake of her head, warning Robby not to say anything.

"Alright boys, load up your plates and pour yourselves a drink. It's every man, woman and child for themselves tonight!" Sharon said as she followed her own advice and put some of everything on her plate.

"Mom, I thought you were on a diet," said Robby as he shoved a fry in his mouth.

"Robert Alan Swain, that is none of your business!" she said, pretending to be offended as she also chomped down on a fry. "Sometimes a girl's gotta cheat and if ever there was a day where I felt like having some comfort food, this is it."

"Here, here," agreed Dale. Everyone munched on their food for a few moments. Dale broke the silence by asking Nicki and Robby, "So, have you guys come up with any ideas about how to solve your little problem?" he asked as he waved a shrimp tail toward Robby's hair.

"Nope, right now we're making notes on what we know so far," said Robby carelessly as he continued to slather fries in ketchup and eat them in quick succession. Nicki kicked him under the table and he tossed her a what-the-heck look. Trying to cover she said, "We don't really know much yet."

"You might be surprised," Dale said as he took a sip of the drink Sharon had cracked open for him and set in front of his place at the table. "Why don't you let me help you think through it. What have you got?"

Robby nodded to Nicki since he wasn't clear on what she was willing to share.

"You know, we can tell that some people have had changes," she started slowly. "Like Robby's hair, and obviously Dom and Rani's too. Marcus's arms and legs are silver."

"Don't forget Marcus and Rani can run like a thousand miles an hour," Robby contributed enthusiastically, earning himself another kick under the table.

"Really?" said Kevin with his eyes wide. "Man, I wish that had happened to me, I'd be on the starting line in football." Knowing that high school football was practically a second religion in Texas, Sharon heartily agreed.

"So the changes weren't strictly visual?" Dale asked, turning back to Robby.

"Nope, I think I have some sort of super-heat vision, but I haven't really figured out how to use it. I've been trying to be careful so I don't accidentally burn anything down with my untested superpowers. You're welcome, mom," he gave her a little wink.

"What were you dressed as?" Kevin tried to remember.

"Well, I started off as Daniel Larruso from the *Karate Kid*, but then I put on a Superman mask so I could go around again without anyone recognizing me. There were a few Karate Kids, so it wasn't obvious or anything. Yesterday, I tried to fly, but we think since I didn't have the cape, I didn't get that power. Still pretty cool though, huh?"

Nicki gave up trying to get Robby to shut his trap and pushed back her chair to get a drink refill. Her chair caught on the grout line in the kitchen tile and started to tip backward, almost knocking her to the floor. She flung herself forward to grab at the table, and as she did, saw a shock of pink hair fall across her eyes. "Oh goodie, this again."

"Whoa!" said Kevin. "How did you do that?"

"We don't know, her Jem costume seems to come back at weird times," responded Robby. "But we should write that down in the notes."

"Dale," began Sharon, "did you ever find out anything else about the hospital machinery? Have you talked to that tech guy who scanned our candy?"

"Yeah, he didn't know anything," Dale shrugged. "And

nobody else ever came into the hospital with anything remotely similar. I'm sorry I can't be more helpful."

"Oh well, let's finish up our food, and then we can go watch a little TV before I put these munchkins to bed. It's been a wild weekend, and I suspect tomorrow is going to be an intense day at school," she predicted. Nicki nodded her agreement while Robby gave a 'whatever' shrug and polished off the last of the popcorn shrimp.

# 8

# THE JUSTICE LEAGUE

The next morning, Rani stepped out of her house just in time to join Robby and Nicki on the walk to school. They were a house ahead, so she jogged to catch up with them, her backpack bouncing up and down as she went. Rani breathed a sigh of relief as she fell in step with her new friends. She zipped up her jacket against the chilly breeze, extremely relieved to have the company so she wouldn't have to walk up to the school by herself with her unexpected and unwelcome new look. When they got to the sidewalk leading to the building, Nicki looked around for Dominique, who usually arrived earlier since her mom had to drop her off on the way to her job.

"Geez, I hope Dom didn't really talk her mom into letting her stay home," said Nicki, still looking around. As her eyes swept the perimeter, Dominique stepped out from behind a tree on the edge of the school property. She was wearing black pants with clear jelly shoes, a Duran Duran T-shirt under a denim jacket, a solid black scarf wrapped around her head and sunglasses.

"Hey, guys," she greeted her friends with a little wave, trying to draw as little attention to herself as possible. "My mom talked to the principal this morning and got the scarf okayed. But just so you know, now the counselor wants to talk to all of us." She made a face showing her displeasure.

"Dominique, what the heck? The counselor?" said Robby, sounding more than a little put out.

Rani put a hand on his wrist and said, "You know, it's actually not a bad idea."

"Psh, well I guess it at least gets me out of class for a little while. I hope it's one I don't want to be in anyway."

Nicki gave him a skeptical look, "Please do share Robby, what class *do* you want to be in."

"That's easy, P.E.," he said as he snapped and pointed at her with a satisfied smirk on his face. While Nicki shook her head, the four of them walked into the school together.

---

The morning started with several kids and even a teacher or two asking Robby, Rani and Dominique about their new appearances. Nicki had so far been lucky that her hair hadn't changed. Javier was similarly pleased that he hadn't disappeared since he got to school, and Marcus covered up his arms and legs with long sleeves and pants. But shortly after the morning announcements and pledge, the counselor came over the loudspeaker and asked for them by name: "Robby and Nicki Swain, Jasmine Drake, Dominique Ross, Rani Gabri, Joel Jacobson, Javier Alanis and Marcus Daniels, please report to the counselor's office immediately."

"Ummmm, you're in trouble!" one smart-mouthed kid in Joel's room taunted. A few kids snickered, but most were too curious to know how to react.

The eight friends waited for each other as they made their way from their respective classrooms and gathered outside the room before they knocked on the door with the nameplate "Nancy Calvert, School Counselor" and entered.

"Hi boys and girls, come on in and please have a seat," she said in a warm voice as she gestured to the chairs in her room, a mismatched set that had obviously been expanded to accommodate the eight of them. They shuffled around and eventually settled down to stare at Mrs. Calvert and wait to see what she was going to say. Mrs. Calvert was a middle-aged woman with shoulder-length blond hair that had been permed into frizzy curls and was held back on the right side with a fluorescent green barrette. She had a kind face with brown eyes and a smile that helped even the most anxious children who passed through her doorway feel a little calmer.

"I've been made aware of your unique situation, and I wanted us all to have a chance to talk about it. First, to make sure that you're all okay, but also to determine how we're going to communicate it to the rest of the school."

Dominique groaned as she envisioned a school assembly

where they were all trotted out in front of their peers on display while Mrs. Calvert did her best Vanna White from *Wheel of Fortune* impression and gestured with her hands at each child while their principal, Mr. Goliber, individually described their transformations into a microphone.

"Please know that I will take your feelings into consideration as we figure out the best way to do that," Mrs. Calvert noted in her reassuring voice with just a touch of a southern drawl. She enunciated each word but spoke slowly so it didn't come across as antagonizing. "But I do think it's important that we address it for a couple of reasons. It will mean that each of you won't need to tell your story repeatedly. And we can also speak to our expectations for how you'll be treated by the other students at this school."

Dominique stared at her for a moment, then slumped forward in resignation. "Fine, but what are you even going to say?" she asked, not looking up from her hands in her lap. "I mean, no one will believe that we ate candy and turned into our Halloween costumes."

"You know, Miss Ross, I have been giving that some thought, but as we just found out this morning, I have not discovered a perfect solution. I was hoping that you all would have some ideas that we could look at together."

Robby informed her, "I already told some of my friends what happened in the hall before school. They didn't really seem to believe me, but maybe if you say it too, they'll have to realize I was telling the truth."

"Are you going to tell everyone about all of us? I mean,

Jazz and Joel don't even have anything obvious," Nicki pointed out.

"That's a great question, Nicki," Mrs. Calvert said in her soothing counselor voice. "Jasmine, were you affected at all?"

Jasmine looked uncomfortably at her friends out of the corner of her eye. "Not really," she said. "Nothing that anyone would ever be able to tell anyway."

Mrs. Calvert studied her for a moment and then decided, "Perhaps we shouldn't share details. Just note that the eight of you were involved in an incident and there are certain side effects of varying degrees for each of you. We will say that we expect our students to be respectful and supportive as you work to resolve the situation. Does that work?"

Jasmine shrugged just her right shoulder almost up to her ear and said, "I still think people will ask what happened to me since they can't see anything. Javi and Joel too. Eventually, they'll probably see Nicki."

"Gee, how tragic," said Dominique, her voice drowning in sarcasm. "No one can tell what happened to you. That must be rough."

"Miss Ross, my note about being respectful and supportive must start in this room with the eight of you," Mrs. Calvert's voice didn't change as she admonished her, but Dominique mumbled a semi-heartfelt, "Sorry," to Jasmine.

"Thank you for your apology," Mrs. Calvert said to Dominique. "Now I understand that Dominique is having a difficult time with these circumstances, and we're willing to make accommodations to our dress code to help her feel more comfortable while she's here in school. While we thought that allowing a hat might cause some resentment if it were only allowed for one person, we will ensure that all of the teachers know that the scarf is okay. Is there anyone else who requires special considerations? Or even some one-on-one time with me to talk through your feelings?"

"Nah, my hair is annoying with this dumb curl always in my face," Robby said as he flicked his Superman bangs, "but I don't really care what people think about it."

After each child gave Mrs. Calvert a quick update on their mental health, they were allowed to return to their rooms. Shortly after, Mr. Goliber's voice crackled over the loud-speaker to deliver the message that they had all agreed upon.

"Hello, students of Ambrose Elementary. I'm sure many of you have noticed that we had a few students involved in an incident on Halloween that had some unexpected results. They did not do anything wrong, they are not in trouble here or at home. Please treat them with respect and understanding. As usual, we will not tolerate any bullying. We hope they find a resolution quickly so we can all get back to focusing on your very important educations. If you have questions, please don't hesitate to reach out to your staff here at Ambrose. Thank you and let's have a great day, Roadrunners!"

Dominique slid down in her chair, her cheeks flaming red and tears burning the backs of her eyes, as every head in her homeroom pivoted to look at where she and Rani sat next to each other in the back of the class. She took a shaky breath and willed herself not to cry while her hands fidgeted with the buttons on her jacket. This was going to be the longest day ever.

---

Later in the cafeteria, Marcus was quizzing Nicki. "So wait, you almost fell out of your chair when your hair turned pink again?" He counted on his fingers, "First when Shmoofy barked, second when your mom said we had to tell everyone's parents, and third when you almost fell. Is that it? The only times the earrings have activated?"

Nicki nodded an affirmation.

"So I wonder if it happens when your heart rate rapidly quickens," pondered Marcus.

"I guess that could be it," said Nicki, not quite sure, but not having any better suggestions. "I'll keep track so we can test that theory."

"Technically it's a hypothesis," said Marcus.

"*Fine*, I'll keep track so we can test that *hypothesis*," said Nicki irritably.

Not helping her prickly attitude, Andrew Sanderson, a sixth-grade boy whose closet seemed to consist entirely of sports jerseys and jeans that he rolled up tight around his ankles, walked up with a swagger to their table and said, "Hey, how's it going Hallo-wieners?"

"Haha, how long have you been waiting to use that?" Nicki glared at him and then looked back at her lunch, not wanting to give him the satisfaction of seeing her ruffled.

"Well, I thought of it this morning after announcements, but then I had a pretty serious debate with myself over what was better: Hallo-wieners or Hallo-weenies. Wieners won in case you hadn't noticed," he said with a fake smile at Nicki.

She looked back at him and gave him a slow, sarcastic clap. "I can tell you're very proud of yourself. Good job, Andrew." Dominique snorted a laugh while Andrew's eyes flared and he turned his attention to her.

"What's wrong Little Orphan Annie?" he spat at her. "Did you get a fur ball from these mongrels who followed you back to the orphanage?"

Dominique hid a laugh behind her hand, which startled Andrew. In fact, no one at the table was reacting how he expected, they were all smiling or laughing, and suddenly he realized that someone was standing behind him.

"Mr. Sanderson, is that your idea of supporting our class-mates?" Mrs. Calvert asked him in a pseudo-pleasant voice. "If so, I'm afraid we need to spend a little time together talking about appropriate ways to treat our fellow students. Why don't you come to my office after your lunch period, I'll notify your teacher that you'll be late returning to class." He threw a venomous look over his shoulder at Dominique and Nicki and stomped back to his own table to tell his friends about the horrible injustice he had just suffered while muttering "freaks" under his breath, just low enough that no adults could hear over the buzz in the cafeteria.

"Are we doing alright here?" Mrs. Calvert asked the group as she placed her hand on Dominique's shoulder.

"Yes, Mrs. Calvert, thank you for checking on us," said Nicki, hoping she would go away quickly so they could resume their conversation. When she did just that, Joel asked, "Why would your heart rate quicken when your mom said that we had to call our parents?"

"I just panicked because I didn't want anyone's parents to be mad at us and tell you guys that you aren't allowed to hang out with us anymore. It's already hard with a single mom, she has to handle all of the battles, so sometimes I just sort of freak out when stuff like that happens."

"That makes sense and lends credibility to my hypothesis," Marcus said in a voice devoid of emotion that seemed out of touch with the confession Nicki had just made.

"Seriously Marcus," said Joel shaking his head, "are you just going to turn into a total robot?"

Marcus blinked rapidly a few times, coming out of his analytical haze and gave Joel a confused look. But then the bell rang and everyone had to scurry to pack up their lunchboxes and get back to their classrooms. "Meet out front after school!" Javier shouted to his friends over the buzz of noise that inevitably bubbles up when a herd of students all start to migrate at the same time. But it was unnecessary because nearly everyone was counting the minutes until they could reunite and talk about their day back in the storm shelter.

Out on the front steps of the school, the sun hid behind a layer of gray clouds and a cooler breeze inspired everyone to put on their jackets for the walk home. The group had just gathered their last member, this time it was Rani who had to stay for a moment after class to learn about an assignment that was already in progress when she had started at Ambrose Elementary. "Thank you for waiting for me, you guys," she said with heartfelt gratitude.

"Of course! You're one of us," said Jasmine with a smile, flipping her curly ponytail behind her shoulder.

"You know, I've been thinking," said Robby.

"Uh oh, watch out everyone," Nicki jabbed at her brother both verbally and with her fingers in his ribs.

"Ha ha, you're hilarious," he responded, swatting her away. "Seriously though, Andrew was being a mega jerk, but I think we should have a group name. Like The Justice League or The Rebels in *Star Wars*."

"Hey guys," interrupted Joel. "I'm totally cool with this idea, but have you noticed that silver car right behind us? I swear it's following us."

Robby, never one for subtlety, whipped his head around saying, "Where?" But Joel didn't need to answer because the old man in the front seat with the crazy gray hair was looking at them as he manually rolled down the window of his older model sedan and gestured toward the group.

"Oh wow, this is like, total stranger danger," said Dominique as the kids sped up and kept walking toward

Joel's house while Nicki sang the chorus of Rockwell's "Some-body's Watching Me" under her breath.

"Hey, um...kids," said the man as he realized he didn't know any of their names and had no more effective way to summon them. Joel turned to his friends and whispered, "Let's split up, he can't follow us all. Either go to your own house first if he follows you or meet at Home Base. Everyone ready?" He received a series of tense nods. "Go!"

As the kids scattered, the man in the car heaved an exasperated sigh and tried to keep an eye on at least one of the children. He swore there had been eight of them, but in the blink of an eye, there were only six. Rani and Marcus had disappeared using their newfound ability to run way faster than your average human. All of the kids ran in different directions, the boys hopping over fences and running through yards while the girls stayed mostly on the sidewalk, but split up to head down different side streets. Within ten minutes, all eight children were back in the bunker, some breathing heavily and sweating profusely. Rani was the first back and sat twirling the end of her long blonde hair as though she had only been out for a leisurely stroll. Marcus, who had taken a more circuitous route, showed up a few moments behind her and the others trickled in as they made their way through the neighborhood and to Joel's backyard.

"Did you lose him?" Rani asked Javier nervously as he was the last to enter the bunker.

"I'm pretty sure," he said, just a few seconds before they heard a tentative knock on the door. Nicki and Dominique screamed, Jasmine slapped her hands over their mouths to muffle the noise, but it was too late. While the heavy steel did make it difficult to communicate effectively, piercing fifth-grade girl squeals were hard to cover completely.

"Guys, I just want to talk," yelled the muffled voice from the other side of the door.

"Robby, did you ever check out those kung fu moves?" Marcus asked his friend.

"A little. I can take this guy," he said confidently. He flung open the door and delivered a swift Karate Kid-style Crane Kick right under the jaw of the man standing there. The man's eyelids fluttered as his brain fought to remain conscious. Meanwhile, the kids dragged him into the bunker and put him in the back corner so he couldn't get away before they figured out what he wanted. After he shook off the effects of the kick, he looked at the kids and said, "Look, I'm here to help you. Or see if you can help me."

"Why would we help you when you're trying to kidnap us?" asked Dominique.

"What? No, that's not what I was doing. I'm trying to help you with your Halloween issue."

The kids all stared silently for a moment. "Who are you and how do you know about that?" asked Marcus finally.

"I work at the hospital with Dale, I'm the one who X-rayed your candy."

Each of the kids studied his face and realized that, while his hair was decidedly different, he did have the same face. And it was a young face, not that of an old man, it was only the hair that gave that impression. Marcus and his ability to analyze data as quickly as a robot was the first to put two and two together. "You ate some of our candy."

Chad nodded slowly as he looked around at the kids who held him captive. "And I want to figure out how to fix it. But I don't trust Dale, so I wanted to talk to you guys first."

"Why don't you trust Dale?" Nicki asked, her voice rising with concern. She didn't particularly want Dale to know too many details about their situation, but it was interesting that a coworker also didn't trust him.

"I don't know, just a feeling I have."

"But you do want to help us?" Joel asked skeptically.

"No, he wants to help himself and he thinks we know something," said Marcus, intuiting the real reason for this conversation. Chad didn't move or speak, so finally Marcus turned to the girls and said, "Dominique, I need you to go get the Lasso of Truth before we interrogate this guy. Nicki, go with her so you can let her in your house and so she's not alone." The girls didn't even question their brother's friend ordering them around, they immediately got up to go get the one tool that would make them all feel a little better about entering into an alliance with this stranger.

Once they left, Javier asked, "How old are you anyway?"

Chad looked surprised at the question, but answered, "I'm twenty-three. I finished college a year ago and I've been working at the hospital since." Javier nodded thoughtfully. "So what else happened besides your hair changing?"

"What do you mean?"

Marcus didn't answer Chad's question but asked one of his own. "What did you dress as for Halloween after you left the hospital?"

"I didn't really, I just left on my lab coat and took a beaker to the party I was going to. I was a mad scientist."

"Original," said Robby derisively.

"I'm not that into Halloween, it was just a party that some of my old college friends were having, and I wanted to pop by after I did all the X-rays."

"How much candy did you eat?" Marcus followed up.

"Just one piece. It was a mini Snickers," Chad anticipated his line of thought.

"So back to my question, what else changed for you?" jumped in Javier.

"Nothing that I know of," he said uncertainly. At that moment, the girls stepped back in with the Lasso of Truth. Chad looked at them and asked, "What's that all about?"

Robby rushed to explain, "Dominique had the lasso with her when she ate the Halloween candy. Now it actually works. And since none of us know you, we thought it would be a good idea to have, what are those lie detector thingies called?" He looked to Marcus.

"Polygraph."

"Yeah, we thought it would be good to have a polygraph test to see what we're working with here."

Chad nodded along. "Okay, fair enough. I have only good intentions, what do I have to do?"

"We'll see about that," said Dominique as she manually

wrapped the rope around his waist (there was no room in the bunker to swing it like an actual lasso).

"Why are you here?" she asked him as she held onto the end of the rope.

"Because I don't know what else to do. And I don't know who to trust."

Javier, a bit obsessed, asked for a third time, "What else changed for you after you woke up on Saturday?"

"Well the first thing I noticed was my hair," Chad looked at each person in the bunker as he told his story. "I was really confused because I hadn't had a crazy night or anything. Maybe one beer. I knew I hadn't dyed my hair and that no one else had messed with it. But I didn't notice any other physical transformations. The only other thing…," he hesitated and Dominique pulled the lasso a little tighter. "It's not a lie, I just don't know how to explain it. It's like my mind operates a little differently?" he said with an upward inflection to his voice like he was asking a question.

Marcus crossed his arms and said, "Like you're more analytical or can see many possibilities all at once?"

Chad slowly shook his head from side to side. "Not quite, it's more like I can look at something and see the chemical compounds that make it up. Or I see math equations. For example, when I drive, I can tell how far I need to go and at what rate I'm driving and calculate exactly how long it will take me to get there."

"So you've basically turned into Einstein," said Joel.

"I wouldn't go that far, but there are things that I can't

explain. Nothing horrible, in fact, if the higher level of math and science aptitude stuck, I'd be okay. But at the very least, I'd like my normal hair back," he said this as his eyes darted to Dominique's red curls and then quickly looked away.

"I saw that," she mumbled.

"So what do we do now?" asked Nicki.

"Before we put the lasso on, you said that you only have good intentions," Marcus resumed the role of interrogator. "Is that true?"

"I don't mean any of you harm. I'll admit, it's mostly selfish reasons. There's a cute nurse at the hospital and I don't want her to see me like this. Geez, can you take this thing off already?" he asked tugging at the lasso. He had never told anyone about his crush and was embarrassed that his mouth seemed to have a mind of its own.

"Not yet," Nicki interjected. "Why don't you trust Dale? He's dating our mom and if there's a problem, I'd like to know about it."

"I honestly can't tell you," Chad shrugged, but looked Nicki directly in the eyes, imploring her to believe him. "He comes across as this nice guy, but he's always kind of given me the creeps. And he's constantly defending the super crappy machinery we have at the hospital. It's all Russian and barely works. I think maybe he got some kickbacks when he bought it."

"What's a kickback?" asked Javier.

"You know, like the hospital gave him a certain amount of money to buy equipment and he bought cheap stuff from some Russian company and kept the difference," explained Chad. "Look, I have no proof of that, so don't say anything to your mom, okay?" Nicki narrowed her eyes at him as she thought this over, but eventually gave one quick nod. Chad continued, "You guys asked what else happened. And you have this lasso. So can I assume that you all have more symptoms than meets the eye?"

"I don't know that I'd call them symptoms," said Joel. "It's not like we have a sickness."

"Really?" asked Dominique with her eyebrows practically meeting her red, curly hairline. "I'd say it's exactly like an infection and we each have our own symptoms."

"Geez Dominique, it's not like you were dressed as a zombie and woke up with green skin and open wounds. You're a redhead, get over it already," said Robby.

Dominique leveled him with a withering stare. "I don't care about the color. My hair was long and thick and glossy. Thanks to that stupid wig, now it's thin and course and ugly!"

Marcus acted as though this exchange hadn't taken place and addressed Chad, "We have some notes. Perhaps if we compared ours to yours, we can come up with some sort of resolution. I know most of us would like to reverse this if at all possible."

"Yes, I have notes back at my apartment. It's not much, but I at least have some information about the settings on the machine that I doubt you have."

"That's great," agreed Marcus enthusiastically. "We need

to compile everything we have and then start to put together some ideas. When can we meet?"

"You can come back to my apartment now," offered Chad.

"Yeah, that's not going to happen," said Nicki. "First of all, we have to be home by the time my mom gets back from work at 5 o'clock, and second, you're kind of a stranger."

Chad mulled this over. "Okay, well I have to work the next few days and it's late for you guys by the time I get off. Why don't I write down my notes and leave them in here for you to see tomorrow after school? I can drop them off on my way to work. Then you can make a copy of your notes and share them with me. We'll get together this weekend to compare and make a plan for reversal."

"This *weekend*?!" Dominique shrieked. "There is no way I can wait that long!"

"Me neither," Rani said, "I'll be at my dad's this weekend."

Marcus turned to them and said, "You might not have to. Once we have…" he turned to Chad as something occurred to him and asked, "I'm sorry, I forgot your name."

"Chad."

"Once we have Chad's notes, we can start to figure some of this out. But we need everyone to meet here again tomorrow after school, and I'll bring the notepad. Deal?"

Everyone was quick to agree. Dominique took the lasso off of Chad and wound it back up around her arm from her palm to her elbow.

"Well Chad," said Jasmine, "It was nice to meet you."

He looked startled at the sudden change in tone, but then

nodded and said, "You guys, too. Although I didn't actually meet you." As they exited the bunker, everyone introduced themselves to Chad and then headed home for dinner, eager to get some rest after one of the most exhausting days of their young lives.

# 9

# PRETEEN MUTANTS

The next morning, Chad delivered on his promise and parked in front of Joel's house. He looked in his rearview mirror and carefully tucked a few loose strands of grey hair under his St. David's Hospital baseball cap. Eyeing the windows and front door for any signs of life, he deemed it empty then quickly walked into the backyard with his head down, hands in his pockets and shoulders slumped trying to look as inconspicuous as possible.

Half expecting the door to the bunker to be locked, he breathed a sigh of relief when it opened easily. He slipped into the shelter and placed the envelope with his notes on the corner of the bench where he had sat the previous day.

Although Chad was in a hurry to get to work, he hesitated a moment and stood looking at the corner of the space, eyes unfocused, remembering the events from yesterday. As strange as it was for him to try to understand what had happened to his hair and thought process, the Lasso of Truth was a whole different level of unfathomable.

Glancing down at his calculator watch, he realized that he needed to hurry to make his shift at the hospital. As he looked down, he caught a glimpse of yellow under the bench. He crouched on his hands and knees to get a better look. Blowing a tuft of hair out of his eyes, he reached out and picked up a piece of yellow notepaper that was lying amongst a couple of dust bunnies. It was folded into a small rectangle (2.75 inches by 2.125 inches he mentally noted) and had his name clearly written in black marker. Carefully unfolding it, he noticed it was actually two pieces of yellow paper. He bent over so he could lay them on the bench and used his hands to press out the wrinkles, making them as flat as possible. Standing back up in the center of the bunker, he read:

*Mr. Chad,*

*If you're reading this, then I'm hoping it means you were able to come by with your notes. I thought it would be most efficient if you also had ours, so here is a copy of what we know so far.*

Chad's eyes skimmed the two pages with increasing awe. Not even through the first page, he reached behind himself to find the bench without taking his eyes off of Marcus's notes. He slowly sank down onto it as he tried to process what he was reading. Physical attributes changed, superpowers, plastic weapons that took on the properties of their television and movie counterparts. How could this be real? Eventually, he realized that he had to leave now and would still be late, so he carefully refolded the pages and pushed them all the way down into the back pocket of his jeans to review more closely when he had time later. Then he rushed out of the bunker, making sure to close the door all the way, and raced back to his car.

---

Chad parked in the back of the hospital parking lot, he wasn't important enough to warrant a designated parking space at the front. He half jogged toward the building using one hand to hold the bill of his cap in place and the other to trap the strap of his workbag against his shoulder.

He flashed his badge at the door behind the receptionist and again at the door to his room, then quickly hung his workbag on the back of the door before racing into the staff room to clock in. He pulled up short when he saw Dale sitting at the table where people took their breaks, sipping a coffee and reading a newspaper.

"Hey Dale," he said, trying to sound casual as he tucked some more stray hair under the baseball cap.

"Hey Chad, I've been waiting for you."

"Oh really? I stopped by my room to drop off my bag and check on a couple of things first."

Dale looked at him, on the verge of noting that Chad was late and wearing a hat that didn't necessarily follow the hospital dress code, but then switched tactics. "So, any other strange occurrences over your weekend?"

"Nope."

"Good, that's great," Dale nodded as he assessed Chad, trying to determine if he was telling the truth. "I haven't heard any other reports of unexplainable happenings, so that's good for the hospital."

"Definitely," Chad shuffled his feet nervously.

"Chad," Dale smiled, trying to look approachable. "You aren't going to sue the hospital for what happened, are you?"

"What? No, I...I hadn't thought about it actually. I've just been trying to figure out if there's a way to reverse it."

"Really?" Dale displayed more interest than he'd ever shown in Chad. He put his coffee down and leaned forward to stare intently at the lab technician with his arms crossed on the table, making Chad even more nervous. "Do you have a plan?"

Chad started walking toward the machine to check-in for his shift. "Not really, not yet. I'm still gathering information."

"Like what?" Dale inquired. Chad could have kicked himself. He really wanted this conversation to end. He moved over to the coffee machine and grabbed a white Styrofoam cup, which he filled about three-quarters of the way full and then added a good deal of cream and sugar.

"Oh you know," he stalled to figure out what to say as he used a thin, red straw to stir his coffee. He finished stirring, licked off the end of the straw and threw it in the trash. "Like what setting the machine was on, what kind of candy I ate, that sort of thing." He shrugged like it was no big deal.

"Sounds promising," Dale said, giving Chad a little smile. "Let me know if I can help."

"Will do," Chad took his coffee and walked back to his room where he shut the door and breathed a deep sigh of relief to be alone again.

---

"Good morning, Roadrunners! This is your principal, Mr. Goliber, here to welcome you to another great day at Ambrose Elementary. Before we get to the pledge, I wanted to start with an announcement about the Texas Sesquicentennial in Grayson Ridge this weekend. As you know, our great state turns 150 years old this year. There will be a celebration in town by the gazebo with food, rides and live performances. As a gift from the mayor, each student in our school will receive one ticket for free admission to the festival for this Saturday. We hope to see you there! Now if everyone will please stand and follow me in the Pledge of Allegiance."

---

A little while later in the school cafeteria, the eight friends once again congregated at their table. Naturally, they were split down the middle of the table by gender.

"I was thinking we could make our group name something after a cool band," Nicki said as they all unpacked their lunches and started eating. "Something like 'The Costume Club' after The Culture Club."

"Look Nicki," said Robby before anyone else could

comment, "no offense, but you got to name the dog and we've been stuck with that stupid name forever. You don't get to pick this name too!"

"Hey, Shmoofy is a great name! Besides, you never even call him by it anyway," Nicki was quick to defend. Robby just rolled his eyes.

"What about The All Hallows League like The Justice League," suggested Joel.

"That doesn't work. All Hallows Day is November 1. All Hallows *Eve* is Halloween," Marcus corrected.

"Well technically we didn't find out about our issue until November 1, so it still kind of makes sense," Dominique pointed out. "Although I think we should name ourselves something a little more fresh."

"Like what?" asked Jasmine.

"I don't know, it just needs to sound choice, to make up for the fact that the actual situation is so ridiculous."

"I like The Punk Squad," Javier exclaimed with his usual gusto and a flourish of his hands.

"But we're not punks," said Rani confused.

"Oh, yeah," his face fell. "I was thinking like short for pumpkins, but you're right, that's confusing."

"That would be The Pumps Squad, which is even more heinous," Dominique said dismissively.

"Harsh! Okay, then what's your idea?" Javier asked a bit testily. He still hadn't forgiven her for the stunt with the Lasso of Truth and wasn't in the mood to take any more jabs from her. "Because I don't know about you, but I'm not getting either of Andrew's Hallo-wiener names printed on a T-shirt."

"Why don't we each come up with a name to suggest by the time we meet at the bunker this afternoon and we'll vote," suggested Rani.

"That seems fair," agreed Jasmine and the others nodded. "By the way, Rani, didn't you say that you're going to be at your dad's this weekend?"

"Yeah, I'm really freaking out too. At least here, I have you guys. At my dad's, I'm not even sure people around there know what happened to us. And of course, there's also the problem of my dad being extremely mad. Mom is supportive, but I have a feeling my dad is just going to spaz out all weekend. I am *really* not looking forward to it."

"I'm sorry, I know," Jasmine said sympathetically. "But I did have a thought during announcements this morning. Do you think you could get your dad to bring you to the Sesqui-centennial? It would get you out of the house and maybe he would see that you have some really great new friends here."

"I don't know," Rani sounded extraordinarily skeptical. "It doesn't sound like something he'd do, but I'll definitely try."

"I would tell him you get extra credit for school if you go," Robby suggested.

"Ha! Don't listen to him," advised Nicki. "He'll get you in trouble. But make sure you take your free ticket when you pack to go to his house. Maybe it will help if he sees that the school is supporting it."

"Thanks guys, I'll do my best. Wish me luck!"

Dr. Kenneth Ashland was a short man in his late fifties who had been the ophthalmologist for Grayson Ridge and some of the smaller rural towns in the area for more than twenty years. He was a balding man with a fringe of graying hair and a matching mustache. He got Kevin situated in a room full of equipment designed to diagnose and solve a variety of eye and vision issues.

"Look through the lens and tell me which one is more clear, A or B," Dr. Ashland guided Kevin.

"A," Kevin determined for the first slide. The doctor went through a series of slides as he tested Kevin's good eye and then moved him to a chair in front of a different machine.

"Okay, please remove your eye patch and set your chin on the brace with your forehead on the other support right here," he directed, tapping the black bar that would hold Kevin's head still for the next assessment. "You're going to feel a puff of air when I count to three."

They continued through the series of tests, moving from machine to machine before ending with Kevin tracking a pin light that Dr. Ashland moved from side to side.

The doctor turned to Dale to include him in his initial assessment. "Well, the good news is there is nothing wrong with the structure of the eye itself. No infection or hardening of the tissue."

"That's good," said Dale. "So what's the problem?"

"That's what's so strange," said the doctor, turning to look at Kevin again. "There is no visible reason for you to be experiencing such an intense irritation. I'm prescribing some drops for you to apply four times a day that will ensure your eye stays moist and it has an antibiotic in case there is an underlying infection. If it's still bothering you, keep the patch on when you leave the house. I'd like to see you again in a week to check how that's working."

"Is this cause for concern? It sounds like you're guessing," Dale had been searching for a more definitive answer.

"I will admit it's very strange. There are very few things that come across my path that I am not familiar with, but it does happen in the medical industry. Viruses and infections are inclined to mutate, even for eyes, so it's possible this is a new issue."

"Mutate?" Dale accidentally burst out loud. The word struck a chord with him that reminded him Kevin had been in the house with the candy the night of Halloween.

"Yes, I'm sure you're used to that coming from the hospital?" The doctor seemed confused by the abrupt outburst.

"Yes, of course," Dale tried to cover. "We'll be sure to pick up the drops and get those started right away. Is that all?" He was suddenly in a hurry to get out of the doctor's office.

"I'll call in the prescription now, and you should be able to pick it up by tonight."

"Thank you, doctor," Dale shook Dr. Ashland's hand and then moved to place his palm on Kevin's shoulder to guide him out of the room quickly.

"What was that all about?" Kevin asked as they walked past the receptionist desk.

"Hang on," Dale instructed his son.

When they were back in the car, instead of turning it on, Dale turned to Kevin and asked him, "Did you eat any candy on Halloween?"

"Um...I don't remember," Kevin responded, perplexed by the odd change in subject.

"It's important. Think!" Dale commanded.

"Alright, geez. Ahhh, I think I had some from Robby's pile. A chocolate bar of some sort and maybe some Skittles."

"And you were still wearing your work uniform?"

"What? Yeah, I guess. Yeah." Kevin gave his dad a look that said he clearly thought the old man was losing his marbles. "Why are you asking me such weird questions?"

"Let's go home, and I'll tell you."

"And what does any of this have to do with my eye?"

"Wait until we get home."

"Why? Just tell me."

"Fine. So there's been some stuff going on at Sharon's."

"Yeah, I know, I saw Robby's hair and the thing with Nicki when we had dinner there," Kevin prompted.

"Oh right, sorry," Dale issued a perfunctory apology as he spun the steering wheel to make a left turn and head toward home. "I'm trying to drive and think and there's just a lot going on. That's why I wanted to wait until we got home. But I think something happened with the X-ray machine that night they came in to somehow alter the candy. I suspect what's happening to your eye is related and has something to do with the pirate uniform you were wearing."

Kevin paused long enough that Dale stole a quick glance at his son to make sure he was still listening before returning his eyes to the road.

"You're serious," Kevin said to his dad, more a statement than a question. Dale just nodded. "So that's why Sharon was asking you about the X-ray machine at dinner the other night. I knew buying that Commie crap was going to get you in trouble," Kevin said referring to the Russian machinery he knew his dad had purchased for the hospital. He crossed his arms over his chest and sank down in his seat with a huff.

"That's not helpful," said Dale, a frosty edge in his voice.

"It wasn't intended to be," Kevin snapped back. "What have you done to me? How do we fix it?"

"I'm not sure yet. I'm trying to figure that out."

"Figure it out faster, I don't want to be some pirate freak for the rest of my life!" Kevin turned away from his dad to look out the window with his one good eye and sulked all the way back home.

———

As the kids filed into the bunker after school on Tuesday, Marcus saw the envelope in the corner and immediately started to open it.

"Okay, so what names have we got?" Javier asked everyone as they squeezed into the available seating in the bunker.

"Hang on," said Marcus, "Chad dropped off his notes."

"Cool, anything useful?" asked Dominique hopefully, looking over Marcus's shoulder at the chicken scratch that Chad had made on a blank piece of white paper for them. "What are all those numbers?"

"These are the settings that were on the X-ray machine."

"Does he have anything else we didn't already know?" Joel directed his question to Marcus.

"He did make a note about Jasmine's crystal ball. He mentioned that there was glass and granite in the machine the first time he ran it on our bag."

Jasmine jumped in to note, "It isn't granite, it's moonstone. I'm not sure that makes a difference."

"It might," said Marcus. "I mean, let's face it, we're dealing with some really weird and unexplainable occurrences, we can't overlook anything."

"Does anyone know what phase the moon was in that night?" Jasmine started thinking out loud.

"What does that matter?" Dominique wanted to know.

"I'm not sure it does, but if Marcus says we can't overlook anything, I was just thinking maybe the moonstone somehow reacted to a particular phase of the moon."

"Didn't you say something about a cat's eye that night when you saw the moon?" remembered Nicki.

"Yes! So what phase is that?" Jasmine turned to Marcus.

"Well, it was probably either a waxing or waning crescent moon. If we can figure out what phase it's in tonight, I can tell you for sure."

"So, if we went at the opposite phase and took all the same steps as last time, do you think it would reverse?" Dominique wondered aloud.

Joel, who frequently took things very literally, asked, "How do we dress as ourselves?"

"What do you mean?" Dominique looked perplexed.

"Well, before we dressed up as our characters to turn into what we are now. In order to take the same steps as we took last time, would you have to get like a long, black wig? And how does Javier dress as 'not a ghost?'"

"Oh, I get it. That's a good question, what do you guys think?" Dominique looked around the room for some words of wisdom.

"We're putting a lot of faith in this whole moonstone theory," said Marcus skeptically, rubbing his chin as he voiced his concern.

"Do you have anything better?" Dominique snapped. "We have to try something!"

"Okay, okay, just let me give it some thought. I need to make sure our plan makes sense before we bother running any experiments."

"In the meantime," said Javier, "what names did everyone come up with?"

"Geez, Javi, obsess much?" asked Nicki laughing and shaking her head, causing Javier to blush bright red.

"Actually, I did have an idea," said Joel. "What do you think about The Atomic 8 since there are eight of us?"

"Hmmm, I was thinking more Halloween related names," said Nicki slowly, "but I like it."

"I like Short Circuit," said Javier. "Like that movie that just came out with the robot that gets zapped in the lab and comes to life since that's kind of like what happened to us!"

"Oh, that's a good one too! Someone should write these down," Jasmine said. Nicki took her Trapper Keeper out of her backpack. The front originally had a rainbow that ended in hearts corresponding to each color, but you could barely see it for all the stickers that she had pasted on every available surface. Many of the stickers were peeling off due to the several times each day it got shoved into her backpack or cubby and then dragged back out. She extracted a multi-colored pen and pushed down the lever to drop the purple ink into place, then turned to a fresh sheet of paper at the back to start keeping track of the suggestions.

"Okay, I've got Joel with Atomic 8, Javi with Short Circuit, what else?"

"Instead of Atomic 8, why don't we call ourselves 8-tomic?" Robby pitched in.

Dominique countered, "I was thinking Dare Devils, because you know, Halloween, Devils, and I seriously *dare* anyone to say a word about my hair to my face."

"Okay, got it," Nicki was writing quickly to keep up with her friends' suggestions.

"What name did you decide on, Nicki?" asked Javier.

"Okay, are you ready for it? Motley Boo," she said with a flourish of the hand holding the pen. "You know, like Motley

Crue? Which we basically are a motley crew right now. Except with a Halloween twist."

"I get where you're trying to go with it," said Dominique rolling it around in her mind, but not committing to anything out loud yet. "Okay Marcus, your turn."

"I'm sorry guys, I was actually still working on the solution and sort of forgot to come up with a name."

"Okay, Rani then," Dominique turned to the one person who hadn't made a suggestion yet.

Rani suddenly looked embarrassed. "Well, you know how X-rays are a form of electromagnetic radiation?" Marcus nodded, encouraging her to go on even though everyone else glanced around with quizzical looks on their faces. "I was thinking we could be something like Radi-ate," she spelled it out on Nicki's paper so they could see how she incorporated the number into the word 'Radi-eight.' "We could even do something fun with a logo like RA-D8."

"That reminds me of R2-D2. Boys and girls, I think we have a team name," said Robby, totally sold.

"Hey, we have to vote," Nicki chastised her brother. She tore a piece of paper out of her notebook, folded it three times and used her fingernail to create hard creases, then tore it into eight pieces. She handed them out and each child passed around her pen to mark their preference. When all of the pieces of paper had been collected and reviewed, Radi-eight emerged as the clear winner.

"Awesome, well are you happy now Javi?" Nicki gave him

a little wink to show she was kidding. He blushed in response but gave her a shy smile back.

"I bet my mom could make us T-shirts," said Nicki as she put away her school supplies. "She's really crafty."

"I would wear one," said Jasmine.

"Me too," said Joel.

"Okay, well how about we all get plain T-shirts that she can work with and I'll talk to her about making them for us," Nicki said to a round of agreement.

"Great, now that's settled, I want to share what I've been thinking," Marcus tried to bring everyone's attention back to more serious matters.

"Yes, go!" said Dominique, hoping he had a foolproof master plan.

"I think there might be something to your moon-stone/moon phase theory," Marcus said to Jasmine.

"Don't you mean hypothesis?" Nicki couldn't resist a snarky comment.

"Yes, exactly," said Marcus. "It defies all scientific reasoning, but so does this whole situation in general. So knowing that this appears to be limited to our group, Shmoofy and Chad, it had to be more than just the machine or everyone who had X-rayed candy that night would be running around with the same problem. And the main difference that we know occurred was the crystal ball inside the bag the first time it was X-rayed. Does everyone agree?"

"So, if I hadn't left my crystal ball in the pillowcase, none of this would have happened?" Jasmine looked near tears.

"We don't know, it's just the most reasonable assumption based on the details that we have available at this time. You do still have the crystal ball, correct?"

"Of course! It's in my room with the rest of my costume," Jasmine assured her friends.

"Okay, then we need to figure out what else is necessary to recreate the exact scenario. Javier, you still have your pillowcase, right?"

"Yep!"

"We'll need to get some more candy."

"Wait, if we're trying to reverse it, should we use the already infected candy?" asked Dominique.

"Interesting," Marcus mulled this over. "There's still enough left for each of us and Chad to have a piece, right?"

"Yeah, remember my mom only let us have one piece of each kind that night, so there's like a whole bowl full left," Nicki responded. "Also, don't forget Shmoofy."

"Aw man, I was hoping to keep Muffin with the moo. It's way cool," said Robby.

"Wait..." Rani lifted a finger to request silence so she could think. "That guy Dale, his kid took some of the candy, remember? I thought about it when you were talking about how much was left and I remember he said we could spare some for his Halloween tax or whatever."

"Yeah, but he wasn't wearing a costume," said Joel.

"Oh my gosh, you guys," Nicki slapped her hands over her mouth and her voice had changed to one that sounded almost frightened, creating a stir among the rest of the group.

"He kind of was," she continued in a hushed voice. "He had on that Black Beard's Fish Tavern uniform and when he came to our house the other night for dinner, he had on an eye patch and said he couldn't take it off because he had some kind of infection."

"You're right," Robby confirmed.

"We already know work uniforms had a similar effect as our costumes, thanks to Chad," pointed out Marcus.

"What does that mean?" asked Javier.

Nicki shook her head slowly back and forth as she tried to figure it out. "I don't know, but Dale must know more than he's telling us. Think about it, his girlfriend's kids, his co-worker and his son all have basically the same issue? Robby, I think we need to talk to mom about this."

No one disagreed.

At the Swain dinner table that night, Nicki tried to broach the subject carefully. Her mom was really tired and looked pinched around the eyes like she hadn't slept or maybe had a headache. Probably both.

"Mom, have you heard anything else about Kevin and his eye?" Nicki asked with a fabricated nonchalance as she took a bite of mashed potatoes drenched in butter.

"No honey, why? What made you think of that?"

"Well, the guys and I were talking and it just seems weird

that he was dressed like a pirate, ate some of our candy and now he needs an eye patch."

Sharon pondered this as she finished making her own plate at the counter and then walked over to the table to sit with her two children. "Yes, I suppose it could be related."

Nicki tread even more carefully as she shared the next bit of information. "We also sort of talked to that lab tech guy who X-rayed our candy. It turns out he took a piece and woke up the next morning with some crazy mad scientist hair since he was wearing his lab coat when he ate it."

"What? When did you talk to him?" Sharon immediately sounded anxious at the idea of her children talking to a virtual stranger without her knowing.

"He found us after school one day. I guess something Dale said let him know that we also had problems and so he came to talk to us. I know we shouldn't talk to strangers, but there were eight of us and one of him and it turned out okay, so I hope we aren't in trouble," she said smiling and batting her lashes in a way she thought was endearing. Sharon stared at her with a severe mom scowl, but then she started drawing the same conclusions that her daughter had.

"Then Dale knows about this tech guy, his son and you guys, and he hasn't said anything to me?"

Nicki hated hearing the betrayal in her mother's voice. "I don't know for sure, but that's what we were thinking. I'm so sorry mom, I know you like him."

"Yeah, I did."

After the dishes had been cleared away, the kids moved into the living room to watch *ALF* on television. Sharon asked her neighbor Alisha to come over for a drink so she could think through the news about Dale with another adult. Rani joined Nicki and Robby in the living room while the ladies meandered into the kitchen where Sharon explained the most recent discovery to her new friend.

"So you think Dale knows all of this and isn't sharing because…" Alisha's voice trailed off and she took a sip from her glass while she studied Sharon across the kitchen table.

"I don't know. Why wouldn't he tell me? He knows I'm going out of my mind trying to figure this out!" The anxiety in Sharon's voice was obvious, she was just barely on the safe side of hysterical.

"Well, maybe that's why he isn't telling you. He knows you're stressed and it sounds like the symptoms of the tech guy and the son are mild at best. Or maybe he's up to something nefarious. I honestly don't know."

"Do you think I should confront him?"

Alisha thought for a moment before answering, tapping her index finger on the table lightly. "I think it makes sense to ask him about the son. We should be careful about the tech. We don't want to get that guy in trouble at work. It sounds like the way he approached the kids was a little sketchy. Honestly, I'm not happy about it, but I guess all's well that ends well. But it is something I'd prefer we not share with

Rani's dad. He's already livid and strange adults following her around after school won't help matters."

Sharon sighed and twirled her glass by the stem as she watched the red liquid swirl around. "I really appreciate you coming over. I get so busy that I don't do a good job keeping up with my friendships and even if I had a close friend, I'm not sure I could talk to them about this unless their kid was one of the infected."

Alisha reached across the table and put her hand on top of Sharon's. "I feel the same way. Moving, even just one town over, was scary. And as much as I hate all of this, the silver lining is that both Rani and I have made some close new friends very quickly." The ladies shared a small, sad smile.

Alisha continued, "You know, Rani was telling me that the kids are working on coming up with a solution. Marcus has an idea, but it requires the use of the same X-ray machine that initially examined the candy. It sounds beyond crazy, but at this point, nothing makes any sense, so why not go with it. I think all of that will be easier if we stay on Dale's good side, so if you want my advice, I'd say proceed with caution if you decide on any sort of confrontation."

Sharon was silent for a moment while she took another sip from her glass. She eventually nodded and said, "You're right, thank you for keeping me sane."

"Well let's not go that far," Alisha said with a tinkling laugh that almost caused Sharon to spit out her beverage as she cracked up.

## 10

## NEWFOUND POWERS

Wednesday morning, the fifth-grade students in Mr. Graff's physical education class were lined up in even rows and columns around the gymnasium. Mr. Graff was still in his small office, just to the right of the door leading into the gym. It was barely large enough for his desk and the obligatory shelf full of trophies. While he wrapped up a phone call, the students were seated and chattering with their closest neighbors. The hardwood floor and high ceilings bounced the sound around, so although no one was speaking particularly loudly, it was noisy in the gym.

Mr. Graff wrapped up his call, walked out of his office, blew his whistle in two short bursts and addressed the students. "Alright class, today we practice for our fitness test. We'll be doing shuttle runs, jump rope and push-ups. I have three stations set up: jump rope and push-ups to the right and shuttle runs along the sidewall to the left. Everyone count off starting with Jessica. Go!"

The students went up and down the rows, counting from one to three and then starting over to determine which activity they would take on first. Once everyone was in their respective groups, Mr. Graff walked around providing pointers on how to build their stamina in preparation for the state fitness test that was required twice per year, the next one coming up just before school let out for the winter break.

Dominique and Rani managed to get in the same group and were next to each other doing push-ups, carrying on a conversation as quietly as possible in the echoing gymnasium. After a full minute of push-ups, Rani was still going at a steady pace and telling Dominique about the new Madonna album her mom had bought her. "So there's this one song called 'Papa, Don't Preach,' and I haven't really listened to all of the lyrics, so I'm not sure what it's about, but when I listen to that part, I totally get why Nicki loves to sing so much. I wish I could tell my dad not to preach to me. I mean, really, this wasn't my fault!" Just then, Dominique fell to the floor gasping for breath.

"You...aren't even tired...are you?" Dominique sputtered out between breaths.

Rani hadn't really given it any thought, she was so preoccupied with telling Dominique about her favorite songs. When she had lived with her dad, she wasn't allowed to get pop albums, so she was especially excited about her purchase. "No, not really," she replied as she lifted one hand off the floor to move her braid behind her back and then continued her task. She cast a glance around and noticed that most kids had either stopped or were accommodating their exhaustion by pushing up from their knees instead of toes or piking their hips toward the ceiling.

Mr. Graff walked over to their group and told Dominique and a couple of other students who were unable to continue to head over to the water fountain and get a quick drink before they moved on to jump ropes.

"Rani," he nodded in appreciation of her endurance. "You're doing great, that's perfect form even after almost two minutes. Great job! Let's save your energy for the other stations, run grab a drink and come right back."

Rani stood up and wiped her hands together to clean off the gym floor grime and went to get in line at the water fountain. After she had taken her turn and walked back over to Dominique, she started a new topic.

"So anyway, I talked to my dad last night. He's still telling my mom that he wants to fight for custody of me. Can you believe it?"

Dominique, wiping sweat off her brow, had just managed to return to a normal breath. She turned to her friend and asked, "Would that mean that you wouldn't live with your mom at all?"

"I don't know."

"Do you miss your friends at your old school? Like if he wins, would you want to go back?"

Rani looked a little uncomfortable. "I didn't really have a

lot of friends at my old school. I was too nerdy and quiet. I had one close friend, Emi. But she and her family moved back to Japan after school ended last summer. I was kind of starting to make new friends at the beginning of this school year, but for some reason, it always seemed like a lot of effort. Not like with you guys."

"Yeah, nothing like getting zapped by a broken Nazi machine and turning into Halloween characters to kick start a solid friendship."

Rani laughed and followed her friend to the jump ropes as Mr. Graff told everyone to rotate stations. "It was Russian, but yeah, I can honestly say I've never made friends in quite the same way before."

Both girls bent down and picked up a jump rope from the floor. When Coach Graff blew his whistle, Dominique started a slow and steady skip, one foot and then the other. Rani's pace was about triple that and she jumped with her feet glued together, bouncing off of her toes.

Dominique looked over and asked, "Can I assume this is a She-Ra thing? Or have you always been a superstar in PE?"

"Oh, it's definitely a She-Ra thing," Rani confirmed. "At my old school, I was always the girl trying to hide in the back and just get by without passing out. But now I don't really feel tired at all. It's actually kind of nice!"

"I figured," Dominique sighed and returned her focus to her slow skip.

---

On the way to Joel's after school, Dominique asked the girls if they wanted to hang out without the boys. Before Halloween, they had not frequently mingled, but since the event, it seemed like there was never any time for just the girls. Nicki, Jasmine and Rani all agreed and the boys seemed relieved to have some time without them as well. So the boys continued on to Joel's bunker while the girls headed back to Nicki's house and went straight to her room.

"So Jazz," Nicki said as she grabbed a square, pink, fluffy pillow from her bed, flopped down where it had been and put it in her lap with her arms folded over it. "Have you seen anything else interesting in the crystal ball?"

"Not really, I've looked in it a few times, but it always just tells me things that are about to happen in the next few minutes. The longest was last night when I saw myself eating dinner like fifteen minutes before my mom actually called me to come to the kitchen."

"Can you ask it questions now?" Nicki persisted as she ran her fingers through the furry pillow, brushing it first one direction and then back.

"I've tried. It only sort of works. Like if it's something that someone is about to do, it will show me. But if I ask it, will I have a date to prom when I'm in high school, it's just blank."

"Really useful," Dominique said sarcastically. Jasmine just shrugged. "What about you Nick? Have you figured out anything else with your situation?"

"Not really, I meant to try to find something that would

make my heart beat fast to test out what Marcus said, but I couldn't think of anything that wasn't dangerous."

"Seriously? It obviously doesn't have to be anything crazy. Oh, hey look there's a spider on your wall," Dominique pointed to a space just a few inches from Nicki's head.

"Do you really expect me to fall for that?" Nicki raised one eyebrow at her friend.

"Suit yourself," Dominique shrugged. Nicki turned around to look at the blank wall behind her head, but as she was turning back to call out Dominique, something flew at her face. Nicki wasn't quite quick enough to snatch the medium-sized brown stuffed hound dog that Dominique had thrown at her and got smacked in the face with it, right as her earrings twinkled and her hair turned pink.

"I guess we answered that question," Dominique snickered.

"Gee thanks," Nicki said wryly as she rubbed the bridge of her nose, which had taken a hit from one of the plastic eyeballs on her stuffed dog.

"Well, now that you're Jem, we can see if you have any special powers to go with the hair," Rani tried to help.

"I don't think Jem really has special powers. She can just project the hologram that changes her from her normal self to her rock star persona and she can sing. Which is why I wanted to go as her."

"That's not entirely true," said Jasmine slowly as she thought back to the cartoon. "She can also project other holograms with her earrings. I know she used it to make their concerts really cool with pretty righteous light shows. But remember how she used them to get away from The Misfits in a couple of episodes too?"

"Okay, let me see if I can project something." Nicki closed her eyes, took a deep breath and pictured her room full of fireworks. About five seconds after she started envisioning it, she heard Jasmine squeal and opened her eyes to see what looked like gold, sparkly fireworks coming out of her earrings and filling her room from floor to ceiling. She slowly waved her hand back and forth through the projection, feeling nothing, but seeing extremely vivid sparks in many bright colors as she moved her hand through them.

"I have got to admit, that is pretty cool," Dominique nodded her wide-eyed approval.

"Yeah, it is!" Jasmine enthusiastically agreed.

"We need to show the boys so Marcus can make a note," said Rani, always pragmatic.

"Not right now, I really just wanted to hang out and talk about something, *anything*, other than what happened to us on Halloween," begged Dominique. Jasmine smiled at her friend and put her hand on Dominique's arm.

"Of course, what were you thinking?"

The girls spent the next hour just being normal, talking about classes, celebrities and music and generally enjoying each other's company.

Meanwhile, the boys were also further testing the boundaries of their newfound powers. Joel asked for complete silence and a moment to collect himself. As everyone collectively held their breaths, he telekinetically moved a pencil from the bench on one side of the bunker through the air to the bench on the other side. When it touched down, Robby jumped up and down and whooped as he patted his friend on the back and congratulated him on having The Force.

"Dude, that is big time," Javier clapped Joel on the shoulder. "I can't believe you'd want to turn back to normal when you can do that, and you don't even look different than you did before Halloween."

Joel was quiet for a moment and then admitted, "I wouldn't be upset if I got to keep The Force. So far I haven't seen any reason that I *should* turn back."

Robby contemplated this different take on the subject. Ever since they had woken up and discovered the change, all anyone had talked about was turning back. "I can see that," he conceded. "I mean, if I had full-on Superman powers, I wouldn't want to change back either. But so far, I have annoying hair and I sometimes accidentally burn holes in things when I stare at them for too long."

"What about the karate stuff though?" Joel countered.

"Eh, I've only played around with that. I should find somewhere I can practice and really see what I can do."

Javier asked, "So would you change back if we figure out how or not?"

"I don't know," said Robby. "If I still looked like myself

instead of some 1950s businessman, I wouldn't even have to think about it. I'd keep my powers and just learn to not stare at stuff too hard. But right now, I'm not sure it's worth it. What about you?"

Javier shrugged. "I've only turned invisible maybe twice that I know of. It's not really a big problem for me. I'd be fine either way."

Marcus looked down at his feet. "Of the guys, I guess I'm the only one who is pretty desperate to turn back."

"Yeah man, but we'll still help you," Robby assured his friend. "And who knows, I might totally want to change back too once I actually bother to think about it." Marcus chuckled a little, realizing it was true. Robby hadn't given it one percent of the thought that he had. Marcus woke up thinking about it and was still contemplating how to reverse it when he laid in bed struggling to fall asleep at night.

"Besides, Dominique won't let you change back by yourself even if we did all decide to stay," Joel reasoned. "I think most of the girls will actually want to stop this."

"Totally," agreed Javier. "Jasmine is the only one who might keep hers because unless she has the crystal ball with her, she's pretty much exactly how she was before."

"So you guys won't be mad if some of us ruin your name? Because you know it will be more like Radi-four the way things are going," Marcus joked.

"We'll just have to make Rani come up with a new name," laughed Robby. "So, do you guys want to help me play around with my powers? Where can I find something that I'm allowed to break?"

"Oh! My dad has some scrap lumber in the garage," volunteered Joel. "We were making a bookshelf a few months ago and there are tons of pieces we could use. Let me run and grab them. We can play around here in my backyard."

---

"Yeah!" cheered all of the boys as Robby demolished board after board with an array of increasingly impressive kicks, jump kicks and then jump spin kicks. His friends took turns two at a time holding the boards out for him with each person securing opposite corners of the board so they could keep it flat and steady. "Okay, now I want to try a double kick while doing the splits, but we need one more person to hold boards if I'm going to do two at once."

Joel was rubbing his raw palms and had to damper his friend's excitement. "Sorry, Robby, but I don't think I can hold any more boards right now. It's really cool how hard you can kick them, but my palms are killing me!"

"Aw, come on, don't be a hoser!"

"Dude, I'm with Joel," Javier set down the half of the broken board that he was holding after Robby's most recent 360 round kick. "We need to work on something else."

"Like what?" asked Robby.

"I have an idea, but I'm not sure how to do it," Joel said.

"What is it?" asked Javier.

"So, I've got this really awesome lightsaber, but no one that I can have a lightsaber battle with. So really all I do is wave it around in my room. Which makes it seem less awesome after a while."

"I can see that," Robby nodded. "What do you want to do about it?"

"I was kind of wondering if Rani's sword would hold up to the lightsaber. At first, I was thinking we could just buy a sword or make one, but I'm pretty sure mine would slice right through it. But She-Ra's sword could turn into something strong enough to battle mine. I'm just not sure if she'd be up for it, or if one of you guys could use her sword."

"I don't think that would work," Marcus started.

"Yeah, I know," Joel interrupted. "I don't remember anyone else being able to use her sword in the cartoon, so it probably wouldn't work. But do you think she'd battle me?"

"I'm not sure, maybe we can ask tomorrow. I don't get the feeling they wanted to hang out with us today," Marcus said.

"When does she go to her dad's?" asked Joel.

"I don't think she said," Marcus tried to remember. "I just know she'll be there this weekend."

"I can ask if the girls are still at my house when I go home," Robby offered.

"That would be great!" Joel's face lit up. "I know The Force is cool, and I've had a lot of fun with it. But come on! You can't have a lightsaber and not have at least one lightsaber battle. That's just wrong!"

## 11

# JEDI VS. THE PRINCESS OF POWER

On Thursday afternoon, immediately after they got home from school, Rani and Joel stood facing each other in the middle of the street, holding their respective weapons in front of their faces while the rest of the group sat lined up on the curb.

"So what are the rules?" Rani asked Joel as she peered at him around her sword.

Marcus stood up from his spot on the curb and walked over to them. "I think it makes sense to test out their resistance to each other first. Why don't you lightly tap them together to make sure one doesn't destroy the other."

"Good idea," Joel said. "I'll hold mine still while you touch your sword to my lightsaber," Joel instructed Rani.

She shifted her feet so one was in front of the other and bent her knees a little. "Okay, here goes!" She ever so gently touched the edge of her blade to the light of Joel's weapon.

There were a few crackles of electricity from the lightsaber, but neither weapon sustained any damage.

"Yes!" cheered Joel, pumping his fist. "I can finally have a lightsaber battle! Or at least as close to one as I'm ever going to get."

"Yeah," Rani agreed slowly, "but let's keep in mind that we shouldn't let the weapons touch our skin. So we can't go all out, we'll still have to be careful."

"I know," Joel assured her. "We should just do basic moves. No spinning or anything that takes our eyes off of the weapons or each other."

"I agree," Rani said. "Let's also not get too fancy with overhead swings or anything. It opens us up too much." She saw his face fall a little. "Unless you want to choreograph something so it looks cool for these guys, but we each know exactly what's coming?"

Joel nodded thoughtfully. "That's probably the best idea. It will look like an awesome battle, but no one will get hurt."

While Joel and Rani proceeded to map out their battle to show their friends, the others continued chatting.

"Wow, she's really great at that," Marcus said as he watched Rani bend and twist to give their routine as much flair as possible.

"Yeah, she told me in P.E. the other day that she's not usually athletic," Dominique agreed. "I guess it's all the Halloween stuff. I bet it will be hard for her to lose that."

"Totally," Marcus nodded emphatically. "I've been thinking about that a lot. I never understood why people were so into sports. Then when this happened, and I felt what it was like to be naturally athletic, I kinda get it."

"Well this is totally different," Nicki cut in. "You never had to train or anything, and you could even beat Carl Lewis in a race. Most sports people have to practice and work out all the time to get to where they are."

"You're right," Marcus said. "It would be harder to lose if we had worked really hard to get here. I guess it's sort of an 'it-was-fun-while-it-lasted' kind of thing."

He pondered going back to his normal self and then wondered what Rani's normal self even was since they had barely met her before. Then Javier broke into his reverie.

"Hey, you guys know we're not that far away from Christmas. What are you all asking for this year?"

"Oh, wow," Jasmine remarked. "I hadn't even thought about it. With everything that's been going on, it doesn't seem that close to the holidays. But I guess Thanksgiving is...what, like three weeks from now?"

Dominique smiled. "Huh, yeah, I guess that means we have a week off soon. Five fewer days to deal with all the jerks at school and by the time we go back, hopefully we're fixed."

Jasmine gave an exasperated sigh. "Dom, there aren't that many people who have been jerks. Just a couple of kids."

"Whatever, let me be happy about the break, alright?" Dominique insisted. Jasmine gave an amused eye roll.

"But really," Javier insisted, "what do you want this year?"

"I want a new cassette player with good speakers for my room," Nicki said.

"I thought for sure you'd want a Jem doll," Javier told her. "I saw a commercial that had dolls for the whole band and a stage that you can play cassettes through."

"Yeah," she nodded pensively, "that would be really cool. But I'm getting more serious about music. I've started writing some of my own. It's not very good or anything, but eventually, I want to record it so I need better sound equipment."

Javier said, "I bet you'd be great at it!" Then remembering that she knew about his crush, he quickly looked away.

Robby, completely detached from the conversation, was watching a black crow walk across the grass under a tree across the street. He asked his friends, "Do you ever get mad when you see birds walking?"

"What? No. Why on earth would you get mad at a bird for walking?" Jasmine asked, utterly perplexed at both the change in subject and the new topic itself.

"Well, you know. Because they can fly! They shouldn't waste time using their stupid legs," Robby explained as though it were the most reasonable thing in the world.

Javier laughed, a little louder than was natural, grateful that Robby had distracted them from his embarrassment. Then he asked his friend, "So what about you, Robby? What do you want for Christmas?"

"I want more Transformers. I asked my mom for some for my birthday, but I only got one of the Decepticons. I really want Optimus Prime since it's basically a three-for-one!"

"I would definitely come over and help you check those out," Javier offered.

"I wish I could get a laser tag set," Marcus told his friends. "They're really expensive though, so I don't think I'll get one."

"I'm going to ask for some clothes and makeup," Dominique said. "Once I'm back to normal, I'm giving myself a makeover."

"Oh, that will be fun, I'd love to help!" Jasmine exclaimed.

Dominique shrugged, "Sure, why not. So, what are you asking for?"

Jasmine scrunched up her face and thought about it. "I don't know. I was originally thinking I wanted a Pound Puppy for my Cabbage Patch kid, but maybe I'm getting a little old for that kind of stuff. Although, I do love puppies, and if I'm not allowed to get a real one, a Pound Puppy would be kind of cool. Or a Monchhichi. They're so soft and cuddly!"

Rani and Joel walked back over to the group and announced that they were ready to put on their show. So everyone turned their attention back to the middle of the street and watched them swing the sword and lightsaber around in huge arcs, tapping them in the middle and then doing overhead strikes and uppercuts. They ended with Joel dropping down to his knees to swipe the lightsaber across what would have been Rani's ankles, but at the last moment, she did an aerial cartwheel over his weapon and landed with her sword tip stuck into the ground. They both stood up and took a bow for their friends who were shouting their approval along with a raucous round of applause.

# 12

# FREAKS OUT IN PUBLIC

"Rani! Over here!" Jasmine hollered enthusiastically as she hopped up and down, waving at her friend to join the rest of the group. It was barely after 8 o'clock on Saturday morning, opening day of the Sesquicentennial festival, but everyone was awake and ready to have fun. The sky was clear, although the air was still brisk at that time of day. The forecast for later was sunny and mid-70s, so nearly everyone had a light jacket that would end up tied around their waists as the day wore on. Javier was the one exception, he still needed his mom to buy him a new jacket since his old one left about three inches of wrist exposed. Sharon had expressed concern when she picked him up at his house, but he assured her that he didn't get cold easily.

Sharon had brought Joel, Marcus and Javier along with her own children and was standing at the entrance holding the free tickets for each child as well as the one she had purchased for herself. Jasmine's mom had dropped off Dominique and Jasmine only a couple of minutes before they spotted Rani walking toward the ticket booth with her father.

"Alright kids," Sharon spoke in a low voice without moving her lips while she smiled at Rani's father. "Everyone on your best behavior."

They didn't need to be told twice. Mr. Gabri was wearing reflective sunglasses that completely hid his eyes, but the scowl on his face was still evident. He was a tall man, a couple of inches over six feet, with short dark hair and a tightly trimmed, stubbly beard. Rani doubled her steps to keep up with her lanky father, although her defeated posture suggested that she was not nearly as excited about the festival as the rest of the children.

As they approached, Sharon stepped forward and held out her hand, "Hello Mr. Gabri, I'm so pleased that you and Rani could join us today. My name is Sharon, I'm Nicki and Robby's mom."

He reluctantly took her hand and gave it two jerky shakes and then pulled back. "It's nice to meet you," he said with forced cordiality. "You can call me Anil."

"It's nice to meet you, Anil. Shall we go in?" Sharon held her hand out toward the gates indicating that the children should go first. She handed each one a ticket as they filed past her toward the entrance.

Each person received a red plastic bracelet proving that they had access to all of the rides. As they formed a huddle while they waited for the adults to get their bracelets, the kids looked around and took in the sights, sounds and smells of the Sesquicentennial festival. They could already smell a mix of sweet and fried foods on the breeze as the festival booths prepared to feed the hungry revelers throughout the day. Music from a few of the rides tinkled, creating a buzz of excitement, although there were no shrieks emitting from their direction yet as the rides were just starting to open for the first guests. Everything from the rides to the booths to the employees working the festival were dressed in red, white and blue, the colors of the Texas flag, and you couldn't look a few feet without seeing big white stars adorning everything, celebrating the Lone Star State. It was a dizzying array of stimuli, and the kids all stood transfixed, not knowing where to start.

Sharon led them toward the bumper cars, which were just to the right of the entrance. The kids paired up with two children per car and set to ramming into each other and laughing hysterically, the passenger of each car shouting instructions to the driver. Meanwhile, Anil stood an unnaturally distant six feet from Sharon. After she did her run-through to make sure each kid was safe and accounted for, she took a sideways step toward Rani's dad and attempted to make conversation.

"I'm so glad you were able to bring Rani here today. It's such a nice day out, and the kids needed a break from school and the...well, you know. Constantly thinking about their situation," she finished haltingly. She knew from Alisha that Anil was aware it had been her house where the incident took place. And while she was by no means eager to discuss it, she also wanted to be transparent if he wished to do so.

Anil turned to look at Sharon, appraising the woman he blamed for what had happened to his daughter (when he wasn't busy blaming his ex-wife for moving in the first place). She had such a warm and open manner that he found it difficult to gripe her out as he had imagined he would if he ever met her. "Yes, well, we didn't have other plans for today, and Rani seemed really excited to come. I don't get enough time with her anymore, so we try to do something special on our weekends together."

"She's such an amazing young woman," Sharon smiled at Rani as she said this. "So smart and so polite. You and Alisha have done a wonderful job raising her."

He turned back to look at the chaos on the bumper cars at the mention of his ex-wife and gave a terse, "Thank you." After a few more minutes of awkward silence, all eight kids came tumbling out of the exit line, bubbling over with commentary about who had bumped whom and who 'won' the session. Above the rest of the chatter, Robby shouted, "What's next?"

Anil cringed a little at the volume, and Sharon reminded Robby that while it was loud on the bumper car track, she could hear him perfectly fine and there was no reason to shout. She took a peek at the paper map that she received at the ticket counter and determined that the most reasonable route was to continue forward from their current location toward the Ferris wheel.

After a couple more rides, including the Tilt-a-Whirl, the Scrambler and the Gravitron, a few of the children complained that they were hungry, so they stopped to grab some snacks: corn dogs, turkey legs and giant pretzels, followed by cotton candy, all washed down with sodas. They found a picnic table to rest and consume their snacks, so they spread out and gobbled down their festival food.

Nicki finished first and asked her mom if she could run across the pathway to where there was a sign-up for the karaoke stage. "You can see it from here, look," and she pointed a few yards away where there was a person taking names and song requests.

"Fine, but stay where I can see you and hurry back," Sharon relented.

While they had taken their break, a rush of new visitors had entered the park and the next couple of rides required somewhat lengthy waits.

"Rani, we should probably get going," Anil said to his daughter shortly after noon.

"But Dad, it's not Nicki's turn to sing on the karaoke stage for about half an hour! We can probably do one more ride and then watch her performance. I'll go with you after that if that's okay?" She had such hope in her voice that Anil felt compelled to relent. "Alright," he nodded curtly, "What ride?"

Rani looked at her friends. Jasmine smiled and said, "You pick, if it's the last one you get to go on, that's only fair!"

A slow smile spread across Rani's face as she said, "I want to go on the Wave Swinger!" The boys whooped their approval while Dominique gave a nervous smile that clearly said she was not jumping at the opportunity to take her turn on the swings that raised up to what seemed like a hundred feet and then swung around in wide circles until each swing was practically parallel to the ground. But never one to chicken out, she followed the other kids to the line at the Wave Swinger.

Unfortunately, after Robby, Marcus, Javier, Nicki and Jasmine walked past the gate toward the ride, a man in a Sesquicentennial uniform pulled the chain back across the entrance to indicate the ride was full. Rani checked her watch and saw that it was still more than twenty minutes before Nicki's performance on one of the side stages, so she stepped back and waited for the next round.

She noticed that her dad and Sharon were talking about his job as an engineer and hers as an office manager for a dentist. Rani smiled, pleased to hear her dad sound like he was loosening up. She was about to try to clandestinely share this observation with Dominique and Joel when she heard a tremendous metallic scraping noise and a change in tone from the screams coming from the Wave Swinger, mingling with new yells from every direction. She whipped her head around, her blonde braid slapping her face. She took in the sight of the ride's giant center pole leaning at an angle. The swings jerked around, nearly hitting the ground as they raced back up almost to the sky while the machine kept rotating.

Everyone stood transfixed for a moment before Joel shouted, "I've got The Force!" and did a flying leap over the gate toward the machine. Rani took just a fraction of a second longer to react, but then was right on Joel's heels and speeding past him toward the center pole.

She vaguely processed her dad yelling her name as she stood underneath the pole and pushed with all her might. Nothing happened except the riders on the machine continued to scream and workers at the festival ran around with walkie-talkies trying to figure out the best course of action. As the swings continued to nearly graze the ground, she heard a sickening crack and a scream of panic mixed with agony. Out of the corner of her eye, she had seen someone's foot make contact with the ground. She knew she had to do something fast.

Rani took a deep breath, closed her eyes and said with great conviction, "I am She-Ra, Princess of Power!" This time when she pushed, the center pole started to right itself and the arc of the swing was almost back in line with where it started. The metal was obviously compromised, but it was holding up the swings.

However, as she pushed to make the final correction, she heard another wave of panicked screams and looked up to see one of the riders clinging to the bottom of his swing, feet dangling high above the concrete. She could tell his fingers were slipping. Just as his grip gave out and he started to fall toward the ground, Joel rushed forward and put his hands in front of his face, slowly lowering them toward the pavement. The pace of the falling rider slowed to match Joel's hand movements and his feet gently touched the ground. The rider's hands stayed out to his side as though he couldn't find his balance until he realized he was firmly back on earth. With a whimper, he ran to his parents.

It took another few moments for the employees of the festival to get the ride stopped and the rest of the riders off. In the meantime, Rani and Joel returned to the line where Anil and Sharon grabbed them and checked them out for any sign of injury. Sharon, already accustomed to the newfound skills, processed what had happened much more quickly than Anil, but she was still anxious to have her kids back with her.

"What were you thinking? You could have been hurt!" Anil had a tight grip on Rani's shoulders and was shaking her, not as a punishment, but because he was so violently trembling with fear. Sharon gently laid her hand on his shoulder. "Anil, I think you might be hurting her now." He swung his head and looked at her with wide, frantic eyes, then took a moment to catch his breath and released his daughter. Finally, he said, "What was that?"

"Sir, ma'am, could you please come with us and bring those two?" A pair of police officers had approached them and were pushing aside the crowd that was forming around them. Both Sharon and Anil had been so consumed with checking on the children, they had completely blocked out the cacophony of people chattering all around.

"We have to wait," Sharon pleaded. "My kids were on that ride, I need to get them first."

"No problem, ma'am, but let's step over here please."

As she did so, she was vaguely aware of one of the riders

getting loaded onto a stretcher while a teenage girl stood next to him sobbing and trying to grab for his hand while paramedics worked to ensure his leg was immobile.

Just then she heard a frantic "Mom!" and turned to see a pink-haired streak that was Nicki racing toward her, tears streaming down her face and the others only a heartbeat behind. Nicki slammed into her mom with the others piling on behind in a rather aggressive group hug, several of them were crying. Marcus stood to the side, stoic with shock.

---

After giving them a moment to connect, the officers ushered the group to a make-shift tent that was set up for some of the policemen and women who were patrolling the event. It also served as a home base for children who became separated from their parents.

The officer who had originally approached them was a man in his mid-forties, slightly overweight and starting to show signs of balding. While he couldn't completely hide the confusion and concern on his face, he had friendly eyes and a gentle smile that he hoped would put everyone at ease while he worked to discover what had just happened. His partner was a slightly younger, short Hispanic woman with her brown hair pulled back into a tight bun that was twisted up just above the collar of her dark blue uniform. She poured water from an orange plastic pitcher into clear cups and passed them around the group.

"Sir, ma'am," the male policeman, Officer Pembroke, nodded to Anil and Sharon in turn, "I need to ask these young folks some questions. Do you mind? You can stay while we talk." They both nodded their assent.

Officer Pembroke turned to Rani. "Can I ask your name?"

Rani nodded, took a sip of water and then looked somewhere around the officer's chin, unable to meet his gaze. She said in a voice barely above a whisper, "My name is Rani."

"Okay Rani, I was over by the Ferris wheel when I heard screaming. When I got to the swings, I saw you pushing on the center post of the ride. Can you please explain what happened before I arrived?"

Anil cut in angrily, "She didn't cause the ride to malfunction if that's what you're insinuating! She saved every one of those people on that ride!" He jabbed his finger toward the broken Wave Swinger.

The policewoman, Officer Velazquez rushed to assure him that was not what they thought. "Sir, we already have several witnesses who say the same thing. We're just trying to understand what happened. Rani, did you see how the ride initially broke?"

"None of us did," Anil once again answered for his daughter, although slightly less angrily. "We only turned around to look when the screams coming from the ride no longer sounded like 'good' screams if you know what I mean."

Sharon agreed. "I'm sorry, officers, we were facing each other, not looking at the ride. None of us saw anything."

Officer Pembroke took back over the interview. "Okay, fair

enough. The people we have spoken with said that this young man and young lady rushed toward the machine. And that you," he nodded at Rani, "reset the pole to a standing position while you," this time a chin toward Joel, "somehow slowed the fall of a rider who had fallen from his swing? Can you talk to me about that?"

This time Sharon responded. "Officers, are you familiar with what happened in Grayson Ridge on Halloween?"

"We had heard that there was some sort of strange phenomenon where the members of a slumber party somehow turned into their costumes," confirmed Officer Velazquez. "But I'll admit, I assumed it was either a rumor or something my kids blew out of proportion."

"Well, it wasn't," Sharon confided with a sigh. "It's bizarre, and I can't explain it, but the eight children that were at my house on that night woke up the next day with properties of their costumes. As you've seen, or at least heard, Joel has The Force like Luke Skywalker and Rani has She-Ra's super-strength, among other things."

The two officers, along with a couple of others who were in the tent eavesdropping on this wild conversation, all just stared back and forth between Sharon and the children.

"I can disappear," Javier said when the silence got to be more than he could stand. But then he shuffled around even more nervous when every face with a wrinkled forehead and gaping jaw swung his way.

Finally, Officer Pembroke shook off his disbelief. Who was he to contradict nearly eighty witnesses, not to mention the twenty or so riders who had also seen the entire event, albeit from a different perspective? He asked a few more questions for his report and then let Sharon and Anil know that they were free to take the kids and go home.

While they had been talking with the police officers, the back half of the festival had been fenced off and shut down. So they walked in a tight group through the rest of the festival, earning more than a few stares, pointed fingers and whispers behind hands. A tall, bulky teenage boy stepped toward them from a line at one of the rides and hollered "Hey freaks, stay away from our ride!" But not a single one noticed anything as they kept a laser beam focus on their path back to the parking lot and away from the nightmare they had all just experienced.

## 13

# POWERFUL DECISIONS

At 8:30 on Sunday morning, the doorbell at the Swain house rang once, then two more times in rapid succession before anyone could answer.

Sharon tiptoed to the door as she tied the belt to her white terrycloth robe around her T-shirt and pajama pants. Depending on who it was, she had no intention of answering. She needed today to just hold her kids and feel grateful they were home safe. But when she glanced through the peephole, she saw Dale standing there, rocking nervously back and forth between his toes and heels on her front porch. She leaned her forehead on the door for a moment, summoning the strength to deal with this unexpected intrusion and then opened the door, still standing partially behind it, not exactly inviting him in.

"Sharon!" Dale exclaimed, his voice full of concern. "I'm so glad you're home. Kevin said he saw you and the kids when he got hurt on that ride yesterday morning. By the time we got his leg cast and back home, I had to finish my shift at the hospital and it was late so I didn't want to bother you. Is everyone okay?"

Sharon looked at him in confusion. She pulled the door wider and moved aside so Dale could walk past her into the entryway. "What do you mean Kevin got hurt?"

Dale took a shuddering breath and said, "He was on the ride at the same time as your kids. He got taken off on a stretcher after his foot slammed into the ground while it was swinging out of control. His ankle was shattered along with several bones in his foot."

"Oh Dale, I can't believe I didn't see him. I knew someone got hurt, but before I could get a good look, the police pulled us aside to ask about Rani and Joel, and I forgot all about it. Why don't you come into the kitchen? Would you like some coffee?" she offered.

"That would be great, thank you," Dale accepted as he anxiously raked his hands through his hair.

Walking toward the kitchen, he could smell a pot already brewing and helped himself to a lemon-colored cup on the coffee mug tree stand that lived on Sharon's counter. Sharon held out the pot and poured it nearly to the top before pulling out a chair at the kitchen table next to her own still steaming mug. Dale took a moment to add some sugar and then sat down across from her, blowing on his coffee to cool it enough for his first sip.

"I was already at the hospital working when I was called

to the emergency room where they had just admitted Kevin. While they were getting his foot set, a mom brought her son in to get checked out. He claimed to have fallen at least thirty feet, but we found no sign of any injury, not so much as a scratch or a sprain. He says that someone used magic to slow his fall and then described a group that sounded an awful lot like yours. What happened?"

Sharon stared at the steam rising from her coffee cup, holding it with both hands while she contemplated where to start. "I was there standing in line when Nicki and Robby were on the ride and it broke. I thought they'd be killed."

"Gah! Sharon, I can't even imagine." He reached across the table for one of her hands. "I have to assume they're okay though?" She nodded an affirmation. "Can you tell me more about what happened? All I was told is that it was old machinery and moving it from town to town probably compromised its structural integrity. It doesn't sound like anyone did anything to cause it other than probably some gross negligence when assembling and inspecting it."

Sharon proceeded to outline how the machine had started up and just as the swings reached their maximum height, the center pole fell askew and then collapsed far enough that the arcs dropped the swings at the bottom to within inches of the ground.

Dale interrupted, "So no one did anything to it that you could see? It just broke?"

"It appears so. It was almost like there was ten times the weight on one side as the other and it just couldn't manage the difference once it got going. But I don't think that was the case. Surely they have rules around that type of thing."

"I would think," Dale vigorously nodded his head, obviously still agitated. Sharon continued with the story of how Rani and Joel had prevented a far worse outcome, then their time with the police, and ended with them leaving the festival and getting everyone home as quickly as possible.

Dale exhaled a long breath, it felt like he had been holding it for the entirety of the story. "I'm so grateful Rani was there. I can't believe she saved all of our kids. While Kevin is in a lot of pain, it could have been so much worse." Sharon had a vacant look in her eyes and nodded numbly.

Dale continued, "So it's definitely not just visual attributes that the kids adopted after Halloween," he stated this more as a fact than a question, causing Sharon to tense up. She shook her head indicating that no, it was not just aesthetic changes as she watched his face.

"Well, it sounds like you have your own little gang of superheroes. Very lucky for everyone on that ride yesterday!" Dale broke into a tired smile.

"Yeah, I guess so," Sharon acquiesced, her face still grim.

"In that case, do you think they'd want to keep their... powers for lack of a better word?"

"Well not all of them have powers," Sharon explained. "Dominique has just changed appearance, and she's pretty antsy to go back."

"Okay, so I know this has been traumatic for some of the kids. But don't you see the potential? What if we could use this technology to take someone in a wheelchair and give them the powers of Superman?"

Sharon was quiet for a moment while she carefully selected her words. "I suppose when I hear the word 'technology,' I think of things that were intentional or at least easily repeatable. I'm not under the impression that's what this is. Unless you know something you aren't telling me?"

"No, nothing like that," Dale attempted to wave off her concerns. "I was just thinking that if that ride had broken yesterday and there was no one there to save our kids…" He left the implication hanging.

"I see your point, but we don't know if there are going to be any negative effects; if this wears off or if it would pass onto their children. The number of things we don't know is substantial, Dale."

"Yeah, I know. I just think it's rash to only think of ways to reverse it when we could also think of ways to…"

"Exploit it?" she filled in for him.

"That sounds so negative. I'm talking about advancing humankind in a way that no one could have dreamed of outside of fiction!"

"Can you promise me something?" Sharon leaned forward to gauge Dale's answer.

"What's that?" Dale said warily. He leaned back slightly, uncomfortable with the intensity of her stare.

"If we come up with a plan to help these kids get back to normal, will you help us? Will you let us use the X-ray machine again?"

Dale hesitated and saw her expression shut down behind her eyes at his reluctance to comply, so he rushed to explain. "It's just that we're talking about using hospital equipment for something other than its intended purpose. If something happens, you could sue the hospital."

"Dale, I could sue the hospital now after what happened on Halloween! And how is this different than what you're talking about? What if you tried to turn someone into some Super Mega Fantastic Man and something bad happened?"

Dale looked down and studied his fingernails. "Let me give it some thought, okay?"

Sharon clenched her jaw but heard Alisha's voice telling her to stay on good terms with Dale so she nodded, granting him some time to come to the right decision.

———

As Dale pulled his keys out of his pocket and walked down the sidewalk in front of the Swain house, he couldn't stop thinking about what Sharon had said. Was it even possible to mix and match a series of costumes to essentially give himself every superpower imaginable? He decided then and there that he was going to have another conversation with Chad.

## 14

## OUT OF OUR ELEMENT

While the rest of Sunday passed without incident as everyone recovered at home, Monday was back to sheer chaos at school. Everyone had heard about the events at the festival, a handful had even witnessed it themselves. From the moment they approached the school on Monday morning, every member of RA-D8 received a constant onslaught of questions, coerced into retelling the story over and over. They were actually relieved when classes started and they had a valid excuse to focus on something else.

Unfortunately, Robby focused a little too hard in his math class that morning. The final class before lunch was taught by a young teacher with short, brown curls framing her slender face. She wore a pair of glasses that highlighted her vibrant blue eyes. Robby studied the chalkboard trying to understand how his teacher had found the answer to an equation when he felt a thump on his shoulder. He turned around with his eyebrows pinched together, and gave Marcus a stern look. But then Marcus tilted his head toward the chalkboard where there was a clearly visible burn hole. Mrs. Maxwell stopped her lecture mid-sentence with a startled look on her face and turned her head a little to sniff the air. "Do you guys smell something burning?"

Robby's face flushed bright red and a few students started to point at the board, which was emitting a thin stream of gray smoke from a pea-sized black hole. Mrs. Maxwell looked at the board then whipped her head back to the classroom, her eyes searching for something flammable.

"Um...Mrs. Maxwell," Robby timidly raised his hand. "I think that was me, but I promise I didn't do it on purpose."

She put her thumb over the hole to ensure the flame was completely snuffed out and wiped her thumb on a piece of paper she had on her desk to remove the soot. She studied Robby for a moment before addressing the class, "If you can please finish the first ten problems on your worksheet, Mr. Swain and I are going to step out in the hall for a moment."

Robby slowly got up out of his seat, his shoulders slumped forward and his arms hanging by his sides to follow his teacher out into the deserted hallway. He shuffled his feet while Mrs. Maxwell held the door for a few moments and every pair of eyes in the classroom watched him make his laborious trek across the room.

"Can you please explain?" she asked Robby after she had softly closed the door, her face etched with concern instead of the anger he expected.

"Yes ma'am. So that thing that happened on Halloween left me with some sort of heat vision, kind of like lasers. Which would be totally cool if I could control it. But sometimes when I look at something too hard, it just happens. I couldn't figure out how you got the remainder on that problem on the chalkboard, so I was really focusing on it and, well...you saw." He shrugged with embarrassment, his hands turned helplessly upward toward the ceiling. "I'm really sorry, I promise it wasn't on purpose."

Mrs. Maxwell laid a hand on his shoulder and said, "I believe you. Do you want to go back into the classroom or head down to Mrs. Calvert's office for the rest of class?"

Robby gave it some thought and then asked, "Do I still need to finish the worksheet?"

The teacher gave him a sympathetic smile, her blue eyes twinkling and nodded her head. Robby sighed.

"Then I guess I better go back to class."

———

Dale strolled into the hospital cafeteria five minutes after he saw Chad head down for lunch. He grabbed a sandwich and a Pepsi, paid at the register and then stopped by Chad's table. As usual, Chad was in the back corner at a table by himself. He had chosen the seat facing the wall with his back to the activity of his more social coworkers, far from the chatter of the other hospital employees who tended to congregate closer to the register at the front.

"Hey Chad, how's it going? Mind if I join you?" Dale gestured to the seat across from the lab tech.

Chad looked up from the book he was reading and gave Dale a tight-lipped smile. "Sure, Dale," he said flatly, making it clear that the invitation was not willingly extended. "What do you need?"

"Need?" Dale, still standing, feigned confusion. "I don't need anything, I just thought you looked like you could use some company."

Chad stared at Dale across the table for a moment, he thought it was quite evident that he was busy reading and in no way looking for a conversation, but he eventually acquiesced, nodding to the open seat and then took another bite of his soup. Dale sat down and after a silence long enough to be uncomfortable, he said, "So, how's it coming with the research on the X-ray situation?"

"What do you mean?" Chad asked uneasily, glancing over his shoulder, his eyes shifting around the cafeteria, making sure no one was within listening distance. But no one was close enough or paying any attention, so he reluctantly looked back at Dale.

"Well, I've been thinking," Dale paused and took a sip of his drink. "You have the settings for the machine, you obviously have ample access to the machine, so what are you waiting for? Why haven't you tried to reverse the spell or whatever you want to call it?"

Chad snapped his mouth shut and tried to think quickly.

Dale misread his reaction and said, "Or have you tried and it didn't work?"

"No, no nothing like that," Chad shook his head to emphasize that he hadn't done anything with the machine since Halloween. "I mean, I did panic a little the first time I had to use the machine on a person. I hadn't thought to cancel any appointments for X-rays, but nothing happened at the time of the X-ray and no one has complained since."

"Oh dang," Dale leaned forward and lowered his voice. "I didn't even think about that. We should have told everyone the machine was broken and rescheduled. But nothing has happened? Have you followed up with anyone that you used it on?"

"No, but I don't usually talk to patients except when I'm X-raying them."

"Okay, can you get me a list of names and phone numbers so I can follow up?"

"Sure thing, boss. I'll do that after lunch."

"Okay, so..."

"So..." Chad wasn't sure where this was going.

"I've been thinking: what if we could use the machine for good? Like what if we could cure someone who can't walk? Or give a blind person not only sight but X-ray vision?"

Chad mulled it over while he took another bite. "I suppose there is a possibility that those things could happen. But there's no way that would be legal. I mean, think of all the rules we have at the hospital. All the tests that have to happen before we can get a new drug or machine approved."

"Yeah, it wouldn't be something we could advertise," Dale conceded, his gaze roaming around the cafeteria.

"I don't think it's something we can do *at all*," Chad was staring at Dale in disbelief. As a hospital administrator, part of Dale's job was to be the one informed about rules and regulations and then ensure that everyone adhered to the guidelines. What he was talking about was a blatant disregard for any sort of precaution and would most likely come with a prison sentence if he were caught.

"Okay, so maybe that's a bad idea," Dale shrugged it off. "But I'm sure Sharon would still like to know if there's some way to reverse everything for those kids she had that night. Not to mention her own kids. So what's the plan?"

Chad quickly considered what was safe to tell Dale and realized that it wasn't wise to share much of anything. So he decided a distraction would be his best bet.

"Well, we've been trying to research what will happen if we go through this process again," Chad said solemnly.

"What do you mean?" Dale asked.

"Come on, Dale. Aren't you worried about Kevin and what's happening to him? Or to Sharon's kids? Or me?"

"Of course I'm worried! I want to help Sharon get her kids back to normal. And I want my kid back to full health."

"Well we have to make sure we're actually reversing it, not compounding it."

Dale nodded in agreement, waiting for Chad to continue.

"Do we zap the same candy? Different candy? If we do the wrong thing, will we just make it worse? Or make it so we can never change back? Do our powers get stronger or weaker with each attempt? There's a lot to consider."

Dale sat back in his chair and exhaled a long breath. "Wow."

"Yeah."

"So what does that mean?"

"I'm not sure yet, that's what's taking so long and why I haven't already turned myself back. I'll let you know when I figure something out."

"Yeah, please do," Dale said. After another moment of staring at the table, processing all of Chad's questions, Dale finally slid out of the bench, gathered his trash and turned back to Chad. "Well, thanks for telling me what you know. Let's work together to figure out how to fix this for you and for those kids."

"Sure thing, Dale," Chad nodded and opened his book back up to finish his lunch in peace.

---

That night at dinner, Sharon was ladling tortilla soup from her Crockpot slow cooker into three bowls. It had finally started to get cold at night, and she took advantage by making one of her family's favorite winter comfort foods.

"Alright guys, come pick your toppings," she instructed her children.

Shmoofy hovered near the counter while Nicki and

Robby added cheese and tortilla strips to the top of their chicken soup.

"Robby, leave some for the rest of us!" Nicki bumped him with her elbow as Robby was putting his second handful of shredded cheddar into his soup. The bump jostled his arm and Shmoofy was rewarded with a few bits of cheese that missed Robby's bowl.

"Hey guys, come on, the vet said Shmoofy shouldn't have too much dairy. Be careful please!" Sharon chastised her bickering children.

"But there's hardly any cheese left and the rest of us haven't had any yet!" Nicki stomped her foot as Robby turned to look at her and licked his fingers with a smirk on his face.

"You're so gross!" Nicki said.

"Robby, that's enough, go sit down," Sharon said as she pulled the cheese grater out of the dishwasher, rinsed it off and grated more cheese directly into the bowls that held her and Nicki's soup. "Alright, satisfied?" she asked Nicki.

"I guess," Nicki mumbled as Sharon finished topping her soup with tortilla strips, a little diced jalapeño and a dollop of sour cream.

"I've been thinking, maybe we should make a little care package for Kevin," Sharon said. She blew on her spoonful of steaming hot soup. "I feel bad that we didn't notice he was the one getting loaded onto the ambulance last weekend."

"We did kind of have a few things going on," Robby pointed out.

"I know, but we could just gather some snacks and maybe

something to entertain him and take it over there. What do you think?"

"I think it's a good idea," Nicki responded. "I would hate it if I couldn't move for that long."

"I wouldn't!" Robby said. "He's lucky he doesn't have to do chores or go to school or anything!"

"Yeah, but he also doesn't *get* to do anything," Nicki pointed out. "If he can't go to school, I bet he also can't go to work, so he's not making money, which is a bummer. And for him, I bet it's torture not to play football."

Robby pondered this as he stirred the stringy, melting cheese into his soup. "If he has a Nintendo or Atari, I still think it would be cool to play as much as you want and not have anything else you had to do."

Nicki opened her mouth to challenge him and then decided it wasn't worth her time. She turned back to her mom and said, "When did you want to take it over? I could make him a mixtape of cool songs for when he's tired of watching TV. But I would need a little time to get it together."

"I was thinking Wednesday since the office closes early. We could go over shortly after you guys get out of school. Is that enough time?" Sharon glanced over at Robby and saw him playing with the stringy cheese again. "Robby, would you please just eat your dinner before you make a mess?"

He dropped his spoon back in his bowl, sending up a little splash that got on his shirt as well as the table. "Sorry mom," he said as he grabbed his napkin and started wiping up.

"Yeah," Nicki said, "I think I can work on it some tonight and then tomorrow after school so it's ready by Wednesday."

"Great!" Sharon said, before turning back to her son. "And what about you? Can you come up with something to contribute for Kevin?"

"Yeah, I'll think of something," Robby agreed. "While we're there, we can also check to see if they're doing anything supervillain-y."

"What?" Sharon said startled.

"You know, like if Kevin has stashes of gold that he pirated away or if Dale has a Superman costume that he's planning to turn into."

Sharon nodded thoughtfully. "You know, I was going to call and let him know we were coming, but you bring up a good point. If they're doing anything crazy, hopefully, we could catch them in the act."

"Mom," Nicki said. "Are you seriously listening to Robby for advice? The world must be ending."

"I know," Sharon smiled at her daughter. "It does seem kind of nuts, but Alisha was right when she gave me advice the other night. We need Dale to let us use the machine, so I can't get on his bad side." Nicki raised her eyebrows at her mom. "I know, that sounds bad," Sharon defended. "But I promise I'm not using him. I'm just trying to make sure I don't do anything rash and, in the meantime, I have enjoyed his company. But I will be careful. Okay?"

"If you say so," Nicki reluctantly agreed. "You know Chad

will let us use the equipment even if Dale isn't around though, right?"

"I know, but still...let's not burn any bridges until we don't have a choice," Sharon said firmly and then changed the subject to ask if anything interesting happened at school.

———————

Dale sat at his kitchen table with a notepad and pen after Kevin had gone to bed. His brain was swirling with ideas on how he could use the machine to make things so much better. Kevin's leg was expected to take a couple of months to heal and then even longer for rehab. During that time, he would lose his football scholarship to college, and Dale couldn't let that happen. He was already thinking that he could have Kevin dress as The Flash or the Six Million Dollar Man so he could restore his leg in far less time and maybe give him a little extra boost on the field in the meantime. He would need to research the merits of each and figure out which one made the most sense for his son. But in the meantime, he hadn't forgotten his plans for himself.

He tapped the pen against the pad as he looked around his kitchen and thought about what powers he would want if he could create his own superhero. Super-strength, flight and mind-reading occupied the first three lines of his paper under a heading that said "Powers." He had written "Invisibility," but then added a question mark next to it. He felt like there was something creepy about an adult man wandering around invisible. Besides, if this worked, he could always go back and add it. He did have unlimited access to the machine that would do the job after all. So for now, he drew a line through it and mentally noted that he would need to rule out X-ray vision for the same reason.

Dale had told Sharon that he wanted to use the machine to help people, but the truth was slightly different. He had to help Kevin get back on track with his football scholarship. His entire future depended on it. But he was also using it as an excuse because he had wanted to fly since he was a little boy. Now, he had the potential to not only do that, but he was basically Charlie unsupervised in the chocolate factory, able to pick and choose whatever he wanted, and he couldn't help himself. He went back to the top of his list and made a new column for "Costume." Next to "Super-strength" and "Flight," he wrote "Superman."

Remembering what Robby had said about his powers being limited since he had only worn the mask, he made an additional note that he would need the full costume. But then he realized he couldn't think of a character who had the ability to read minds. He'd have to talk to Kevin in the morning to get some help on that one.

Most of what he could think of, Superman already had. In addition to flight and strength, he was super-fast and bullet-proof. There was always immortality, but the more he thought about it, that one just didn't really have any appeal. He would outlive his son, Sharon and everyone else he knew.

He added "Control elements" and "Thor," but then he got

stuck again. He stood and paced between the kitchen and living room. This had sounded so easy when Sharon first mentioned Super Mega Man. But now that he was actually trying to figure out the logistics, it was more complicated than he expected. If he needed a full Superman costume, it limited how much else he could feasibly wear at one time. On his third trip through the living room, he had his aha moment and raced back to his chair at the kitchen table.

A grin spreading across his face, he wrote in a third column, "Accessories," then added a line for The Force under Powers and scratched in "Lightsaber" under accessories. He started to add Captain America and his shield, but then realized that if he were bulletproof, that was redundant. He looked back over his list. Satisfied, he hid the notepad at the back of the junk drawer so he could add to it if he thought of anything else. Smiling to himself, he went to his own room to get ready for bed.

# 15

# THE CARE PACKAGE

On Wednesday afternoon, Sharon stood outside of Dale's apartment and shifted the basket in her arms so she could use one hand to rap lightly on the door to apartment number twenty-three. After a moment, Dale opened the door and said, "What a nice surprise! To what do we owe the pleasure?" He stood aside for Sharon, Nicki and Robby to pass into the space he shared with Kevin.

It was a small apartment for two grown men, with a kitchen that scarcely had enough room for a refrigerator, stove, microwave and a toaster on the avocado-colored Formica countertop. She noticed that there was no dishwasher unless you counted the sink. The only other visible space was a living room that held a couch, a love seat and a large TV sitting on the floor next to what was clearly a fake plant. Two closed doors concealed what she assumed were their bedrooms and another that was slightly ajar showed a glimpse of the bathroom. Sharon knew that when Dale's ex-wife had left the country to join Doctors Without Borders two years ago, he and Kevin had moved out of their house and into this smaller space so Dale had less to keep up with when he suddenly found himself raising a teenager alone.

Sharon held out the basket and said, "We made a little care package for Kevin to help with his recovery. I hope we aren't intruding?"

Kevin turned awkwardly from the spot on the couch in front of the television that he had occupied for the past few days. Once he had cranked around enough to see his guests, his face lit up, and he motioned for them to join him.

Sharon walked over and set the basket on the coffee table next to a few empty soda cans, a *TV Guide,* a box of tissues and a jumble of hand weights. "Hey Kevin, how are you feeling?" she felt his forehead with the back of her hand.

Kevin squirmed a little and said, "You know I'm not sick, right? It's just my leg."

"Oh, I know, sorry, it's a mom habit! And a fever could be a sign of infection, but you feel fine."

He grinned at her and then said, "So what did you bring me?"

Robby jumped in to show him each item in the basket. "We thought you'd probably want some snacks that would be easy and not messy. So here's some popcorn, chips, crackers and cookies. There are also a few pieces of fruit because Mom thought we should add some healthy stuff. We got things that don't have to go in the refrigerator if you eat them in the next few days. Like apples and oranges. I also added some of my comic books. Those are just to borrow though, I want them back!"

"Robby," Sharon admonished.

"What? I do! I thought he might want to do something besides watch TV, I was trying to be nice!"

Nicki rolled her eyes and then stepped forward and lifted a cassette tape out of the basket.

"I made you a mixtape," she explained. "Which you can keep, by the way." Robby countered her snarky look by sticking out his tongue at her. She ignored him, turning back to Kevin. "The quality is not amazing because I was trying to record off of the radio and some of my own tapes. Side A is almost all Casey Kasem's Top 40. There are a few songs where the DJ talked for a really long time after the song started. But if the song was good enough, I left it on. Side B is a bunch of my favorite songs that I think you'll like. I played them from my own cassettes on Robby's tape deck and recorded from my jam box."

"Hey! I never gave you permission to use my tape deck!" Robby was indignant.

Nicki put her hand on her hip and gave him a pointed look. "If you didn't know that I used it, it obviously didn't bother you. I only did it when you were over at Joel's."

Robby harrumphed but closed his mouth after his mom gave him a warning look not to be rude.

"Anyway, I picked songs that should get you in a good mood. I hope you like it," she said sheepishly.

"Thanks Nicki, I do love listening to good music. I'll let you know what I think after I have a chance to check it out," Kevin said appreciatively. "This is so nice, y'all. I was getting really bummed out. I should be practicing for football, not sitting here watching the tube for hours every day. In the next week or so, they think I'll be able to at least sit on the bench and watch practices. But this will give me something else to focus on in the meantime."

"Yes, we really appreciate you bringing all of this over," Dale agreed. "I've been a little scared to leave to go to the store in case he needs anything, so we're running low on food. For now, the doctors don't want him moving at all, and I'm already gone so much at work, I really want to be here as much as I can."

"What's this for?" Robby asked as he picked up what appeared to be a straightened-out wire clothes hanger. "Are you studying how to break into cars in your spare time?"

"Haha. No, that's how I scratch under my cast. It gets really itchy under there."

Robby dropped the hanger onto the green shag carpet and looked at his hands, horrified. "Ew!"

"Hey, you asked!" Kevin was clearly enjoying tormenting Robby and making Nicki laugh.

"Alright kiddos, I think we've taken up enough of their time," Sharon motioned for her kids to follow her to the door.

"No!" Kevin said quickly. "Really, I'm enjoying the company. Could you stay and maybe play a board game or something? We have so many games that we hardly ever play anymore. Monopoly, Scrabble, Clue, Life, Mastermind."

Sharon looked at Dale, who smiled and nodded that he'd be happy to have them stay. "And actually, if you guys stick around, I might make a grocery store run," Dale said.

Sharon considered for a moment. She was still skeptical that she could trust Dale, but finally decided that Kevin needed the company and staying in Dale's good graces would help her children. So she took her purse off her shoulder and set it under the coffee table as she found a spot to sit on the love seat. "Okay, what game are we playing?"

# 16

# DECISION TIME

On Friday night after dinner, settled in on the couch at home, Sharon flipped off the TV and turned to face her kids. "Are you guys ready for tomorrow night?"

"Yeah, we have our list of things we need to do to recreate Halloween night," Nicki said as she tucked herself under her mom's arm and snuggled her. "We still aren't sure if it will work because we're taking a chance that the opposite moon phase will turn us back the opposite way. Marcus thinks we need the same moon phase, but we all agreed to try it this way just in case. I'm afraid Dom is going to spaz out if it doesn't work though."

Sharon bent down to place a kiss on Nicki's head and then rest her cheek there. "That's possible. You just have to be there for her if it doesn't work out. You know Dominique is like a second daughter to me, she's practically lived here since her mom started that new job. I hope it works, but we'll be here for her if it doesn't. What about you, Robby, are you okay with our decision to reverse your situation? I know you've really been enjoying your wicked new karate moves."

Robby shifted around in the beanbag next to the couch. "Mom, stop trying to sound cool. It's just weird."

"Fine, but my question stands. Are you going to go through with this?"

"Yeah, I can always take classes to get good at karate if I want. But this hair has got to go, and I'm tired of burning all my stuff since I can't seem to control my heat vision. I accidentally burned through three of my best comic books just this week!"

"I won't lie, I'll be glad to have my babies back to normal. I'm glad you've chosen to do that."

Robby groaned, "Mom, I'm not a baby."

She reached across to where he was sitting, ruffled his hair and informed him, "You'll always be my baby."

"Could a baby do this?" asked Robby as he pushed himself out of the beanbag and did a flying side kick into the entryway. He turned back to face her in a fighting stance with an expression that challenged her to disagree with him.

Nicki sang "Kung Fu Fighting" to Robby as her mother laughed and shook her head, marveling at the resilience that her kids showed after all that had happened.

"Okay guys, so this is it. Time for final decisions," Marcus said as all eight members of RA-D8 huddled in the cold bunker in Joel's backyard late on Saturday morning. The nights were starting to drop down near freezing and the underground shelter was much colder than it was outside.

"Can we do this in the yard? I'm turning into an iceberg," Dominique shivered with her hands shoved into the pockets of her coat and her chin tucked down under the scarf wrapped around her neck.

"Yeah, it's warmer out there, let's go," Jasmine, who had been bouncing her feet up and down to keep warm, immediately agreed with her friend. As they filed out, she turned to Javier and commented on his new jacket. "You finally got a jacket, Javi?"

"Yeah!" he was excited that someone noticed. "My mom felt bad that it was already November, and I didn't have one that fit. I think she also still feels weird about our whole thing, so she got me a Members Only jacket, do you like it?"

"Yeah man, it's totally rad," Robby said.

Jasmine gave him a smile and a thumbs up to indicate that she too thought it was rad.

Once everyone was out in the yard, Dominique started walking in circles kicking at the brown leaves that were now piled on the ground. Joel leaned against the tree where his old tire swing dangled on a drooping branch to his left and informed his friends, "I've decided to stay the way I am. I'll go with you to the hospital tonight, but I can't think of any reason not to keep my powers."

Dominique glared at him for a moment, but she really didn't have a solid argument for why he shouldn't follow her lead and move as quickly as possible toward a resolution. She set her jaw and turned to Javier, "What about you?"

Javier looked up at the wispy clouds that floated lazily past the sun, casting shadows across the lawn and said, "I actually don't know yet."

"What?" Nicki looked truly surprised. "But we're doing this in a few hours. You have to decide."

He held his hands out in defense, "I know, I know. But I feel like Jasmine and I don't really have that much that changed. And what is different could actually be helpful someday. I don't want to just sit around and talk about how cool it would be to fly or disappear. I want to be able to do it! Well, disappear at least. And mine is so easy to control. Actually, it's kind of hard to make it happen unless I'm asleep."

Dominique folded her arms and shifted most of her weight to one foot with her head cocked to the side. "Of course, it would be for you. The boy who never sits still." She pursed her lips and continued, "So someday, your poor wife is going to wake up and never know if you're in bed or not."

Marcus jumped in, "He would still occupy mass. There would be an indentation in the bed and she could always reach out to feel if he's there or not."

Dominique rolled her eyes. "Okay, so Joel and Javier are going to stay freaks. Anyone else?" She looked around the circle of friends, daring anyone else to opt-out.

Marcus hesitantly looked at Jasmine, "So you're going to change back? Even though you're still mostly the same?"

Jasmine nodded. "My dad is worried that there might be some sort of long-term effects and he wants me to just get it over with."

"Long-term effects? What kind?" asked Javier, his face creased in worry.

She shrugged and picked at the furry edge of her coat, not looking up at anyone else in the group. "I don't know. He said he thinks it's better to go back to normal just in case."

Javier and Joel made eye contact, each one thinking the same thing. What if it was, in fact, better to not take any chances and go back to normal. Finally, Joel broke the silence, "This isn't a foolproof plan we have. I'm still going to hold off in case going through with it causes problems."

"Why would you say that? Are you trying to jinx us?" Dominique shrieked at him.

"No," he met her hysteria with calmness. "But there isn't exactly a rule book for all of this, is there? For me at least, it's not worth trying something that we don't know will work or might even cause more problems."

Dominique's face contorted while she considered this new possibility.

Rani looked at Joel and said, "I can see why you would think that. My mom and I actually talked about the same thing last night. What if it's safer to just leave it? But after I outlined everything that we're doing, we couldn't come up with any scientific reason why this would cause more issues. What's more likely is that we're doing this in the wrong moon phase and nothing will happen at all." She turned to put both of her hands on Dominique's shoulders. "Which is a real possibility. You *have* to prepare yourself for this taking another fifteen days to fix. I know we both want this over with, *trust me*, life with my dad will be a million times easier if we can make all of this go away. But I don't have a lot of confidence that it will until we cycle back and recreate everything exactly as it was."

Dominique finally looked up into her friend's unnaturally blue eyes with her own green ones swimming in unshed tears. "I hope you're wrong." And she walked over to the porch to sit on the swing hanging from the awning to brood by herself.

---

That night at 8:30, Chad unlocked the door to the room with the X-ray machine and held it open for the rest of their crew: all eight kids as well as Sharon and Alisha. The rest of the parents had conceded to wait in the lobby as the room was already jam-packed. After everyone had filed in, he took the pillowcase full of candy and the crystal ball from Javier and set it on the X-ray machine.

"I wanted to meet early in case this piece of garbage had trouble getting started," Chad explained why he had asked them to meet and get started approximately half an hour earlier than everyone else expected. They nodded that this was a good idea, no one was willing to take any chances.

Chad flipped some switches and pulled out his notes with the settings so he could be absolutely certain that everything was set up accurately. Miraculously, the machine started up without any trouble.

"That's a good sign, although it means we have half an hour to kill before we can do anything," said Javier.

"Is it though?" Marcus wondered aloud.

"What do you mean, Marcus?" Sharon looked at him with a furrowed brow.

"Well, remember on Halloween how it was acting up, turning itself on and off, emitting sparks, Mr. Chad hit it with a wrench at least a few times."

Chad nodded and said, "Good thinking. Let me turn it off and then turn it back on like I did that night." And he proceeded to do exactly that. The second time, the machine did give a little cough and sputter as it started up. So Chad thwacked it with the wrench in the same place he recalled doing it two weeks previously. The minutes ticked by, marked by the sound of the clock on the wall that seemed to echo unnaturally loudly as everyone sat in silence.

Finally, at about five minutes before 9 p.m., Chad jumped up.

"What did we forget?" Marcus asked nervously.

"Nothing, I'm sure it's not important," said Chad. "But just in case, I forgot I pulled the first X-ray that we had done that night and I wanted to position the crystal ball exactly where it was the first time." He put the X-ray print out on the light board and shifted around the candy and the crystal ball inside the pillowcase in his best approximation of how everything was situated the first time.

"Okay," Alisha put her hands on Rani's shoulders and gave them a reassuring squeeze. "I think it's time to do this."

Chad took a deep breath and then hit the button to start the X-ray. When it was done, he turned back to everyone to see if they were satisfied.

"Do you think you should do it again without the crystal ball since that's what happened last time?" Sharon asked.

"I don't think it was the second time that did it," Chad looked at her uncomfortably. "I took those couple of pieces for myself when I removed the crystal ball. The ones I ate didn't go through a second time. I'm happy to do it again if you want, but I don't think it will make a difference."

"Okay, well, then everyone who is turning back, take a piece, and let's do this," Sharon said as she reached into the bag to grab a handful and pass them out. Joel and Javier both passed on taking a piece. Sharon asked if they were absolutely certain, to which both nodded yes, so she continued around the group. She lingered as she gave the last piece to Dominique and smoothed down the hair of the long, dark, silky wig that Dominique was wearing. "Oh honey, I hope for your sake this works. I know it's been hardest on you." Dominique gave her a weak smile and then anxiously opened her candy bar as fast as she could. She went so far as to lick the bit of chocolate that had melted onto the wrapper.

Alisha turned to Chad and said, "Thank you so much for doing this for everyone."

Chad blushed and muttered something that sounded like, "No problem," as he polished off his own piece of candy.

Alisha turned back to the group and clapped her hands together once. "Now all that's left to do is get everyone home for a good night's sleep."

"Absolutely," agreed Sharon. "Tomorrow morning, breakfast at our house. Regardless of what happens. Okay?" She pushed Dominique's wig hair behind her ear and gave her a smile of encouragement.

"No matter what," said Marcus, and he surprised Sharon by rushing at her and giving her a big hug around the waist. Sharon hugged him back, realizing that now the process was done and all they could do was wait, Marcus didn't really know what to do with himself. He was definitely happier when he had a problem to solve. She looked around at all of the kids, most of whom she had at least lent a hand in raising, and closed her eyes to say a little prayer that they'd wake up and everything would be back to normal.

# 17

# MUTANT FREAK WEIRDO MONSTERS

Nicki was the first to rise on Sunday morning, even before the sky had done much more than turn to a less dark shade of gray. She reached for her earrings and tried to pull them apart without any luck. Only marginally discouraged, she tiptoed down the hall to get a peek at what would be a more effective test, looking at Robby's hair. But when she sneaked up to his bed, she still saw a mass of tangled black hair, not his normal brown locks. Realizing that the experiment hadn't worked, she flopped down on his bed in a huff.

"What the..." Robby fought his comforter to sit up where he found his sister perched on his bed in the still dark room. "What exactly are you...oh, OH! Did you change back? Did I change back?" Robby reached up to touch his hair and realized it didn't feel right. Coupled with the glum look on his sister's face, he knew their attempt had failed.

Robby fidgeted with his hair and then let his hands drop to his lap. "Are you okay?" he asked Nicki.

"Yeah, I mean honestly it's not a huge deal for me. I'm just worried about Dom and Rani."

"And Marcus," Robby added.

"Yeah, of course. And Marcus. I know they all wanted this to work so badly."

"Yeah," Robby said quietly.

"Well, do you want to get up and watch some TV? I don't think I can go back to sleep right now," Nicki looked at her brother hopefully. She wanted some company while she sorted through her feelings.

"Sure," he threw back his covers, then padded down the hallway to the living room behind his sister.

---

About an hour later, the phone rang and Nicki raced to her room and picked up the receiver on her orange and black Garfield phone, which triggered the cat's eyes to open.

"Hello?"

"Hey," Dominique said sniffling.

"Hey," Nicki replied. "Are you okay?"

"I guess."

"Do you want to come over?"

"I have to go to church first, but we'll be over for your mom's breakfast right after."

"Sounds like a plan. And hey, we're going to try again in a

couple of weeks. Marcus didn't think this time would work anyway. We were just making sure we tried everything. It will be okay."

"Yep. See ya."

———————

At 11 o'clock that morning, Sharon was straightening a stack of napkins that she had set out next to a selection of muffins, cinnamon rolls and donuts as well as coffee and orange juice when the doorbell rang, signaling that the first guests had arrived. Over the next fifteen minutes, the rest of RA-D8 and their parents along with Marcus's two younger sisters arrived at the Swain house and milled around the kitchen and living room, chatting while noshing on a late breakfast. When the last of the guests arrived, Sharon called everyone into the living room.

"Thank you, everyone, for coming this morning. I thought it was important for us to get together and talk as a group about what happened last night as well as our plans for what we'll do next."

She paused as James Ross snorted softly.

"James," she addressed him. "Did you have a question?"

He gave Sharon a sardonic smile and said, "I'm just not sure I'd call what you guys have a 'plan' per se." Which earned him a slap on the shoulder from his wife, Elizabeth, Dominique's mom.

"I'm sorry, did you have some other thoughts we should

consider?" asked Sharon, who sounded deceptively agreeable, but was actually seething inside.

"For starters, I think we should sue the hospital. Then we could use the money from that to hire medical experts instead of listening to some twelve-year-old."

Dominique glared at her dad but didn't say anything out loud in front of everyone, knowing it would mean an argument at home later. Marcus however, had no qualms.

"I assume you're talking about me?" he asked James.

"Are you the one in charge?" James countered.

"I mean, no one is really in charge," Marcus said. "But I am the one who has been documenting everything and working with the lab technician to try to isolate the issue and make a plan for reversing it."

Alisha stepped in to clarify another point, "I would also like to address your comment about hiring medical experts. I've been a doctor for fifteen years, my daughter is one of the children who was affected by this. And I can definitively tell you that there are no experts for this. The size of the settlement wouldn't matter, you aren't going to find someone with experience here. I've already tried a few things, like a round of antibiotics. But so far, we haven't achieved any desirable results. So, what the kids and Chad, the lab tech, are doing is more than what you'd get bringing in an outsider."

"Speaking of outsiders...," James turned his glare on Alisha.

"James." Sharon started and then stopped, taking a deep breath before continuing. "You know I love your daughter like my own. She spends as much time at our house as she does yours." She held up a hand when he started to object. "Which of course I don't mind. She's a lovely girl and welcome here any time. But I do expect everyone to be respectful here. This is a tense situation and accusations aren't going to help anyone. We all have the same goal."

Marcus's youngest sister, Destiny, crawled into her mom's lap and hid her face as the adult's voices became sharper and more aggravated. Sharon noticed and adopted a much more kid-friendly tone. "Nicki, honey, could you and the girls take Destiny and Aliyah back to your room and show her your Teddy Ruxpin?"

"Sure Mom," Nicki jumped up and lifted Destiny into her arms, then took Aliyah by the hand and led them down the hall to her room saying, "How would you girls like to see a singing bear?" Jasmine and Dominique followed, but Rani stayed seated next to Alisha, sliding her hand into her mom's as though to anchor herself in the adult conversation.

When they heard the door to Nicki's room click shut, Antonio Alanis, Javier's dad, jumped in. "I've always thought we should sue the hospital. I still don't see why we shouldn't."

Sharon looked at him for a moment and then said slowly, "Didn't Javier decide not to change back? If he's not unhappy with the results, then I think that makes it a little more difficult to argue your case."

Cristina, Javier's mom, spoke in a soft voice while looking at her son but addressing Sharon. "We haven't all agreed in our household on what Javi should do about that. I would like for him to change back. His older brothers of course think it's hilarious and don't want him to, but honestly, their opinion doesn't count for much in this case. Antonio isn't sure if more X-raying is a good idea. Javier changes his mind depending on the day. So we're really quite unsure, but it has caused a great deal of stress in our home."

Sharon looked at Cristina with sympathy. "I know, I'm sure we've all been having our own conversations and chasing the same questions that don't seem to have answers. That's part of why I wanted us all to get together. To support one another and have an open forum to talk."

James Ross jumped back in with a question. "So, if the little experiment last night didn't work, what makes you think it will work when you try it again in a few weeks?"

All of the children remaining in the room turned to defer to Marcus.

"Well, it's a little difficult to explain," he said.

"Try me," James said.

"James!" Elizabeth Ross took exception to his tone. "Please remember you're talking to a child and not cross-examining someone in a courtroom!"

James tried again, "Please Marcus, share with me your infinite wisdom on the matter."

Marcus ignored his sarcasm and outlined what they knew about the moonstone, the moon phase, and why he hadn't expected it to work the previous night, but also why they had moved forward with the trial anyway. He filled in the other adults on all of the notes they had made about the circumstances of that night, the candy and the X-ray machine. Then he admitted, "I still feel like we're missing something. Maybe something important. But we have a couple of weeks to analyze and figure it out. And Chad, the lab tech Dr. Gabri mentioned before, he's helping too. He had a piece of our candy, so he was impacted. He's very interested in helping us find a solution."

Sharon took charge of the conversation again, "As you can see, we're being very deliberate with everything that we know so we can get all of our kids back to normal. Or at least the ones who want to get back to normal. Speaking of which, can we please talk about Javier and Joel and their decision not to go back?"

Robby jumped up from his spot on the floor and said to Marcus, Joel and Javier, "Hey guys, you should come to my room. I want to show you something."

---

"What did you want to show us?" Joel asked, looking around the room as he walked in, but not seeing anything interesting.

"Oh nothing, I just didn't want to listen to the adults argue anymore," Robby said as he flopped on his bed.

"That works for me," Marcus said. "I had something I wanted to talk to you guys and the girls about anyway. Can we go get them?"

Robby disappeared down the hall and came back with Nicki, Marcus's little sisters and Nicki's friends, minus Rani who was still in the living room with the adults. Destiny walked over and sat in Marcus's lap and popped her thumb in her mouth while Aliyah stayed with Nicki and sat in hers, clutching Nicki's Monchhichi. "What's up?" Nicki asked. "Robby said you wanted to see us?"

Marcus addressed the room, "Yeah, so I was thinking that we should set a list of rules."

"Get real," Dominique interrupted. "You with your rules and action plans all the time! Who died and made you king?"

"Yeah, what was that about? Mr. Ross saying you were the leader?" Robby wanted to know.

"I'm not trying to be the king or the leader. I just think that with everything being so uncertain, it's nice to have some rules to keep us all safe, you know?"

Jasmine, always the mediator, stepped in and asked, "What kind of rules were you thinking?" She gave Destiny a smile and a little wave. The little girl smiled around her thumb and ducked her head shyly.

"Well, for starters, I don't think we should use our powers in public anymore. It's starting to get too much attention and not all of it is good."

Joel took exception to this and asked huffily. "So, you don't think I should use my lightsaber outside? I don't agree with that one. I'm not allowed to use it inside, so that means I wouldn't be able to use it at all!"

"I'm not necessarily saying not to use it outside," Marcus clarified. "I just think we should check to make sure people aren't around first."

Joel huffed again and sat back on the beanbag chair with his arms crossed, not making eye contact with anyone.

Dominique asked Marcus, "What else?"

Marcus was nervous now to share the rest of his thoughts since the first one hadn't gone over so well. So he tried a different approach. "You know we already have some rules, right? Like that we aren't telling anyone about Jasmine's crystal ball? I'm really just trying to think of more things like that where we should consider it now before it's too late. I'm afraid if people know too much, they'll try to exploit us. And I don't want to end up being somebody's dancing monkey."

"Is that because you don't have any really cool powers other than being fast?" Joel narrowed his eyes at his friend.

Robby put his hands up between his two friends. "Dude, what is up with you guys? We're not enemies."

Jasmine added, "And I think we should use nicer voices while the girls are in here," she nodded her head toward Marcus's sisters.

Marcus gave Destiny a little squeeze and then said, "Fine, we'll forget formalizing the rules. As long as we stick to the main ones. We always have each other's backs, and we don't tell anyone anything that isn't already public knowledge."

His words were met with a round of agreement from everyone, including Joel.

No one who was used to fickle Texas weather was surprised when they woke to a rather warm Monday. That afternoon was sunny with a light breeze as all eight members of RA-D8 were out on the playground during recess, sitting in a circle at the top of the monkey bar dome. All eyes were on Rani while she provided a recap of the parents' discussion from the day before during the time that the rest of the group had been in Robby's room.

"It was pretty much what you'd expect," Rani said, shrugging. "Nicki, your mom explained more about what happened Saturday night at the hospital. Just a step-by-step explanation of what we tried to recreate. They talked a lot about who does and doesn't want to change back."

Joel was quick to ask for details, "What did they say?"

Rani pursed her lips trying to remember the specifics. "Well, it sounds like your parents want you to change back. They agreed with Jasmine's parents that since we don't know if this will ever fade or get worse or cause us to have other illnesses, they think we should all change back."

Joel looked livid but didn't say anything.

"Did you know that's how they felt?" Rani asked, unnerved by his reaction. "I'm sorry, I assumed you knew. I shouldn't have said anything."

"It's fine," he said, not sounding fine at all. "I just don't know why they never talk to me about this stuff. I'm not a toddler, and I should get a say in what happens to me!" He slapped his hand against the metal bar beneath him to emphasize his point.

Rani felt a red heat creep up her neck and tried to recover. "I don't know, Joel. I don't think they're going to force you or anything. They just said that's what they wanted. Please don't be mad."

Joel stared at her for a few seconds, eyes burning with anger, and then took a deep breath. "I'm not mad at you. I'm just sick of my parents acting like I'm still five years old."

"Did mine say anything?" Javier wanted to know.

Rani seemed hesitant to cause any more friction, but she knew everyone expected her to share what she heard.

"Mostly your dad," she started.

"That's not surprising," Javier gave a little chuckle. "What did he say?"

"He's still pretty mad. And I guess some people where he works have been asking about his 'mutant' son, which obviously he's not happy about."

"What?" This was clearly news to Javier. "I had no idea he was getting dissed at work."

Rani nodded sympathetically. "Apparently it's like, all the time too."

Dominique spat out, "People think we're freaks. This isn't exactly breaking news."

"Yeah," Javier agreed. "But it's one thing from an elementary school bully. You would think adults would act more...I don't know. Like adults! It's not like we asked for this."

"They don't care!" Dominique burst out, loudly enough to turn some heads on the playground. A couple of girls nearby gave them odd looks before they ducked their heads together to whisper.

Jasmine shushed her friend, "Please Dom, let Rani tell us what else she heard yesterday."

Dominique snapped her mouth shut and all eyes turned back to Rani.

"The mutant, freak, weirdo, monster thing actually came up a couple of times," she continued as she fidgeted with the end of her braid. "It seems that more than just Javi's dad has had people say something pretty rude."

Dominique looked down at her hands. "Yeah, I came out of youth group at church yesterday and overheard a couple of the adults saying they were glad their children weren't friends with us. They think we're unholy or something."

Jasmine, who knew how important religion was to Dominique and her family, let out a gasp. "Dom, that's so bogus! You're still the same person. A *good* person who has been true to her faith as long as I've known you. Which is almost as long as we've been alive!"

"I know," Dominique choked out as she tried to hold back tears. "I mean, I know now. I talked to my mom about it for a long time when we got home after breakfast yesterday. At first, I did kind of wonder if there was something really wrong with me."

"No!" Nicki said firmly. "This is something that happened to you because you did something that normal kids do. There's nothing sacrilegious about eating candy!"

Dominique gave her a little half-smile. "Well, there are some people who think trick or treating is bad."

Nicki doubled down on her defense of her friend. "Well, those people don't understand that we're just kids having fun, dressing up and enjoying life and not summoning the devil to sacrifice goats or whatever it is they think we do when we trick or treat."

The tension in the group lessoned at this outburst as everyone laughed.

"Seriously though," Nicki continued. "We're just good kids trying to do our school work and help our parents make dinner. We want to go for bike rides and to the movies. We're not monsters or freaks or whatever it is that those idiots are saying." She crossed her arms and gave a little huff to emphasize her point.

After a pause, Marcus reminded everyone that recess was almost over if Rani had anything else to share.

"Oh yeah, I can't remember who it was, but Dominique or Jasmine, one of your moms asked why we aren't working more closely with Dale since he works at the hospital. That was kind of awkward."

"What did my mom say?" Nicki asked.

"Nothing actually," Rani assured her. "My mom jumped in and told them that she had been talking to Dale to work through any medical stuff and that we would have full access to the X-ray machine the night we need it. She pointed out that Dale isn't actually a doctor so our plans with him are more about coordinating time with the machine. Then she changed the subject and no one followed up."

The distant sound of the bell drifted across the playground and the fifth- and sixth-grade classes started migrating back to where the teachers were lining everyone up in their respective groups.

Jasmine smiled at Rani and thanked her for sharing what she had heard. She reached out and gave Rani's hand a little squeeze and then they all got lost in the shuffle of chatter, laughter and the squeaking of shoes on the tile as they walked back into the school.

# 18

# DANCING MONKEYS

"Sure, Mrs. Sanderson, I'll talk to the other parents and get back to you as soon as I can," Sharon was on the phone in her living room, where she had been watching *Who's the Boss* with her kids after dinner on Tuesday night. "Of course, have a good night. Goodbye." She untangled the phone cord before placing the receiver back in the cradle on the side table next to the couch.

"What was that all about?" Robby asked his mom. He and Nicki had heard their names mentioned as well as those of their friends and wanted to know what was happening.

Sharon took a moment to respond, not sure how her kids would react. "That was Mrs. Sanderson. Her daughter Jenny is having a birthday party next Friday and wants to know if you kids would be interested in...I think the word she used was performing."

Robby turned to look at Nicki, his eyes slits as he asked

her, "Jenny Sanderson, isn't that Andrew's sister?"

Nicki rolled her eyes and nodded.

"Mrs. Sanderson said she sent home an invitation with all of the girls from your grade," Sharon looked at Nicki.

"Yeah, I mean, her brother is a jerk. He's the one who called us Hallo-wieners. Jenny is alright, but I hadn't really planned on going since I'm sure he'll be there too," Nicki told her mom.

"What did you tell them?" Robby asked. "I was only sort of paying attention."

"I didn't want to make the decision unilaterally, so I told her that I'd talk to you guys and the other parents and get back to her."

"What's uni-lateral-ly?" Nicki stumbled over the word.

"That's what would happen if I just answered for everyone and didn't take your opinion into account," Sharon explained. "She said the party is at ShowBiz Pizza Place. Do you guys have any interest at all in going before I talk to the other parents?"

Nicki and Robby looked at each other, flooded with thoughts and not knowing where to start.

"I mean, I could sing and do a little hologram show. That could be kind of fun since I didn't get to do it at the Sesqui-centennial," Nicki offered, but without much conviction.

"Yeah, and I could do a board-breaking demo and then end with kicking Andrew in his stupid face," Robby said with more enthusiasm.

"Somehow I doubt Mrs. Sanderson would sign off on that

last part," Sharon gave Robby a mock stern look.

"Fine, just the boards then," he rolled his eyes as he conceded with a dramatic sigh and then all three of them dissolved into fits of laughter. "But I'm warning you right now, some of the kids in RA-D8 really don't want to be put on the spot with their powers. It's kind of a touchy subject."

Nicki nodded with wide eyes, emphasizing her brother's words of caution.

"Okay, I'll call the other parents while you guys finish up this show and then go get ready for bed."

---

The next day, all eight members of RA-D8 were gathered in front of the school to discuss the offer before they headed inside where they might be overheard.

"There is no way that I'm going to go be a dancing monkey so Andrew Sanderson can make fun of me. Now I don't even want to go at all," Dominique had her arms firmly crossed over her chest and stomped to emphasize her animosity toward the birthday girl's brother. These days she wore the wig that her mom had broken down and purchased for their experiment. It didn't quite have the luster of her regular hair, and the red curls had a tendency to sneak out, but it did help her regain some of her confidence and a lot of her sass.

"Yeah, I wasn't sure at first either," Nicki assured her friend. "But I did think it might be kind of cool to do an actual performance. When else would I have the chance to sing and do the hologram light show for an audience?"

Dominique just shrugged, but she was still pouting.

"I wouldn't mind putting on a lightsaber slash sword battle. Rani, what do you think?" Joel asked hopefully.

"I don't think my dad would be cool with that," she wrinkled her nose. "He doesn't want me in public too much after the Sesquicentennial thing."

"What about your mom?" he tried again.

"It won't matter, I'm with my dad that weekend," she said.

"Wait, what?" Jasmine interrupted. "That's the weekend we change back! Is he going to bring you to the hospital?"

"Oh yeah, he's pretty much counting down the minutes for that. He can't wait to have this over with."

"Whew, that's a relief," Jasmine smiled at Rani.

"I think we all know about me," Javier couldn't wait to give his two cents. He was bouncing on the balls of his feet with his usual energy, even this early in the morning.

Everyone chuckled a little as Robby pretended to think hard and finally held up a finger and said, "I'm guessing you're a yes?"

"Of course! I'm planning to disappear and bring the cake to the table so it looks like it's floating!"

Robby's eyes widened. "Hey, if you're invisible, maybe you could mess with Andrew! Pay him back for always being such a jerk." Javier gave a non-committal shrug and turned to Marcus. "Would you do anything?"

"I don't know what I would do. It's not like I can run

super-fast around ShowBiz, that place is always a clown house. And no one wants to hear me solve math equations."

"Hmm," Javier was forced to agree that Marcus's talents were far less useful in an entertainment setting than they were for helping to solve their group's problems. He gave up and turned to Jasmine, "What about you?"

"We haven't told anyone about my crystal ball, remember?" she said.

"Oh yeah, too bad, that would be a fun trick," Javier lamented. "Okay, so we've got Nicki, Robby, Joel and me as yeses. Rani is a maybe. Marcus, Jasmine and Dominique are nos. Is everyone still going to come though?"

Marcus shook his head, "The boys weren't invited, remember? Not as guests to the party anyway. We were only invited to perform. So if I'm not going to perform, I don't feel like I should go."

"Rad," Dominique jumped on his response. "If Marcus isn't going, I'm not going."

Nicki scoffed and said, "Marcus has a better reason than you. You should come, I really want you to see me perform. Pretty please with sugar on top?" She batted her eyelashes at her friend and gave her an enormous megawatt smile.

Dominique and Nicki stared each other down, but were interrupted by the bell before either would give in. "We'll talk at lunch!" Nicki said as they all hitched up their backpacks and ran toward their respective first classes of the day.

Chad was in his lab on Thursday afternoon when Marsha, the hospital receptionist, knocked lightly on the door and poked her head in.

"Hey, what's up?" Chad said as he looked up from his microscope, surprised at the interruption.

"There's a call for you at the front desk. I would have just sent it through, but the caller wanted to make sure you were available and had some privacy. Which it looks like you do, so I'll go ahead and transfer it if that's okay?"

"That's odd, but sure, thanks Marsha," Chad rolled his chair away from his microscope and toward the wall with the phone. It rang a few seconds later and he snatched it up.

"Chad Stevens, how can I help you?"

"Hey Chad, it's Marcus."

"Hi Marcus, is everything okay?"

"Yeah, we wanted to meet up with you, but I didn't know your last name until you said it just now. So I didn't know how to look up your number or how else to find you."

"Of course," Chad assured him. "Wow, for smart people, I can't believe we didn't plan better for our next meeting."

"Yeah, I know. I guess we've all been a little preoccupied."

Chad snorted at the understatement. "So where would you like to meet? And when?"

"We're going to the park after school tomorrow. You know, the one with the creek and the waterfalls?"

"Yeah, I know the one. I'll tell Dale I have an appointment and meet you there...ummm, around 3:30?"

"That would be perfect," Marcus sounded relieved. "We

park our bikes by the big boulder just past the playground and then walk straight down to the creek."

"Great, I actually have some information that I wanted to discuss with you. I'll be there," Chad said and then hung up. He spun in his chair and bent back over the microscope, which held a tiny sliver of a very specific Snickers bar pressed between the slide and the glass cover. Based on what he was seeing, he was more eager than ever to solve this mystery.

————————

The four boys had arranged with their parents to spend some time at the park on Friday after school. It was the last day before Thanksgiving break, and they wanted to celebrate. When the final bell rang, they met up at the bike racks and raced each other to the park. Once there, they left their bicycles at the boulder Marcus had mentioned to Chad and then traversed the path down to the creek.

It was a favorite spot of theirs, they had all been here with their parents when they were little and continued to go as a group now that they were older. Even though it was less than a mile from their school, the creek area was a world away from the flatlands of Texas that they saw in their neighborhood every day. A serpentine trail of water had carved out deep notches in the ground, creating an elevation not seen in town. Enormous trees towered on either side, meeting to form a canopy over the brook, many of their roots exposed where the ground had eroded away to form the deep bed of the creek. Large rocks were scattered throughout the water and adventurous children for generations would hop from one to the next, making their way down the little valley to explore. Those who were more observant noticed the many layers of the large stones along with the holes that created pools where entire ecosystems lived. The land that the stream wound through gently sloped downhill so that every few yards or so, there was another small waterfall, bubbling the water down the rivulet. This time of year, much of the top of the water was covered in yellow and orange leaves.

Joel asked, "Hey Robby, do you want to have a stick race while we wait for Chad?"

"You know it!" Robby agreed, already searching for the perfect stick to float down the creek.

Marcus and Javier hiked a little way down the bank to the spot where they would serve as judges for the race. Javier started skipping rocks, shouting with glee when he managed seven skips with the same smooth stone. Marcus found a stick and drew in the dirt on the flat space where he and Javier waited. At first, it was just doodles, but then he had an idea, smoothed the sandy dirt back over with his tennis shoe and started drawing a stylized RA-D8.

"Dude, that's wicked!" declared Javier. "We should get Nicki to have her mom put that on the shirts. I wish we had a camera so we could take a picture and show her."

"Okay, we're ready!" Robby's voice carried downwind to where Marcus and Javier stood. Robby and Joel were each standing on a rock in the middle of the creek, a few feet down from one of the waterfalls where the water rushed more quickly. They were both crouched down, a stick in each boys' hand ready to drop it in the water when given the signal.

"Okay," Javier shouted back from his spot on the bank. He held both arms straight up in the air. "Ready, set, go!" He dropped his arms on the last command just in case his friends couldn't hear him.

Simultaneously, Robby and Joel dropped their sticks in the water. Joel's caught a swirl of the current and was swept out to an early lead. Robby's stick took a more casual approach, floating slowly toward the imaginary finish line, spinning lazy circles in the water. Robby rolled his eyes and groaned at his stick's lack of urgency. But then Joel's veered to the right and got stuck in a tangle of tree roots. It ended up half submerged, pointing straight up and barely moving.

"Aww, harsh!" Joel yelled as he dropped his head and pounded his fists onto his knees.

After another few leisurely moments, Robby's stick passed Javier, who declared him the winner.

"Alright, guys come check this out!" Javier yelled to his friends. "Marcus drew a really cool design for our team."

In the time that it took Robby and Joel to pick their way over to where the other boys stood, Chad had arrived, found the bikes and cautiously inched his way down the path. He held onto tree trunks for support, edging toward the small flat space where the boys were looking at Marcus's drawing.

"Hey guys," he was slightly out of breath. It turned out

that sitting in a lab all day and playing video games most of the night didn't keep him in tip-top shape.

"Hey, Mr. Chad," Marcus waved him over. "Thanks for coming to meet us."

"Of course, what do you have there?" he asked, cocking his head to get a better look at the drawing.

"Oh, I was just working on a logo for our group. We call ourselves RA-D8."

"That's really clever," Chad nodded his approval. In his mind, 11-year-olds were still practically babies, but these kids sure seemed more mature than he remembered being at that age.

"Rani made it up," said Joel, giving credit where credit was due.

"Come on, we can all fit on this rock over here," Marcus led them to a spot just behind the flat space where a long, low rock jutted from the ground under the trees and out over the water. "So, what new information did you have for us?"

Chad looked at the eager faces staring back at him and tried to figure out where to start.

"Well, do you remember when I told you that I can see chemical compounds?"

He received four nods of acknowledgment, so he continued. "It's almost like it pops up in white text over the thing I'm looking at if I concentrate on it even a little. I was lying in bed the other night, and I couldn't sleep. I started to wonder if I looked at a regular candy bar and the one I still have from that night, if it would look any different. I didn't actually have another candy bar, so I had to wait until the next morning when I could run to the gas station and buy some more Snickers. I took one of the new ones and the infected one, unwrapped them both and looked at them. Sure enough, there was a difference. I took another of the new ones and laid it next to the first two. The two new ones looked exactly the same, but the infected one was clearly the outlier."

Marcus was quick to ask, "So what is the element that's different in the infected one?"

"That's where things get tricky," Chad paused. "Here, let me draw it for you."

The four boys and Chad walked back over to just past where Marcus had been drawing and picked up another stick to show them what he was talking about.

"I don't remember when you start learning this stuff in school, so stop me if this is something you already know," Chad drew letters connected by lines in the dirt with the stick. "Chemical compounds are when you have atoms from two or more different elements. So for example, the water in that creek is $H_2O$ and it looks like this." He drew an O with two Hs, both slightly below the O, one on each side and then connected them with diagonal lines.

"For the candy," he continued, "there are a few different compounds, I won't bore you with the details. The part that affects us is the missing element." He drew a series of letters and numbers, chained together with single or double lines. In the middle of the chain was a space with no letter or numbers. Marcus immediately picked up on the omission.

"What's that?" he pointed at the empty space.

Chad looked up from where he was squatting next to his drawing. "That is our problem and unfortunately, I don't have an answer." He stood up to stretch his legs and looked at the four pairs of eyes staring at him with confusion and concern. "When I look at the candy bar that went through the X-ray machine, I see the molecules like I normally would, but there's a blank spot in the middle of this chain. I tried to look up known chemical compounds that have these other elements," he pointed back to the areas where he had written the elements comprising the molecule in question. "But I haven't yet found anything that matches this combination and even if I could, I still wouldn't be able to explain the hole. It's almost like the X-ray mutated the element into something that hasn't previously existed on Earth. Or at least hasn't been discovered and documented by any scientists yet. My guess is that I can't see what it is because I don't know the sign for that particular element, so my brain can't render it."

"Wow," Marcus whispered on an exhale.

"Yeah," Chad agreed. "Which makes it really difficult to determine how to reverse it if we don't know what *it* is in the first place."

Robby scrunched up his face trying to understand. "So the lasers and the moonstone made a new element?"

"That's not technically possible," Chad shook his head. "At least I don't think. I know they're working on some really advanced stuff in labs to try to basically smash atoms together, but that requires equipment way more sophisticated than anything we have at our hospital."

"So what do you think happened?" Joel asked.

"Honestly, I have no idea. I do wonder if those green sparks had anything to do with it. I've tried to research that as well, but didn't really find anything helpful."

All five of them sat silently for a moment, listening to the babbling of the waterfalls below and the birds chirping in the rustling leaves above.

Finally, Marcus broke the silence. "I think we have to make some assumptions at this point. It sounds like something during that first X-ray with the crystal ball and moonstone somehow created a new molecule that found its way into the candy. Eating and processing that molecule resulted in the reaction that caused this," he waved to his silver arms. "So we need to get that molecule out of our bodies. Which does make me think that running the same process on the candy that is already infected has the potential to reverse our situation. I think if we use new candy, it will just do the same thing it did the first time."

"Sure," Joel conceded. "But if the people who wanted to change back dressed like themselves instead of in costumes, they would at least look normal, right?" He looked back and forth between Marcus and Chad, neither one offering an immediate answer.

Marcus spoke first, "I suppose we would look normal, but..."

Chad picked up where Marcus left off, "Our bodies would

still have something in us that isn't right. And we don't know if it would ever wear off. Or what the other side effects might be."

"Or if it would happen again any time we wore a costume?" Javier asked.

"Who knows?" Chad gave a small mirthless laugh.

Joel offered another potential issue, "So if we use the already infected candy, what's supposed to happen? The X-ray machine creates an entirely new chemical?"

Chad jumped in to explain his thought process, "Well, that is certainly a possibility. But I think it will act more like an antidote, sort of like a vaccine, but not exactly. Do you know how those work? Basically, something new is introduced into the body and your body learns how to fight it off. Then when it gets exposed to the same virus, it already knows how to kill it."

"But our bodies are just accepting this, not fighting it off," Marcus said as worry lines etched his forehead.

"Right," Chad agreed, nodding slowly. "That's why I'm hoping the second 'dose' from the machine to the candy and then to our bodies could theoretically kick start our immune systems, effectively acting more like an antidote." He stared around the small circle of hopeful faces. "I have to admit, it's all a guess at this point. I can take a look at the candy after we X-ray it and before we eat it to see if my thoughts pan out."

"Great," Robby said and then bent down, scooped up a handful of pebbles and threw them all as hard as he could into the creek.

While the boys were at the park, the girls walked back to Nicki's house. Once everyone had peeled off their backpacks and shoes, which were left by the front door, Nicki heated up a package of microwave popcorn. Jasmine, Dominique and Rani went to the refrigerator and each selected a can of soda for their movie afternoon.

"My mom got us *Top Gun*," Nicki announced.

"Yes!" cheered Jasmine.

"You've already seen it like three times, why are you so excited?" Dominique asked her friend.

"Because it's still good every time," Jasmine said with a little smile and a sheepish one-shoulder shrug.

The microwave beeped and the girls all piled onto the couch in the living room, their drink cans lined up on the coffee table in front of them. Nicki held the popcorn bowl in her lap where everyone could reach while they watched Tom Cruise and Val Kilmer trade barbs in the locker room and on the sand volleyball court.

Nicki sang along with every song until they got to "Take My Breath Away," which she deemed gross and tried to fast forward through.

"Hey!" Dominique protested.

"What?" Nicki asked.

"Quit deciding which parts of the movies we get to watch," Dominique said grumpily.

"Oh come on, Dom, this part is gross."

"Fine," Dominique harrumphed and crossed her arms over her chest. She wasn't quite ready to admit to her friends that she didn't actually find this part gross like she did the first time she watched it in the movie theater.

While the credits rolled at the end of the movie, the girls started to chat about their weekend plans. Before they got too far into their discussion, the boys burst through the front door like a tornado. They joined the girls in the living room and proceeded to tell them about Chad's discovery.

"So you're saying there's some weird molecule floating around my body causing this?" Dominique asked, horrified.

"Basically," confirmed Robby.

"Ewwwww!" she shrieked.

"Oh come on Dom, what did you think was happening?" Nicki chastised her friend before returning her attention to the boys. "Does this help us at all?" She looked between Marcus and Rani, the mutually agreed upon smartest members of their group when it came to scientific matters.

"Maybe," said Marcus, who had been able to spend more time processing the new information. "To be honest, it's really uncharted territory. It's not like I can look in a science book and find anything about this. So I have some thoughts, but no way to know if they're accurate until we run our test."

Dominique seemed to deflate at this news.

"But," he emphasized to her, "it does help me think through some of the decisions we were trying to make. Like whether to use new candy or the infected stuff."

She gave him a small smile, realizing that he was trying to keep her spirits up.

"Alright, well we have a little more than a week until we try this again," Jasmine calculated. "We should spend some time thinking of all of those questions and making sure we have the best answers we can. And in the meantime, we're on Thanksgiving break, so we won't be distracted with school stuff while we try to figure it out!"

"Yeah, totally," Nicki said to a murmur of assent from the rest. "Thanks for meeting with Chad, guys. I feel like we're finally starting to get somewhere."

---

With school officially out for the week of Thanksgiving and Sharon also taking some time for the holiday, everyone in the Swain house was operating at a slower pace. It was nearly 8 o'clock on Friday night and the scent of teriyaki was just starting to permeate the kitchen as Sharon prepared to serve stir fry for dinner. While her kids set the table and poured drinks, Sharon fluffed the rice with a fork, then divided it up between what she and her kids affectionately called "plowls," shallow bowls or plates with high edges, and topped it with a variety of seasoned veggies and shrimp. She finished it off with a sprinkle of sesame seeds and then brought the meal to the table.

While they ate, Nicki and Robby explained to their mom everything Chad had shared with the boys that day. She nodded her head, encouraging them to go through the details while they were fresh on their minds before she started asking questions, most of which they weren't able to answer.

"I'll ask Alisha to come over tonight or tomorrow so we can run this past her," Sharon said when they had finished. "She's definitely got the more scientific mind, and it's been helpful to brainstorm with her. And, of course, as a doctor, she'll know more about antidotes and how they might possibly work in this case."

Nicki was quick to agree, "Rani told us that she's so good at science because her parents talked about stuff like that with her since she was really little." She took a couple of bites of her stir fry and then looked back up at her mom. "Hey, I was thinking since we're out of school for Thanksgiving this week and you took some time off of work, maybe you could take me and the girls to the skating rink? Since we're just staying here this year, I want to do something to make the week special. Rani will be with her dad because her mom can't get off work, so it would just be me, Jazz and Dom."

With everything that had been going on, and the next attempt at reversing their condition on the horizon, Sharon had decided to stay in town for Thanksgiving and just invite over a few people who also didn't have travel plans. Typically, she took her kids to see her parents a few hours north and she hated missing the time with them. But she was hoping that everything would be resolved in a week and they could try again at Christmas.

Sharon mentally pictured her schedule and then replied,

"I think Tuesday would be best. I need to go into the office Monday morning for a couple of hours. I figured you and Robby would sleep in, so you can just stay here. But Tuesday I'm off and planned to run some errands in town to start getting ready for our guests on Thursday. Robby, why don't you see if one of your friends would like to come along? You can play video games while the girls skate and I take care of a few things."

"Sure mom," Robby agreed as Nicki beamed and said, "Thanks, Mama!"

It was Monday morning, less than a week before their plans to reverse the curse, and Chad whistled to himself as he crossed the parking lot toward the hospital doors. He realized that he had left his coat in his room the last time he had been at the hospital and it was dipping down near freezing at night. He wanted to grab it before he met up with a college friend for a beer and a couple of games of pool that night.

As he approached his room, he heard a rustling sound from within and tiptoed closer to see who was messing around with his stuff. He peered cautiously around the corner and saw Dale hunched over his desk rifling through papers. His first instinct was to back away, but then he felt a surge of anger and instead cleared his throat as he entered the room. "Can I help you?" he asked, his voice scathing at the intrusion into his personal things.

Dale whipped around, hands held up in front of him as though expecting to find that he was being held at gunpoint.

"Hey Chad, what are you doing here?" Dale laughed nervously as he dropped his hands to his sides.

"What are *you* doing here?"

"Well, I...um...you see...," Dale stammered as he raced to find a plausible excuse. "I thought you were off today and I promised Sharon I'd get your notes to share so the kids had a little adult supervision with their plan. They have all these ideas, but we thought it would be smart to have them run it past us. And Alisha. And of course, in order to make the wisest decisions, we needed all of the information. Since it's your day off, I didn't want to bother you."

Chad stared at him for a few very uncomfortable seconds and then said, "You can stop wasting your time. I keep my notes at home."

"Oh," Dale's face fell with disappointment.

"Besides, Marcus already has all of my notes. If Sharon wants them, she's welcome to ask him. Or I'd be happy to make her a copy." His voice was still frosty and Dale seemed lost at this reversal of authority coupled with the news that what he was seeking was not in a place where he could access it.

Finally, Dale walked toward the door and gave Chad a single nod as he said, "I'll be sure to tell her."

Chad watched Dale with narrowed, suspicious eyes and then called to him as he reached the midpoint in the hallway between their offices.

"Dale, what are you planning?"

Dale stopped but took a beat before turning around to face Chad. "What do you mean?"

"I mean, you've made references to exploiting this glitch in the machine, you're digging around in my office, giving me excuses that don't make sense. You're obviously planning something. I need to know that you aren't going to interfere with our plans to turn the kids and me back."

Dale paused to consider how much he could tell Chad. Then he walked back into Chad's room, waited for Chad to follow and closed the door.

"Look, Kevin really got hurt on that ride. His recovery is expected to be long, painful and will ruin his chances of going to college. I want to use the machine to fix him."

Chad softened ever so slightly. The more he thought about what Dale had said at lunch and the vibe that he put off, Chad was convinced that Dale was planning to turn himself into some megalomaniacal villain and terrorize the town for his own gain. He considered carefully what to say next. "Dale, I'm really sorry about Kevin and his injury. But what will you do if it doesn't turn out the same or actually makes him worse? We're dealing with so many unknowns. It's irresponsible to try this out on your own son! This type of thing takes years of tests on smaller organisms before moving to human trials. What you're talking about is insane."

"What would you know? You don't have kids!" Dale exploded, his already red face moving more toward a purple hue.

Chad was quiet for a moment. He wasn't good with confrontation, but he knew he had to stand up in this case.

"If you insist on moving forward with your plan, I'll be forced to report you to the hospital board," the quaver in Chad's voice somewhat undermined the fierceness of his conviction, but nonetheless, he held eye contact to let Dale know he was serious.

Dale retorted, "How is what you're doing any different? You want to experiment on the kids to perform something that's never been done! I'm at least re-creating something that we've seen success with once."

Chad stopped for a moment to consider what Dale was saying. It was true, he should find a way to safely conduct some tests before doing anything else to himself or the children, but eventually he held firm. "In our case, we have concerns that there could be long-term damage. We're working to prevent further problems. In your case, you're causing issues where there are none."

"You think Kevin's shattered foot isn't a problem?" Dale asked incredulously.

"Broken bones are something that we know how to fix, Dale! Sure it takes time, but it's been done successfully literally millions of times throughout history with repeatable results. We don't even know all of the variables that potentially caused this issue and missing one could net wildly different results. It's not the same thing."

Dale's jaw clenched along with his fists and he finally muttered a terse "Fine" and stalked out of the room.

# 19

# CONVENTION OF MISFITS

Sharon pulled into the parking lot of Grayson Ridge Skateland just after noon on Tuesday and waited for the gaggle of children to exit her van so she could lock up. As soon as the doors to the skating rink opened, Sharon and her charges were assaulted with the sounds of Huey Lewis singing about the power of love. Nicki beamed as she sang along, bobbing her head in time to the beat.

Wafting along behind the jarring sound was the mingled scent of popcorn and old leather skates. Jasmine inhaled deeply and a rush of memories from skating parties past flooded her mind. She gave a little smile as she looked forward to an afternoon of carefree fun.

Meanwhile, Sharon paid the entrance and skate rental fees while the woman at the counter placed bright blue stamps with a picture of a skate on the hand of each child. Then Sharon handed Nicki and Robby a few dollars each to cover the cost of snacks and games. She kissed Nicki on the head, patted Robby's shoulder and told them she'd be back in about two hours.

Nicki, Jasmine and Dominique turned right and went to the counter to pick out skates. They lined up in a row with their hands on top of the counter that came up almost to their chins and requested their respective shoe sizes. Robby and Marcus went left and made a beeline for the video games. Today was more about the girls, so Sharon had asked her son to invite just one friend and he had chosen Marcus. Robby was a little uncomfortable with the way Javier and Joel talked about staying in their current state, and he didn't really want to get cornered by one of them today. He knew Marcus would want to chill and play games just like him.

By the time the girls got their skates on, "How Will I Know" by Whitney Houston was blaring from the speakers. For the next hour, the girls skated in circles, enjoying a break from school and thinking about their situation. They were transported back to an easier time, and Dominique finally seemed to relax and slip into her old personality. She entertained her friends with the skating tricks she knew, squatting down on one leg with the other out straight to "shoot the duck" and spinning in circles in the middle of the rink, the hair of her dark wig swinging out in a wide arc.

Meanwhile, Nicki sang almost every lyric to A-ha, Tears for Fears, Prince, Michael Jackson and Madonna while she flew around the rink. When she wrapped up "Girls Just Wanna Have Fun" by Cyndi Lauper, which Jasmine and

Dominique had joined in to sing, she asked if anyone needed a snack. Jasmine said, "I'm not really hungry, but I'm dying for a drink!"

The DJ had moved onto "Say You, Say Me" by Lionel Richie and announced couples' skate anyway. The girls filed past a handful of high school students who had been sitting off to the side. The older kids took the opportunity to skate onto the rink in pairs, holding hands, for the slower song.

The girls skated awkwardly on the matted carpet over to the concession stand where Dominique and Nicki bought popcorn and sodas, and Jasmine ordered just a drink. On their way to the tables to consume their goodies, they passed Marcus and Robby, who were at video games next to each other, quarters stacked in groups of four on top of their machines. The girls sat at one of the old, rickety tables, nibbling on their popcorn and telling stories. They burst into peals of laughter as they heard Robby declare in disbelief that Marcus had his initials in every single top score slot for *Galaga*. "You really are a robot!" Robby exclaimed, which sent the girls into another fit of giggles. Having conquered that game, Marcus moved over to the newest game, *Arkanoid*, and started annihilating bricks by bouncing tiny white balls off of a little paddle that slid left and right, keeping the balls from falling into the abyss, which would result in losing a player. Even though it was his first time, Marcus was very adept at the new game, too.

When the girls finished eating, they cleaned up their snacks and went back for another round of skating. Jasmine and Dominique stepped from the carpet back onto the hardwood, but as Nicki went to do the same, her skate caught on the transition strip between the two surfaces and she had to throw her hands out to catch herself on the low wall that outlined the skating area. As she stood back upright, she could see her hair had changed to a shocking pink. Dominique and Jasmine were already a quarter of the way around the rink and didn't notice until they heard someone shout, "Look, it's the freaks!"

Nicki's heart pounded in her chest and her face flushed as Dominique looked back in horror to see her friend's transformation. Nicki stood rooted to the spot, unsure what to do as Jasmine and Dominique cut through the middle of the rink and came to stand stiffly by her side. By then, two high school couples had approached Nicki. One of the boys lifted her hair between two fingers, holding it as though it were something vile, an exaggerated look of disgust on his face. Nicki slapped his hand away, causing his girlfriend to laugh.

"I didn't know the freaks were allowed to go out in public," the boy who had touched Nicki's hair said with a self-satisfied smirk.

"At least not since you caused all that trouble at the fair," another backed up his friend with a snide comment.

The girls stood frozen with uncertainty as another couple skated up, effectively surrounding them. From behind Nicki, a girl about the same age as the people harassing them walked up and leaned over the waist-high wall that separated the rink from the rest of the building.

"Jimmy, lay off," she said calmly, but loudly. "They're just kids who had an accident. You think everyone who isn't just like you is a freak."

"Says the freak with the spiky, orange and yellow hair," Jimmy scoffed. "Go pretend you're Cyndi Lauper somewhere else." He dismissed her with a wave of his hand.

"Thanks for proving my point." She chewed her gum slowly and stared him down with such an intense gaze that he shifted on his skates in discomfort for just a moment. But then he turned his attention to Dominique and Jasmine. "Are you guys in the freak squad too? Or maybe you're just doing charity work taking this one out for the day? We should call Ghostbusters so they can bust these guys outta here!"

Dominique's eyes flashed as she lurched forward and poked him in the chest while shouting at him to back away from her friend. She was shaking with rage and gave a little squeal as her skates refused to cooperate under her and she fell toward her bully. The commotion caught Robby's attention, and he glanced over his shoulder from his game to see what was going on. Noticing that his sister and her friends were in the middle of what was clearly not a friendly group, he abandoned his game, shoved his remaining quarters in his pocket, grabbed Marcus and they raced out onto the skating rink in their tennis shoes to stand by Nicki.

Jimmy looked down at Marcus's arms, which had been exposed when he pushed up his sleeves without thinking while playing video games. The glinting silver was hard to miss under the flashing lights and disco ball of the rink.

"Ah, so it is a convention of misfits we have with us today, guys!" Jimmy jeered as his friends laughed along.

Robby jumped into a fighting stance and was about to lash out with a round kick when Marcus put his hand on his friend's arm and warned him to stop.

"Dude, it's not worth it. You're too strong. You could really hurt one of them and end up in juvie," Marcus muttered in Robby's ear.

Just as the group of high school students tightened around the elementary school kids, Kevin stumped into the skating rink on his crutches, looking for his girlfriend who worked at the concession stand. He noticed the gathering, but didn't register the tension and started to look away. But then he saw Nicki's pink hair pop up between the shoulders of two larger guys. He hobbled over and casually asked, "What's going on here?"

"Hey, Kevin," said one of the girls in the group who recognized him from the football team at school. She gave him a little wave and smile, which clearly didn't make her boyfriend very happy.

"Hey," Kevin replied. "Is there a problem?"

"Nah, no problem," Jimmy looked at him to find out if he was an ally or not. "We were just telling these freaks they should probably find somewhere else to hang out."

Kevin kept his face impassive while he studied Jimmy. Finally, he asked in a deceptively calm voice, "When did you start working here?"

"Huh?" Jimmy was caught off guard by the question.

"I asked when you started working here," Kevin said and everyone noticed a dangerous edge to his voice this time. "I wasn't aware that you were able to decide who could or could not skate here."

"Hey man, just because you play football, don't act like you're the king of this place," Jimmy snapped as he turned to fully face Kevin. "We come here all the time, this is our spot. And we don't want these losers here taking up our space." He jerked his thumb toward Nicki. Dominique, who had had enough of being in the spotlight after enjoying a moment of anonymity, grabbed his thumb and yanked it back. Since he was on skates, he briefly lost his balance, but recovered quickly and grabbed her by the arm to retaliate.

Kevin immediately swung the crutch from his good side up and around his head, like a sword, brought it back down and then swooped upward with the end underneath Jimmy's chin, forcing him to stop his assault on Dominique. All sounds other than Chaka Khan serenading her inattentive audience and an occasional beep or bloop from the arcade games ceased at that moment. The clacking of the roller skate wheels on the wood floor stopped, all chatter went silent as every person in the building stopped to stare at the spectacle.

Kevin ordered Jimmy's friends to take a step back and then looked at Jimmy menacingly and said through clenched teeth, "You're the one who's going to leave now." Jimmy rolled backward, barely out of range of the crutch that Kevin still wielded like a weapon, but laughed and said, "Oh yeah, who's going to make me? The gimp on crutches with an eye patch and his army of kid circus freaks? Try me, Blackbeard!" Kevin braced himself on the leg with the cast, leaned forward, then took his crutch and swiped Jimmy's feet out from under him. Even over the music, everyone could hear the loud thump he made as he landed on his rear end with his feet in the air.

"Someone get the manager! This guy is attacking me!" Jimmy roared.

"Funny how the bully becomes the victim as soon as someone pushes back," Kevin said without an air of concern. He turned around and started to use his crutches to get off the rink, but then looked over his shoulder and said, "Sadly for you, I know the manager here and I don't believe you'll be welcome back."

---

When Kevin walked into the apartment he shared with his dad that night, his olfactory senses were inundated with the scent of the pepperoni pizza his dad had picked up for dinner, and he immediately started salivating.

"Hey bud," Dale looked over his shoulder. "You're just in time, I was about to grab myself a slice. I'll get you one too if you want to sit down."

"That would be great," Kevin said with a weary sigh. He placed his crutches against the counter near the table and then maneuvered his way into one of the chairs, sitting down with an audible thud.

"Dad, I have to talk to you," Kevin placed his hands on the table in front of him as he broached the subject carefully.

"Uh oh, sounds serious," said Dale as he brought two steaming plates full of gooey pizza and set them on the table.

"Well, hopefully not," Kevin tried to assure him. "But I'd rather you hear from me than someone else."

"Okay, hit me," Dale said and took a generous bite while he looked Kevin in the eyes, showing his son that he had his dad's full attention.

"Earlier I had my friend Will drop me off at the skating rink so I could see Misty at the end of her shift. But when I got there, some of the guys from my school were messing with Sharon's kids and a few of their friends."

"Oh?" Dale's voice had an edge of fury, but he kept it tamped down in order to let Kevin tell his story.

"Yeah, some of the kids at my school keep saying they're freaks and they need to leave town or stay home, or ... I don't really know. Everything they say is stupid, so I don't really pay attention," Kevin shrugged. "Anyway, I pushed one off his skates with my crutch and I thought you should know. I'm pretty sure he wasn't hurt and I don't feel bad about it. There were six high school kids ganging up on a couple of the girls. They deserved it." He thought for a moment and then continued, "I mean, I guess because I know Nicki and Robby, I don't think of them any differently. Just that this thing happened to them. To us, really. Although I guess the kids at my school don't realize that what happened to me is the same thing."

Dale nodded, deep in thought. "It's probably best to keep it that way."

Kevin looked less sure, "You think?" He pondered this for a few more moments while they each chewed, lost in their own thoughts. "On the one hand, I really don't need more crap at school. The patch, the crutches and sitting on the side to watch practices has been torture enough. But on the other, if the kids saw that I'm still me, maybe they'd lay off of Sharon's crew."

Dale slowly shook his head and said, "The problem is, you see those kids at school every day. And who's to say they won't think that your eye and foot are evidence that you're turning into a freak? It's easier for Sharon's kids to avoid them. I think you should stay quiet."

Kevin looked discombobulated as his mind flew back and forth between trying to figure out how to make people understand what seemed so obvious to him and not wanting to draw more attention to himself. His father let him brood for a while as they each finished their pizza. When Dale stood up to get another slice for each of them out of the box on the counter, he changed the subject to one he had been meaning to discuss with Kevin for a while.

"Kevin, I need to talk to you about something, too. And I need you to keep an open mind," Dale said as he set their reloaded plates on the table.

"Uh oh, sounds serious," Kevin said with the hint of a smile as he parroted his dad's earlier words back to him.

"I'm afraid it is," Dale didn't smile back.

"Okay, what is it? You're making me nervous."

"It's about what happened to you guys, and what I think we should do next," Dale started slowly, but with an air of confidence that he hoped would help Kevin understand what needed to be done. "I think we should use this as an opportunity to fix your foot."

He had Kevin's interest now. He cocked his head to the side, furrowed his brow and asked, "How?" His voice was threaded with tentative hope.

"I think we could use the machine, the same way it was used before, but we dress you in a costume that would help you. For example, The Flash. Think about it, in order to run super-fast, you'd have to have two working legs, so presumably, you'd wake up the next day fixed." He watched his son carefully to gauge his reaction.

"Have you talked to anyone else about this?" Kevin wondered aloud. "Or is this just a guess?"

"Well," Dale knew he had to tell the truth to get his son on board. "I've talked to my tech, Chad. He ate some of the candy and experienced a change as well. So he's been working on a solution with the kids."

"And..." Kevin prompted. "What does he think?"

"Honestly?" Dale saw the results he wanted to gain from the conversation slipping away from him so he gave a version of the truth. "He's more focused on turning everyone back. Which would fix your eye, but not your foot. I'm looking at the bigger picture and trying to help you with both."

"What about Sharon?" Kevin pressed.

"What about her?" Dale wanted to avoid sharing Sharon's thoughts on the subject. But Kevin was a reasonably smart kid, so he guessed, "She doesn't want you to do it."

Dale used a napkin to wipe some stray sauce off of his upper lip while he considered what to say. "She's also really just focused on getting her kids back to normal, Kevin," Dale leaned forward across his empty plate on the table as he begged his son to see his view. "No one else cares about this the way you and I do. They have a different plan for a different problem. If we want to fix you, it's up to us."

A shadow stole over Kevin's face as another thought occurred to him. "So what if I decide to go back someday. Would my foot be broken again?"

Dale looked at him perplexed, "Why would you want to go back?"

"Why wouldn't I?" Kevin countered. "I just want to be normal! I don't want everyone to think of me as a freak my whole life, even if some of the effects would be kind of cool."

"I'm not sure. Maybe we'll have more information after Sharon's kids change back. We only know about this going in one direction, right? So why not use that direction to our advantage?" Dale was practically pleading now.

"What would be different for me this time? Couldn't I just put on a costume and eat some of the already infected candy if that's what we're doing? I'm sure they have some left," Kevin reasoned.

Dale shrugged and let his shoulders drop to his side. "I suppose you could try it. I don't know though. I'd rather be safe than sorry. My plan was to exactly mimic everything that happened that night." Secretly, Dale didn't think Sharon would let them have the candy to try out that variation of the plan and he didn't really want to ask.

Kevin pressed on with his questions, "So would I just eat the same candy the kids are eating to change back? That doesn't make sense. Except I guess I'd have on a costume and they'd do like they did before and just dress as themselves?"

"Well, that's where things get a little difficult," Dale admitted. Kevin tensed up for what he sensed was to come. "I think we'd have to use new candy. And there's this crystal ball that we think was part of what changed everything last time that we'd need to get." Kevin snorted a wry laugh.

"I know how it sounds," Dale admitted. "But I'm serious. And I don't think that we can use it at the same time on old and new candy. I think we'd have to get the crystal ball and do this ourselves."

"There is literally no way in the world Sharon is going to let you do that," Kevin erupted.

"I know, I said it would be difficult!" Dale responded just as loudly. "But the alternative is waiting another month to fix you. None of those other kids are actually hurt. They're fine, just minorly annoyed."

"I seriously doubt some of them would call it minor," muttered Kevin.

"Look, Kevin, I've given this a lot of thought. I don't want to deceive Sharon, but I don't see another way. This is only time-sensitive for one person: You. We need to get you fixed or you could lose your scholarship and your life is basically over." Dale sat back with his arms crossed on his chest, looking as though he were trying to physically protect himself from Kevin's response.

"Is that what you think?" Kevin asked softly. "That all I'm good for is high school and college football?"

Dale took a deep breath and got up to walk around the table to put his hands on his son's shoulders. "Of course not," he said in a more sympathetic tone. "But this is what you've worked toward for years. And it's ridiculous to let it all just slip away because of one little accident if we don't have to."

Kevin considered waiting another month to fix his injury. And then he thought about waiting for nature to heal him. By then, he would have been completely replaced on the football team. In fact, by then his whole senior year would be over. The likelihood of him regaining use of his foot, training to get back to where he was and keeping his scholarship was next to nothing if he let nature take its course. And the thought of hobbling around on crutches for another month with the hot, itchy cast wasn't thrilling. But still, defying Sharon and taking away her chance to fix her kids faster wasn't something he was willing to commit to yet. "I'll think about it," he finally conceded.

"That's all I can ask of you, son," Dale gripped his shoulder. "I just want what's best for you."

## 20

# TURKEY WITH A SIDE OF ETHICS

"Welcome, and happy Thanksgiving. I'm glad you could make it!" Sharon extended a warm greeting to Chad as he stood awkwardly on her front porch with a casserole dish in his hands.

"Thanks for having me," he said with a shy smile.

"Of course!" Sharon beamed at him. "We'll have an odd assortment of people today, but I didn't think it made sense for us all to celebrate alone." She took the dish from him and peeked under the lid where the scent of butter and spices wafted upward as she inhaled deeply. "Oh, your stuffing smells fantastic!"

"Thanks," Chad stood with his hands in his pockets in the entryway while Shmoofy gave him the ritual sniff test. "My mom felt bad that she and my dad were going on a cruise and leaving me alone at Thanksgiving, so she bought all the stuff and left me her recipe. I hope it turned out okay."

"Based on how it smells, I'm sure it's delicious," Sharon assured him. "Come on in, the adults are in the kitchen while the kiddos watch TV."

Chad gave a little wave in the general direction of the living room where Robby and Nicki were sprawled on the couch watching what appeared to be a replay of the Thanksgiving Day parade that had been broadcast earlier that morning. "We didn't want to get up early, so we taped it, and now we're watching," Nicki explained.

"Cool," Chad said and then followed Sharon into the kitchen where Alisha sat at the table with a bubbly orange beverage. Seated across from her was Kevin. Dale leaned against the counter, relishing his role as designated turkey supervisor. Sharon reclaimed her space at the counter where she had been carefully laying pecans across the top of a pie when she paused to answer the door. Chad looked nervously at Dale, they had barely spoken since their encounter in his room at work earlier that week, but Dale seemed content to pretend it had never happened. At least in present company.

"We'll be ready to eat in about fifteen minutes," Sharon informed Chad. "The turkey is almost ready, and then I can slip the pie in the oven to bake while we eat."

"Sounds groovy," he said before turning to Kevin. "I heard about your injury. That sucks, big time."

"Yeah," Kevin nodded in agreement. "I'm getting used to the crutches, but the cast is still a huge bummer. By the way, I just found out a couple of days ago that you had been infected too. I'm sorry to hear that, but I'm glad you've been helping out Nicki and Robby. They're good kids."

"Yeah, they've been really helpful. Way smarter than I remember being at that age," Chad chuckled. He sat down in the chair between Alisha and Kevin as Shmoofy padded into the kitchen, nose held high while he took in the scents of the Thanksgiving feast.

"Alright," Sharon spoke over the conversations taking place around her. "I need Dale and Chad to grab the table leaf out of the pantry and get this extended. We'll be bringing over the food in just a few moments, and we have more food than I expected with all of the dishes that you guys brought!"

Nicki and Robby came into the kitchen to help set the table. Everyone filled their plates with turkey, green beans, stuffing and potatoes covered in cheese and corn flakes, then settled into a spot at the table.

"Hey Kevin," Nicki said with an uncharacteristic shyness in her voice. "Thank you for what you did for us at the skating rink the other day. I was so scared."

"Of course!" Kevin said as he gathered turkey, potatoes and stuffing all on his fork to take one giant bite. "It was no big deal. Those guys are wastoids anyway," he said around his big bite of food.

"Well, it was a big deal to me," Nicki said solemnly.

"No problem, kiddo," he said and chucked her on the shoulder. "I was curious why you guys didn't use your super-powers though. Seems like a few losers like that would be no match for your super-team."

"I was going to!" Robby rushed to explain. "Marcus stopped me. He said I could go to juvie."

"Thank goodness for Marcus," Sharon said.

"Robby has some things he could have used," Nicki explained. "But none of the rest of us have skills that would really be useful. Jazz didn't have her crystal ball with her, and I don't know what good it would have done anyway. Dom doesn't have anything other than the Lasso of Truth, which she also didn't have with her, and it's not like I could sing them away. Marcus's powers are really more intellectual."

"Yeah, but mine would have been awesome," Robby said wistfully. "I could have used my heat vision and stopped them in their tracks." He paused. "Well, assuming I didn't blow them up."

This comment earned him a startled look from Alisha.

"Because I can't really control it," he assured her. "Not because I've turned into some sort of murderous supervillain." This brought a few laughs from around the table.

When the chuckles died down and everyone had resumed eating, Alisha shared something that had been on her mind. "You know, I have been wondering about the ethical implications of using your powers."

"What do you mean?" Nicki asked, intrigued.

"Well," she considered how to start as she took a sip of her drink. She set down her glass and then looked up, her gaze shifting between Sharon and her children as she spoke. "After the Sesquicentennial, Anil mentioned that the police seemed slightly accusatory. Although he is pretty uptight, he might have just imagined it."

Sharon stepped in to clarify, "It did come across that way at first, but it seems enough people had already made statements by the time we talked to them that they knew Rani and Joel were helping, not hurting. I think they were just very formal, and we were overwhelmed."

"That's good," Alisha acknowledged. "And I think as long as the intent is always good, hopefully, there are no problems. But we did talk about what would have happened if Rani got accused of causing the damage. We even wondered for a bit if the person who got injured on the ride might sue us, but then we found out it was you, Kevin, and that you guys knew she would never do that."

"No way, I owe my life to her," said Kevin. "We all do," he nodded at Robby and Nicki to include them in the statement.

"But I see where you're going with it," said Chad as he pushed his fluffy gray hair off his forehead. He usually wore a baseball cap these days to hide his hair, but wanted to be polite at Sharon's and not wear a hat to the table. It was making him somewhat self-conscious. But it was kind of nice to be around other people who were like him, at least in the sense that they had characteristics that were also out of the norm. "If there were ever a question about intent, or if the result had been disastrous, there's really no legal precedent for how we'd be treated."

"Why would we be treated any differently?" Robby asked

through a mouthful of stuffing, although his gaze was on the pie his mother was sliding out of the oven.

"Robby, think!" said Nicki. His attention snapped back to his sister, although he was barely aware of what they were talking about. "What?" he asked, his eyes wide and his forehead wrinkled.

"We *are* different, so of course they'd treat us differently," Nicki explained with feigned patience. "They would literally have to make new laws for people with heat vision if someone worse than you had this power."

"Worse than me? What's that supposed to mean?" Robby asked defensively.

"I just mean, you aren't a bad guy. But what if you were?" Nicki challenged him.

Alisha interjected, "Robby, she's right. That's what Anil and I have been talking about. We're worried about Rani and how she might be treated if something were to go wrong with her powers in public. All that to say..." she hesitated. "We decided that we aren't comfortable with her doing anything with her powers at the birthday party tomorrow. In fact, she's probably not even going to attend. Rani understands, I hope you guys do as well."

Robby gave it some thought and then said, "I don't think she ever agreed to do it anyway. We talked about it, but she said her dad probably wouldn't let her. Right?" He turned to Nicki for confirmation.

"Yeah, that sounds right," she agreed as she used her fork

to scrape up the last evidence of her potatoes. "I'm not even sure she ever planned on going."

Alisha breathed a sigh of relief. "I'm glad it won't be a problem. I just think we need to be really careful until we can get this all worked out."

Chad was fidgeting with his napkin, trying to gather the courage to bring up another topic. He finally decided it was now or never. "Speaking of legal issues," he paused while he stole a glance at Dale. "Dale and I were talking earlier this week, and now I'm wondering if we should proceed with more caution."

"I thought we were being as careful as we could, given the circumstances," Sharon countered gently as she set down her fork. She put her elbows on the table, laced her fingers together and put her chin on her hands, giving Chad her undivided attention.

Chad nervously chewed on his lower lip before pressing on, "Well, when Dale and I were talking, it came up that typically in order to get something approved at the hospital, we'd have to go through some pretty rigorous testing. Generally, there are several rounds of clinical trials, starting with animals and moving on to humans. We'd be the human guinea pigs in this case since there's such a small sample size of people infected. But it might be prudent to test it out on an animal first." His voice trailed off as he saw several faces turn stony, causing him to lose what little confidence he had started with.

"Well you aren't testing on Muffin," Robby interjected.

Chad looked to Sharon with a silent plea for help. She considered what he was saying and then turned to Alisha. "What do you recommend?"

Alisha had an immediate response. "Our family has talked about this. Obviously, Rani's safety is our first concern. We've weighed the threat of doing something unknown against the potential harm in letting this continue to survive in her body. Ultimately, we decided that if there is any chance this mutates, we need to move forward and stop it as soon as possible. It's tough because we usually make informed decisions based on mountains of scientific data, but we just don't have that here. And we're not going to." The table was silent as everyone considered what Alisha had shared.

Eventually, Dale cleared his throat, "So, um, does that mean everyone has decided to reverse on Sunday? I know Sharon said there were a few kids who might not want to." He was fidgeting with his fork since his plate was empty and the pie was still cooling.

"I'm not sure," Robby said. "A couple of the guys are way into their powers. Their parents don't always agree. So who knows?" He shrugged.

Alisha looked back and forth between Kevin and Chad. "Can I assume you'll be joining on Sunday?"

Chad nodded vehemently. Kevin looked at his dad and then down at the table and nodded.

"Kevin," Sharon sensed his discomfort. "What's wrong? Aren't you tired of that eye patch?"

"Oh yeah, definitely," he responded quickly. "We're just not sure what will happen with my other injury."

Sharon's eyes narrowed suspiciously as she cast a quick glance at Dale and then back to Kevin. "What do you mean?"

Dale interrupted. "Well, if he's wearing a cast when he tries to reverse, will that be interpreted as a costume? Will his foot be damaged forever?"

Kevin looked horrified. They had not discussed this possibility, and he hadn't considered it. He knew his dad was going to try to justify doing things his way, he just had no idea this was how he was going to try to approach it. The other adults hadn't noticed Kevin's reaction because they also hadn't considered this possibility and were now mulling it over. It seemed no one had any answers.

Robby's face turned from creased worry to a tentative smile as he suggested, "Maybe you wait and see how it goes with us, and then you can try it out whenever you get your cast off?"

Kevin nodded slowly, realizing that he had fewer options than he thought. Either wait and live with both an eye patch and a cast for a couple more months, or go with his dad's plan and try to solve it all in a couple of days. As he looked around the table and saw six pairs of worried eyes looking at him, he didn't see how he could take away the opportunity to fix Chad and all the kids. But the thought of waiting a couple of months was nearly unbearable.

# 21

# SHOWBIZNESS

On the Friday of the birthday party, Sharon held the door open for her own kids and Dominique to walk into ShowBiz Pizza Place where she planned to ensure they were settled before she escaped the mecca of overstimulation. They were quickly assaulted by lights, sounds and the shrieks of what seemed like hundreds of children, but in reality, was probably fewer than fifty. Before they made it very far, Jasmine ran up and hugged Nicki and Dominique and then stepped back to say hi to Sharon. Robby had already run off to where he saw Javier standing by the Rock-afire Explosion, an animatronic band of animals including a bear on bass and a gorilla on keyboard. Nicki turned to give her mom a quick awkward side hug, and then she too ran over to the area where the party guests were congregating. Sharon saw Jenny's mom, with her shoulder-length permed brown hair, laughing and talking to another of the moms doing drop-off.

Satisfied that her children were with the right party, she made a hasty exit.

Meanwhile, each of Jenny Sanderson's guests was handed a small cup filled with tokens for the games as they arrived.

"I call dibs on *Pac-Man!*" Robby shouted the moment he had his tokens and raced off to find his favorite game.

Javier paused as he took the tokens from Jenny's mom and then asked sheepishly, "Mrs. Sanderson, am I allowed to have a drink yet, or do I have to wait for the pizza?"

"Oh sure, hon, let me grab you one of the cups. You'll need to keep track of it though, we only get a certain amount, so don't lose it!"

Once he had the paper cup with a picture of Billy Bob the bear smiling from it, he went over to the soda fountain and filled it with just a few ice cubes and then a little squirt of every soda option. "Check out my 'suicide' drink!" he showed Joel the muddy-colored mixture.

"Cool," Joel said, although he barely looked, he was scoping out the games to see what would be worthy of his first token. *Spy Hunter* caught his eye, and he smiled as he dropped his coin into the slot and then got set up with his hands on the wheel and his right foot on the gas pedal.

After about half an hour of frenzied running around to claim time on their favorite arcade games, the boys gathered to enter the shadow room. Each person in the room pressed themselves against the wall in crazy poses, waiting for a light to flash that would preserve their shadow for a few seconds before fading and allowing for another round of posing.

Javier stood on his hands and pressed his head, back and legs against the wall for his first flash. The obscenely bright white light flashed and everyone moved back to assess their shadows. Robby was pleased with his roundhouse kick, Joel had a pose reminiscent of one of the Charlie's Angels with his fingers pointed toward the ceiling on his right side like a gun. But Javier was confused. His shadow was only a light outline instead of the solid block that everyone else had, and it was difficult to tell how he had posed.

Thinking that maybe he hadn't been close enough to the wall since he was upside-down, he tried again on the second flash, pressing himself extra hard against the surface of the wall in more of a jumping jack pose, with his arms up high and his feet wide apart. But again, his shadow was a wisp of what everyone else had. He moved to another location in the room, thinking maybe there was something wrong with the space he was in, but nothing changed.

"Hey guys," he called to his friends who were too busy with their own poses to notice he was having difficulty. "Check this out," he said. "I think my shadow is broken." And he demonstrated.

"What's happening with it?" Joel asked.

"I don't know, I've tried different things, but it's like a..." he paused and looked significantly at his friends. "It's like a ghost shadow."

Everyone exchanged wide-eyed stares.

"Do you feel weird," asked Joel. "Like Marty when he was disappearing at the end of *Back to the Future*?"

"No, I feel totally normal," he was adamant. "I mean, other than a little freaked out, I guess."

"Yeah, I can see why!" said Robby. "We should take a Polaroid picture and see if your hand disappears like Marty!"

Joel tried a more pragmatic approach because he could see the distress etching its way across his friend's face as he considered this possibility. "I'm sure you're fine. But we should probably talk more about whether or not you want to change back if there are weird things going on that you can't see. And we can get Marcus to add this to his list so he and Chad can help us figure out what it means."

"Yeah," Javier nodded, subdued for him.

That's when they heard the announcement that it was time for Jenny Sanderson's party to gather at the table for pizza and cake.

"Oh dang it!" Javier exclaimed as he walked out of the shadow room. "I can't remember where I put my cup!"

"I've got it right here," came a voice from behind him where Mrs. Sanderson was holding it out for him. "I thought you might need a little help keeping track of it."

"Thank you!" he grabbed it from her and dragged his two friends over to the fountain machine to demonstrate the proper way to create a "suicide" beverage.

———

Meanwhile, a teenage ShowBiz Pizza employee with curly hair, acne and a bad slouch led Nicki over to the stage where lights were starting to fire up, illuminating the Rock-afire Explosion band. She could hear the gears in the background begin to churn and saw the twitch of a drumstick from Dook LaRue, the dog on drums. Just thinking about getting a chance to perform as Jem was enough to do the trick. She felt her heart rate accelerate, immediately followed by the gentle tinkling sound of her earrings as she saw a couple of stray wisps of hair turn pink in her peripheral vision. A couple of the kids closest to the stage saw her transformation and gasped, which caused a ripple to go through the crowds at the nearby tables. There were two other birthday parties in the same room as Jenny's, and soon every face in the room was turned toward Nicki.

She nervously cleared her throat and then spoke into the microphone that the employee had handed her before scurrying out of the bright lights.

"Welcome everyone, to Jenny's birthday party," she said with a small smile. There was a smattering of cheers for Jenny, but most people's attention was still firmly on Nicki. "Your mom asked me to sing a song to celebrate, so the Rock-afire Explosion and I are going to sing some Beatles. I hope you enjoy it!"

Nicki turned around with her back to the audience and held the microphone in a tight grip at her side to wait. After a few seconds, the band on stage twanged out the first few bars of the "Birthday" song while she bounced her knee and nodded her head with her back still to the crowd. When the vocals kicked in, she turned around and sang, shimmying during the guitar parts and pointing to Jenny when she said the word "birthday."

By the time it got to the drum break, she used her earrings to throw a hologram of fireworks out over the tables, which sparkled down before fading out. Jasmine stood up from the table where everyone had sat down to wait for pizza and started to dance in the aisle between tables. Then the song morphed into another Beatles hit, "I Saw Her Standing There," at which point several other girls, including Jenny, joined Jasmine in the dancing, and a few even sang along.

When the song ended, Nicki gave a little curtsy to a roaring crowd while the lights went out and the animatronic band powered back down. She ran to nestle herself between Jasmine and Dominique, who congratulated her while she blushed furiously.

"It was so fun, but now that it's over, I'm so nervous!" She sat on her shaking hands to get them under control.

"You're supposed to get nervous before," Dominique's laugh tinkled out over the table.

"I know, but I was mostly just excited then. Now people are looking at me, and it's freaking me out!" But after a few comments about her singing and the fireworks display, everyone clustered back into their own little conversations and grabbed slices of pizza from the pans that had been distributed across the table.

Once everyone had their fill of pizza, Javier went to the kitchen area with Mrs. Sanderson and told her to give him a minute. He stood in the corner, closed his eyes and took a few slow, deep breaths. Then he focused on disappearing. When he heard Mrs. Sanderson gasp, he knew it had worked.

"Will you please hold out the cake so I can take it from you?" he asked.

"Yes, I was just trying to figure out how to hand it to you," her nervous laugh mingled with the sound of the games. "This will definitely be a birthday to remember!" She held out the sheet cake with "Happy Birthday, Jenny" written in icing next to a piped Rainbow Brite and a green Sprite. Javier took the edges of the board that the cake rested on and waited for her to let go. When she didn't he prompted her, "Mrs. Sanderson? I've got it."

"Yes! Of course. I could feel it, but I couldn't see anything, and it just seems like it will drop if I move my hands. Okay, here I go." And she slowly moved her hands away but kept them nearby for a few seconds as if she were preparing to grab it when it fell. Once it stayed steady long enough for her to feel confident it was okay, she pulled a lighter out of her pocket and lit the eleven candles that were scattered across the top around the decorations. "Okay, let's go!" she said when she finished the last one.

Javier turned around and saw that the path to the table was not clear. He turned back over his shoulder and said, "Could you please walk in front of me so I don't run into anyone since they can't see me?"

"Yes! Of course," she jumped to the side and scooted in front of him. As she approached the table, she started a round of "Happy Birthday" and then moved out of the way so Jenny could see her cake floating toward her. There was a mix of reactions: a scream, some nervous laughter, a few people remembered to join in for the song, but everyone moved out of the way of the cake as it approached the table so Javier could set it down next to Jenny. She stared at the cake for a moment, then reached out her hand in front of her face into what appeared to be empty space and inadvertently put her hand on Javier's nose and mouth. She pulled her hand back as if she had touched fire, and he smiled as he reappeared in the empty space next to her. "Make a wish," he reminded her. She snapped out of her reverie, looked back at the cake, silently made a wish and then blew out the candles.

Jenny's brother, Andrew, who had run out of his tokens and eaten seconds on both pizza and cake, was getting bored. He sidled up behind where Dominique sat picking at her cake and talking to Jasmine.

"Hey there, little orphan," he said with a smirk.

Dominique gave him an exaggerated eye roll and then turned back to Jasmine, ignoring him.

"How rude!" he said as he sat down on the bench next to her, straddling it so he was facing Dominique head-on.

"Come on, Andrew, leave me alone. I'm not in the mood

for whatever witty comment you spent all afternoon coming up with."

"Now is that any way to treat the only brother of the guest of honor?" he asked with mock hurt in his voice.

"Fine, what can I help you with?" she turned to him and pasted on a fake smile.

"I was hoping you could tell me where you got your amazing wig," he feigned sincerity.

Her fake smile faded as she glared at him, trying to figure out his angle. Then, quick as lightning, he reached over and snatched the wig off of her head. Her hands flew to her smashed down red curls as she screamed at him, "Andrew, what is wrong with you?"

He stood up and held the wig above his head, laughing hysterically as he waved it just out of her reach.

Joel walked over to where they stood and calmly said, "Give it back."

Andrew barely spared Joel a glance as he turned back to Dominique and started to say something. Joel stepped up to where he was practically standing on Andrew's toes, even though the top of his blonde head barely came up to the bully's chin. "Give it back. Now."

"Or what, Puke Skywalker?" Andrew scoffed at him. At that moment, he saw his mother returning from the bathroom, a frown creasing her face as she walked toward him, and he hesitated for a moment with his arm still in the air holding the wig. Before he could decide what to do, he felt his feet lift off the ground as Joel used The Force to restrain him.

Andrew turned his head wildly around and saw Joel with his hand out, palm facing Andrew, who was now rising in the air toward the ceiling. Legs flailing, Andrew felt himself turning so he was effectively lying on his back, but in the air, now mostly right over the table with all of the uneaten pizza, cake and about a dozen half-filled cups of juice or soda.

Mrs. Sanderson raced up next to Joel, begging him in a desperate whisper to let Andrew down. But Joel couldn't hear her because Andrew was screaming threats and obscenities at him as he tried unsuccessfully to flip over so he could face his adversary. People from all over ShowBiz gathered around watching the sight with a mixture of awe and horror. Then a security guard raced up and grabbed Joel by the shoulders, causing him to lose his focus. Andrew came crashing down onto the table, spraying everyone within several feet with a sticky combination of juice and soda.

Everyone stood frozen in time for several moments. The silence that followed was incongruous with the cacophony of the music and games still blaring in the background. Finally, Andrew broke the spell when he stood up and stomped away, his arms straight at his sides ending in clenched fists. Tomato sauce and frosting painted his clothes and hair as he pushed past the stunned crowd while he dripped a trail of fountain drinks in his wake.

"So um, guys," Sharon started as she stood looking at the crowd of kids in the ShowBiz parking lot. "Who is going to tell me exactly what happened here?"

Sharon had passed Andrew as he stomped out of the door, covered in the remnants of the food and beverages from the party. She walked into the pizza place where she nearly bumped into the security guard who was taking Joel back to the main office. After a quick conversation with the security guard where Sharon promised she would wait with Joel outside until his parents arrived, the members of RA-D8 who were at the party (everyone except Marcus and Rani) had congregated outside to defend their friend.

"Mom," Robby said with grave sincerity as he held his hands out in front of himself to punctuate his words with insistent movements. "Andrew was being a butt. He teased the girls and stole Dom's wig then waved it around where she couldn't reach it."

"And..." Sharon prompted.

"And so Joel just picked him up with The Force," Robby finished lamely, his hands falling at his sides. In the moment, Andrew had seemed so much more threatening, everything so much more intense. But as he was telling the story, Robby realized that things went too far. For a moment, everyone stood looking at the ground, listening to the traffic that passed on the street next to the pizzeria.

"Mrs. Swain," Joel's face had lost all color when the security guard dragged him toward the office and he had yet to recover fully. His hands were shaking as was his voice when he tried to help Sharon understand. "I wasn't going to hurt him. I just wanted to make it so he couldn't run away, and we could get the wig back. Then that security guard grabbed me and my concentration broke, and Andrew just fell."

Sharon looked at Dominique who had silent tears streaming down her face. Her eyes were almost as red as her hair. "So where is the wig now? You're going to need it soon," Sharon pointed out.

"I don't know," Dominique hiccupped as she realized how much she was going to need it when they tried to change back in just two days. "Everything happened so fast. Did Andrew have it when he left?" She looked wildly around the group to see if anyone had noticed. But before she had a chance to run off to find her nemesis, Mrs. Sanderson walked out of the building, holding the wig delicately between two fingers. It too had suffered in the fall. The dark strands were covered in a marbled orange swirl of frosting and tomato sauce. It was dripping soda and one rogue pepperoni was tangled in the end.

Dominique rushed toward her and grabbed it with both hands, thanking her profusely. Mrs. Sanderson stood there, a flurry of emotions racing across her face. Everyone was frozen still, collectively holding their breaths as they waited to hear what she had to say.

Finally, cheeks a crimson red, she looked Dominique in the eye and said, "I'd like to apologize for my son's behavior. I was coming back from the ladies' room when I saw him take your wig. I promise that's not how we raised him. He will be apologizing to you in person after I have a moment with him." And she walked off toward her car to find her son.

"Wow," Robby exclaimed under his breath. "I kinda thought she was going to yell at us."

"Me too," Sharon heaved a sigh of relief. "Ah, here come Joel's parents," she said as she pointed to their station wagon pulling into the lot. "Jasmine, Javier, are you okay waiting inside for your parents? I'd be happy to give you a ride home, but I'm not sure the employees here would let me since you didn't come with me. I'm kind of surprised they let you come out here at all, but I guess there was a lot of commotion."

"It's okay Mrs. S," Javier said. "I haven't used all my tokens yet anyway. Come on Jasmine!" and he turned to run back into the building. Giving Dominique a little hug, Jasmine turned to follow Javier back in to wait for her parents and tell Jenny happy birthday one more time.

Sharon walked over to the Jacobson's car to explain the events that had just taken place and then loaded up Dominique and her children to return home.

## 22

## POSITIVE VIBES

"So then what happened?" Marcus's friends were giving him a play-by-play of the previous day's events at Show-Biz. Sharon had invited everyone over for a last-minute planning session. Since Chad, Dale and Kevin were joining as well as Anil, it was too crowded in her living room, so she was serving snacks in her backyard on the patio.

"Nothing," Robby said. "My mom showed up, got Joel out of ShowBiz jail, and we all went to the parking lot to wait for the parents."

"Well, Jasmine and I went back in to wait for ours after Joel's parents got there," Javier corrected.

"Oh, that's right!" Nicki exclaimed. "What happened after you went back?"

Javier looked around, a bit anxious as he realized that the adults were listening in to their conversation. "Nothing really, our parents came before Andrew or Mrs. Sanderson came back in."

"Yeah," Jasmine confirmed. "I watched Javier play a couple of games, then our moms came. So we went and told Jenny thanks for inviting us and left."

"Wow," Marcus said. "I mean, I hate to say I told ya so..." he began.

"Look, Marcus," Dominique cut him off. "You were right. No one should be using their powers in public."

Marcus's jaw snapped shut, not sure how to respond. He wasn't used to people agreeing with him when he tried to follow the rules, much less when he tried to make new ones.

"Besides," Dominique continued, her voice growing more tense, "now there's just one more story for everyone to tell about the freaks."

"Dominique," Alisha addressed her daughter's friend. "You know things that are different scare some people, right? If they can't explain it, they lash out at it. It's not right, but it's human nature."

"Maybe for the dumb humans," Robby muttered.

Alisha gave him a fond smile. "You aren't entirely wrong. For some, it's easier to try to make something go away than bother to become educated about it. Honestly, this isn't the first time that Anil and I, or I'm sure Marcus or Javier and their families, have experienced this lashing out. Not everyone likes people of different races living in their neighborhoods. Especially in the south."

"Why?" Robby asked innocently, but emphatically. "You guys are great neighbors!"

"Well thank you, back at ya kiddo," she smiled. "But you know me. Just like I know you. And I don't know Joel as well, but I understand his situation better than anyone outside of this yard, and I know he didn't mean to hurt anyone. But do you see how someone who hasn't been around this, or doesn't know you, might have seen Joel as the bully? I'm talking more about the guests at the other birthday parties and the employees. I know most of Jenny's guests know you guys from school, and they witnessed what Andrew did to start the whole thing. You just have to keep in mind that not every situation is the same. Not everyone has the same information. And it's important to try to help people understand so they know your heart."

Robby nodded thoughtfully as he worked to process everything Alisha had said. Everyone sat in silence for a moment listening to the breeze rustling the branches of the barren trees. A squirrel nervously glanced over his back on his race to the big oak tree at the back of Sharon's yard.

Shmoofy caught sight of the squirrel and raced after him mooing a warning of his approach, which garnered a few curious looks from the parents who weren't aware of the dog's transformation.

"Well," Sharon said when it was quiet again. "I'm just grateful that Debra Sanderson saw what Andrew was doing and hopefully no one presses any charges."

"Could they do that?" Javier asked, shocked that this was even a possibility.

James Ross was quick to reply, "Definitely. It sounds like there was assault and destruction of property."

"Dad," Dominique rolled her eyes. "He assaulted me and stole my wig first."

"And that's why they probably won't press charges," he assured his daughter. "But technically they could."

Robby glanced at Joel who suddenly looked like he was being strangled by his own fear. "Hey, nothing broke. It's not like you threw him into the puppet band. All that happened are the tables got a little messy."

"Joel," Jasmine asked softly. "Does this change your mind about wanting to stay as you are?"

Joel looked up at his parents. "I mean, I don't want people to call me a freak for the rest of my life. But guys, I have The Force. What kid wouldn't want that? How do I give that up?"

No one had any answers. Eventually, his mom said that they could talk about it that night at home and help him make a decision. He smiled at her, grateful that she was going to include him in their discussions.

After a moment, Dale changed the subject. "Okay, so what do I need to do for Kevin? We'll have him wear normal clothes and take his eye patch off. There's really nothing we can do about the cast. What else do we need to do?"

Chad was still skeptical that Dale's intentions were good, but for the rest of the group, he wanted to ensure everyone had their instructions straight, so he led the conversation.

"We'll arrive at the hospital at 8:30 tomorrow night. The procedure will take place at 9 p.m., just like the first time this happened. Each person needs to dress how they would on a normal day. We'll leave all of the accessories at home. I'm not sure if it makes a difference since they weren't with you guys at the hospital last time, but we're not taking any chances. Of course Jasmine, you're the one exception. You'll bring the crystal ball?" he asked to confirm. She nodded so he continued, "And Javier, you'll bring the pillowcase full of candy? The old candy that we already X-rayed." He received more nods from Javier and Sharon, who currently had the infected candy at her house. "Okay, then there isn't much for anyone else to do. I'll handle the X-ray machine. You guys just need to show up with those few items, and we'll get this done."

After another half hour of chatter, people started to gather their things and leave to go home for dinner. When it was just Sharon, Nicki and Robby alone in their backyard, Sharon gathered her kids on their porch swing and hugged them tightly.

"Mom," Nicki said in a small voice. "I wish Dad was here."

"Oh honey," Sharon choked out around tears that had instantly sprung to her eyes, but that she tried to suppress. Once she thought she had herself together, she confided in her children. "Every night when I go to bed, I look at the ceiling and ask your dad what I'm supposed to do. I knew being a single parent would be hard, but my goodness!"

All three of them laughed at the absurdity of their situa-

270 • STEVIE ALEXANDER

tion and how comically inadequate her statement was to fully convey the magnitude of their circumstances.

"What do you think he'd tell us?" Robby looked at his mom with his still childlike blue eyes, even though he and Sharon were almost the same height.

"I have decided that he'd be happy you're changing back," she offered as a start. "I think he'd be worried, but he'd give you big hugs and tell you everything was going to be okay."

"Is it?" Nicki asked and then slapped her hand over her mouth. "I'm sorry, I didn't mean to say that out loud! I've been trying to remain positive. I feel like if I just keep saying positive things in my head that it will all go the way we planned. I hope I didn't jinx it."

Her mom smiled at her and said, "We'll just get back on track. Robby and I will help you think positive thoughts. I'm *positive* that everything will go according to plan tomorrow. I'm *positive* that we'll all get back to normal and enjoy Christmas with your grandparents. And I'm *positive* that you two are about to offer to help me with dinner!" She squeezed her giggling children and then led them inside to continue their evening.

## 23

# THE TRANSFORMATION

Sunday arrived with a cold front in tow. Between the biting wind and low dark clouds, the day never brightened enough to fully feel like daytime. Although the weather invited a cozy day in bed with a good book or curling up with a blanket to watch TV all afternoon, there was a nervous energy amongst everyone planning to participate in the evening's events. People spent the day checking and rechecking that everything was lined up as expected. However, the list was short and the repetitive actions actually heightened the sense of anxiety instead of assuaging it.

Throughout the day, parents and their kids arrived at Sharon's house to drop off costumes and overnight bags. Although Thanksgiving break was officially over on Monday, a couple of the parents had requested that the school allow their kids to remain home the following day and were granted their wish. Regardless of how things turned out, no one thought that the kids would have a productive day of learning. And so, it was agreed that, with the exception of Rani, everyone would spend the night at Sharon's so they had moral support in the morning. Sharon had made a valiant effort to get Rani permission as well, but Anil was reluctant to lose any time with his daughter, and eventually Sharon was forced to relent.

At 7:30 that night, Dale drove Kevin to the hospital where they made a beeline for Dale's office, giving the night shift receptionist, Donna, only a brief nod as they passed her desk. Kevin sat in one of the chairs that faced Dale's desk while Dale paced the room going over the plan again.

"Okay, one more time. When they start to arrive, they're supposed to meet in the parking lot so I can come let them in. I need you to join the crowd after a few of them get here and make sure you get that crystal ball."

"Yeah, I still don't see how you think I'm supposed to get that," Kevin said as he wedged a pen from his father's desk under his cast to scratch an itch. He was growing more doubtful of the entire plan as the time to execute drew closer.

"Kevin, you're a pirate for Pete's sake. Figure it out!" Dale's pacing became increasingly agitated.

Kevin rolled his eyes and moved on to his next question as he wiped the pen on his pants and put it back in the penholder next to his dad's keyboard. "So I'm outside with the kids, and you're in here waiting to grab Chad and make him adjust the settings on the machine?"

"Yes," Dale sat down in his chair, his hands gripping the

arms and his nervous energy flowing into his foot tapping on the floor. "He'll definitely come in beforehand to do that. He won't want to take any chances that someone else used it or even bumped into one of the controls. He's very meticulous."

"And then once I have the crystal ball, you want me to go to Chad's room, help you secure the door, and then we zap that new candy," Kevin pointed to a small pillowcase with a handful of candy bars that Dale had on his desk.

"Exactly," Dale confirmed. "Don't forget the secret knock. I'll keep things as quiet as I can in the room until I hear it. Then we sneak out the back and meet at my car if we get separated. I already have a motel room booked in Waco. We'll go there to put on our costumes, which are in the trunk of my car now, eat the candy and sleep for the night. I don't want to go back home in case someone comes looking for us."

"Wait, what?" Kevin's ears perked up.

"What?" Dale asked, not sure which part of the plan Kevin was questioning.

"You said 'put on our costumes' just then," Kevin repeated Dale's words back to him. "Why do you have a costume? I thought we were just fixing me?"

Dale pressed his lips together, upset that he had let this detail slip during his paranoid rambling, and tried to figure out how to keep Kevin on board with the plan. He took a deep breath and then pressed forward with an explanation, if not an entirely truthful one. "It's nothing, I just wanted to see if I could get rid of the pain I have in my arm where I broke it in elementary school. You know, it still bothers me every time it rains." He rubbed the spot on his forearm where he did in fact have a recurring throbbing sensation during certain weather conditions from a previous break. "Besides," Dale continued, "I couldn't find a whole costume in my size this far after Halloween. So it's really just a Superman shirt, a mask and a red cape. I'm hoping it's enough."

Kevin looked at his dad through narrowed eyes and said, "We can talk about that on the drive to the motel. For now, I think we should start keeping an eye out for Chad."

"Good idea," Dale flicked a glance at his watch while he leaped back out of his chair like a tightly coiled spring that had just been released and walked over to crack open his door so he would hear Chad when he approached.

---

As Sharon pulled her minivan into the parking lot, her headlights swept over a few figures, all of whom squinted and blocked the bright lights with their hands. She parked and got out to greet Rani, Anil and Kevin while her kids piled out of the backseat and slammed the door before walking around to huddle with the small group.

"Hi Anil," Sharon greeted Rani's dad. "Thank you for bringing Rani, I hope it's not too far of a drive for you."

"Not at all," he said, his face creased with concern, nervous about what was about to take place. "It's less than twenty minutes from our house to the hospital, and I'd drive a hundred times that far to help Rani."

"Of course," Sharon agreed before turning to Kevin.

"Hey, where's your dad?" she asked him, her teeth starting to chatter slightly.

"He's inside, he had some paperwork he wanted to catch up on as long as we're here. Donna will call him to let us in when everyone gets here," Kevin said as he shuffled to find a comfortable position on his crutches.

Sharon exhaled deeply and her breath created swirls of fog in the cold air as two more cars rolled up to their spot in the parking lot. Eventually, all of the kids were dropped off and their parents left, making Sharon promise to call them with an update first thing in the morning.

Large groups in close quarters, such as the X-ray room, were not comfortable for Anil, so he returned to his car to read while he waited for Rani to complete her task and return to him for the ride home.

After a few minutes of chatting, Sharon pulled her hands out of her coat pockets and slid up her left sleeve to check her watch. "Chad should be here by now," she said to no one in particular as she stomped her feet to bring warmth back to her legs. She was trying to remain calm for the sake of the children, but her instinct told her something wasn't right. There's no way Chad would be late for this, of all things.

While Sharon scanned the parking lot for any sign of Chad, Robby leaned toward Dominique and sniffed, then stifled a laugh.

"What?" Dominique's eyes glared daggers into Robby.

"It's nothing," he tried to compose his face unsuccessfully.

"It's just that your wig still smells like pizza," he said as he burst out laughing. Dominique smacked him on the shoulder and moved over to stand between Nicki and Jasmine.

"Mrs. S, I'm getting cold," Jasmine's teeth were chattering audibly. "Can we go inside?"

"Yeah," Sharon said distractedly. "I'm just trying to figure out where Chad could be," her eyes roamed the dark parking lot once again as she said this.

"Why don't we use Jasmine's crystal ball to see?" suggested Marcus.

"That's a great idea!" Sharon said.

Jasmine had the ball in a velvet pouch that was tucked in her jacket. She very carefully removed the ball, stuffed the pouch into her pocket and took a look to see if she could find the lab tech. She held the ball in two gloved hands and asked it, "Please show me Chad Stevens!" She squinted into the ball, trying to make sense of what she was seeing.

"What is it?" Sharon asked, aware that Jasmine's posture had changed into a defensive pose, her nose nearly touching the ball as her shoulders hunched and gloved fingers gripped the ball tightly. Her jaw hanging open, Jasmine turned to Sharon, eyes unfocused.

"Jasmine," Sharon grabbed her by both shoulders. "What is it?" The side conversations in the group immediately halted and everyone looked to Jasmine for an answer.

"It's Chad," Jasmine whispered. She cleared her throat and said more clearly. "He's tied to a chair. I think it's his office. I saw a computer in the background like the one he had when we were here for the X-rays. I also saw the light board thing that he put the X-rays on to see them."

"Tied to a chair?" Sharon asked, utterly confused.

"Yeah, there's a rope that's wrapped around him and his arms look like they're behind his back," Jasmine elaborated.

Sharon asked her, "Do you see anyone else? He couldn't have tied himself to the chair."

Jasmine's eyes flicked to Kevin whose face immediately turned red and he looked away.

"I don't know," she muttered.

"Well look again!" Sharon begged her, panic rising in her throat. "Please."

Jasmine's gaze returned to the crystal ball, but only for a second before she looked back at Sharon with pity and fear mingled on her face. "It's Dale," she said flatly.

Kevin feigned surprise before asking, "Is he helping him? Like is he trying to untie him?"

Jasmine looked miserable to have to tell Kevin that his dad was holding Chad hostage, but she didn't have a choice. She shook her head and said, "Definitely not."

"Alright, we've got to get inside and see what's going on," Sharon demanded. "Jasmine, put the ball in Javier's bag so we don't lose it."

Other than Kevin, who was still on crutches, almost everyone else wasted no time as they raced for the front door of the hospital. Javier held out the pillowcase for Jasmine to drop in the crystal ball. "Hey wait for us!" Javier shouted.

At the moment that Javier and Jasmine looked toward the

crowd of friends, Kevin's hand stealthily sneaked below the crystal ball and caught it when it dropped. Balancing himself on his crutches with one hand, he gave the bottom of the pillowcase a little tug, so Javier would think the ball had fallen in, then slipped the ball inside his zipped-up coat. He gave Javier a nudge and said, "You guys go ahead, I'm right behind you."

---

In the lobby, Sharon and the children huddled around Donna's desk shouting over each other that they needed to get back to the X-ray room. Donna, used to panicked people yelling demands at her when she was on the job, held up a hand and reminded the crowd, "We are in a hospital. I must insist that you lower your voices. Now, one at a time, please tell me what you need."

Sharon took the lead, "We need to get back to see Dale and Chad. It's an emergency."

"I'll call them to come get you," Donna said as she lifted the receiver.

"No!" Sharon's voice echoed in the hospital atrium.

Donna slowly lowered the receiver back to the cradle as she maintained eye contact with Sharon. "Can I ask why?"

Sharon clamped her mouth shut, unsure what to say at this point. She couldn't explain to this woman that her boss had kidnapped her coworker without either sounding crazy or eliciting a call to the police. They needed to get to the machine soon, and the police would definitely want to file a report. They just didn't have time.

Donna broke the silence that had fallen while Sharon contemplated her options and explained, "Look, either Dale or Chad comes to get you, or you can't go back there. It's against hospital policy. So what will it be?"

Sharon took a shaky breath and nodded her assent.

"Okay, could you guys please step back from my desk while I call?"

The group migrated toward the cluster of couches in the waiting area and each took seats, except Kevin who stood leaning against the wall with his crutches. While they waited, people started stripping off their gloves and scarves.

"I have a plan," Marcus said under his breath so Donna wouldn't hear in the echoing space, hoping the sounds from the removal of winter gear would further muffle his words.

"Oh, bless you, Marcus," Sharon nearly wept with relief. "Tell us!"

"I know we agreed not to use our powers in public, but I think we can all agree this is one of those times we should make an exception." He was met with a round of fervent nods, so he continued.

"Javier, do you know if you can walk through walls when you're in ghost mode?"

Javier looked stumped. "I don't know, I've never tried."

"Okay, well I'll work on a Plan B, but let me tell you Plan A first," Marcus said. "Javier, you'll turn invisible and see if you can walk through that door. If you can, you can crack it open for us. You only need a badge on this side, people who have already accessed that space back there don't need one to get out."

"Okay," Dominique nodded solemnly. "Then what, we can't all just walk past her through the door. I think she would notice."

"Right," Marcus agreed. "Joel, that's where you come in."

"Yes!" Joel pumped his fist. "What can I do?"

"Have you tried using the Jedi mind trick on anyone?" Marcus inquired.

Joel's face fell. "Why are you just now coming up with all these things we should have been trying for the past month? I have no idea!"

"It's fine, we'll save that for later, we need to move quickly now," Marcus waved his friend's question away. "Nicki, we'll use you instead. Can you create some sort of diversion with your holograms, and we'll take that opportunity to slip through the door?"

"I can definitely do that!" Nicki was relieved to have something productive to do.

Sharon interjected, "Would it mess up your plan if Joel, Robby and I tried to go around back and get in that way? Dale brought me in through a back door by the employee parking lot once when we came here after we had lunch together. I know where it is, and it's reasonably close to the X-ray room, but I'd need the boys to help me figure out how to get through the lock. I also think splitting up might increase our chances of someone getting in."

"That's fine," Marcus said after a brief moment's consideration. "It won't mess with my plan since we've got Nicki."

"Okay," Sharon nodded before adding one more detail to the plan. "Javier, if you guys make it through before us, can you stay invisible and walk straight back from the X-ray room, then turn right at the end of the hall and then an immediate left at the next opportunity? There's a door there that leads to the parking lot where we'll be trying to get in."

"You can count on me Mrs. S!" Javier agreed enthusiastically, giving her two thumbs up.

Sharon looked back to the desk where Donna was furrowing her brow and apparently trying multiple numbers to reach Chad or Dale. She caught Sharon's glance and shook her head with her palm turned up to the ceiling and a shrugged shoulder indicating that she couldn't explain why no one was answering her calls. Sharon jingled her keys with one hand, pointed to the door with the other and said, "I forgot something in the car. I'll be right back!"

Sharon, Robby and Joel walked back out into the frigid night air and stayed as close to the building as they could to avoid the bitterly cold wind while they made their way around to the unguarded, but locked door. There were a few dim lights in the parking lot, but the area was mostly deserted and cast in dark shadows.

"I'm not really sure what you guys can try," Sharon admitted as she tried to restrain her hair, which was getting whipped around fiercely by the wind. "I'm just hoping that

Joel, you can use The Force to open the door. Worst case scenario, Robby, maybe you have to burn it open."

Joel stepped forward with a fierce look on his face. He held out one hand, closed his eyes and concentrated with all of his might on opening the door. Sharon and Robby stood by, willing the door to open, but nothing happened.

After a couple of minutes, Sharon turned to her son. "You know that it's never right to intentionally destroy someone's property, right?"

Robby heaved a deep sigh and rolled his eyes. "Mom, I know. We're trying to save our friend."

"Okay kiddo, give it all you've got," she stepped back and put a hand on Joel's shoulder to pull him out of harm's way. "I'm sorry I couldn't do it," Joel whispered to Sharon. She gave him a little one-armed hug and smiled to let him know it was okay.

Robby stood with his feet a little wider than shoulder-width apart and clenched his hands in fists by his sides. He stared at the lock on the steel door and concentrated with all of his might. Slowly, the lock started to turn a faint orange, but once it got going, it quickly flamed into a bright, glowing red. He stepped back, carefully grabbed the handle below the lock and gave it a little tug. He let out a quiet cheer as he felt it loosen and then yanked it open so he, Joel and Sharon could race through it.

Their joy, however, was short-lived. As they tip-toed through the corridor, making as little noise as possible, they heard a voice through a walkie-talkie coming from just beyond the bend in the hallway. It was difficult to hear through the static and from a distance, but they got the gist. Their fears were confirmed when they heard a security guard speak back into his two-way radio and say, "Copy that, I'll keep an eye out for a brown-haired woman and any children roaming around."

Sharon put her finger to her lips in a shushing gesture and then, as quietly and quickly as she could, she back-tracked to a couple of doors and opened the one on the left. The three of them slinked through the door and closed it with a soft click. Once inside, she realized they were in a stairwell. They could hear the security guard as he investigated the charred exterior door and reported it back to another member of his security team and then again to Donna at the front desk.

After what seemed like an eternity, the hallway was quiet again, and Sharon went to open the door from the stairwell so they could make their way toward Chad's room. Her breath caught as she realized the handle wouldn't budge. That's when she noticed a panel next to the door and concluded that it would require a badge to open. Sharon whispered their predicament to the boys.

Robby was ready to burn a hole in this door too, but Sharon stopped him. "I think we've done enough destruction here tonight. Let's not get ourselves into any more trouble. Besides, it sounded like that guard will be back to fix the door soon. We'll go up to see if we can get out on the second floor."

But it was no use, the second floor also required a badge

to exit. They were able to get up onto the roof, yet a quick look around revealed that it would be of no help when it came to accessing the interior of the building or even assist them in getting back to the ground. However, they had learned their lesson with the stairwell door, and Robby stood holding this one open while Sharon investigated. But eventually, they all made their way back down to the first floor to try to formulate a new plan.

---

Meanwhile, back in the lobby, Javier made his way to a corner that wasn't visible from Donna's desk and took a few deep breaths to calm himself. He closed his eyes and focused on turning invisible. When he opened his eyes, he saw Jasmine give him a thumbs up from her spot on the couch. The fact that she was staring slightly to the left of where he stood, confirmed for him that he must have turned fully invisible.

Javier slipped off his shoes to avoid making any squeaking noises on the shiny floor and moved as quickly and quietly as he could toward Donna's desk. He slowed down to a silent, sock-footed tip-toe as he passed her and approached the door. Although no one could see it, he screwed up his face as he fixated more intensely than he could ever remember on maintaining his ghost status.

Finally, he took a quiet, but shaky breath and moved forward toward the door. He almost cheered as he passed through it, but recalled just in time that he needed to remain silent. As Marcus had said, the door wasn't locked from the inside and he was able to cautiously rotate the handle and push it open. He stuck his head around the side of the door to motion to the group, but then decided it would be best to remain invisible. Javier saw Jasmine poke Marcus in the ribs and point toward the door, indicating that she had witnessed his success.

Since he didn't know how long he could stay invisible, he pulled back out of sight and stuck his foot between the door and the frame so it wouldn't close all the way.

Back in the huddle on the couches, Marcus gave Nicki the signal to start her distraction while the rest of them readied themselves to race for the door as soon as Donna wasn't looking. Kevin surreptitiously moved his crutches back under his arms, although he remained leaning casually against the wall right next to the sliding glass doors at the entry. He shifted to his right and tapped the bottom of his crutch on the floor mat in front of the doors, triggering the pad that would cause the doors to slide open.

Donna looked up from her computer expectantly. When no one walked through the doors, she glanced around in confusion and then looked at the children who all shrugged.

Then, without warning, a small capuchin monkey ran in on its hind legs, dragging his arms at his sides. His white face looked from side to side around the lobby as he chattered indistinguishable monkey talk. He was followed by a fox, who poked his head around the corner first and then raced in behind the monkey.

Donna sat at the desk, her jaw wide open. She had just started to gather her wits and stand up when a duck waddled in, flapping its wings and quacking behind the fox, which caused her to pause again, albeit just for a moment.

As soon as Donna ran around the desk toward the melee, Marcus and Rani used their super-speed to propel themselves to the hallway in the space of a heartbeat, almost crushing Javier in their rush to avoid detection. Leaping out of the way, Javier's concentration broke and he returned to full visibility. Dominique was not far behind as she sprinted across the lobby. Kevin took longer, although as an athlete who had been using the crutches for three weeks, he was able to shoot forward with surprising speed and agility to join them in the hallway.

The monkey, now standing on the back of one of the couches, stuck his tongue out at Donna and waved his hands in her direction, effectively keeping her attention while this took place.

Jasmine looked back and forth between Nicki and her friends in the doorway. Nicki couldn't leave without the hologram animal disruption disappearing, so she was stuck. Jasmine wasn't sure where she was more needed, but Nicki caught her eye and mouthed, "Don't leave me!" So Jasmine stood by her friend and waved to the others to go on without them, then turned back and pretended to help Donna corral the fake animal fracas.

In the hallway, Marcus, Dominique, Kevin, Rani and Javier moved quickly toward the door to the X-ray room. Kevin tried the handle, but it was locked. He stood back and looked at it for a moment, then made a decision.

"Javier, you go find Sharon, Robby and Joel," he delegated. "Do you remember where she said the door was back that way?" Kevin pointed him on the right path.

"Yep," Javier bounced with nervous energy. "I'm on it!" And he took off racing, nearly slamming into the wall before managing to adjust his speed and trajectory to careen around the corner.

Kevin turned back to the door and knocked lightly on the door three times in rapid succession. There was no response.

"Does your dad have a key?" Marcus asked Kevin.

"To Chad's office?" Kevin asked, then shook his head. "No, I don't think so. But if he did, he'd probably have it locked up in his desk. And he has the key to the desk."

"Ugh, that makes sense," Marcus pounded his fist on the door in frustration.

At that moment, Javier came whizzing back around the corner, his face a mask of despair. He whispered frantically to the group huddled around the door. "I can't find Mrs. S or the guys. There are a couple of security guards at the door she said they would try to come in, and it looks like they're trying to fix something on it. But no sign of our people. Can you guys help me find them?"

Marcus looked at his watch and grimaced. "It's already almost 9 o'clock. We need to figure this out quickly."

Rani volunteered to help since she was fast and could look more rapidly than Dominique, ideally without getting caught. Marcus didn't entirely trust Kevin, so he decided to stay and help get inside the X-ray room. Dominique was too anxious to stray very far from the machine, so she also stayed.

Javier and Rani ran back in the direction they thought Sharon and their friends had likely gone. As soon as they were out of sight, Kevin rapped three times and then again four times with the last two delivered as quick half beats. The door cracked open and Dale ushered Kevin inside. Marcus caught on quickly that the knock was a signal and used his super-speed to sneak past Kevin into the room. He ran straight to Chad and assessed the knots used to tie the rope. Dale made a quick decision and yanked Dominique into the room so she couldn't yell for help.

Dale then shifted his attention to securing the door. He took the brunt of the work, moving a heavy filing cabinet in front of it while Kevin used the shoulder from his good side to help push and speed up the process. They positioned it right in front of the door and then turned to see Marcus working to untie Chad.

"Marcus," Dale said calmly. "I can't let you do that."

Marcus looked up and they eyed each other for several tense moments.

Dominique looked horrified as she came to the conclusion that Kevin had betrayed them.

"How could you?" she asked, her eyes sparkling with unshed tears.

"Dominique, you've got to understand," Kevin pleaded.

"I don't 'got' to do anything," she screamed at him. She snatched his crutch out of his hand and swung it back to strike him with it when she felt it lift out of her hands. Dale had rescued his son before turning his attention back to Marcus, who had resumed working on the ropes the moment Dale's attention was diverted. Dale swatted his hands away from the knots and then led the two children to another chair and asked them to sit down.

"Guys," he used his most authoritative voice. "You need to stay there so I don't have to tie you up as well. We don't want to hurt anyone. But we're going to fix Kevin's leg, and we're going to do it tonight."

"That's what you think," Dominique scoffed. "Do you even know how this works?"

Dale gave her a sad smile. He legitimately didn't enjoy taking away her chance at happiness. But he wasn't going to let his son suffer any longer. "I do," he said quietly, but definitively. "Before you got here, Chad and I took care of the settings. Once he double-checked those, that's when I...well I restrained him."

Everyone turned to look at Chad. He hadn't moved since shortly after they entered the room. As Jasmine had seen in her crystal ball, he was tied to his office chair, his arms snuggly behind his back. Dale had tied multiple knots to avoid the risk of Chad letting himself loose. Chad's head hung in misery. He shrugged as he turned his eyes up to take a peek at the innocent faces silently begging him to tell them that Dale had it all wrong. But the dejected look on Chad's face confirmed everything Dale had said.

Dominique stuck her chin out defiantly and said, "So what? You still don't have the main thing that gets this whole deal to work." But the smugly confident look melted off of her face as Kevin removed the crystal ball from his jacket. While he truly did look apologetic, Dominique was having none of it.

"There is no way on this planet that I'm going to let you take this away from me," she said through clenched teeth and a deepening red face. The hair from her wig swung back and forth as she sized up Dale and Kevin, trying to figure out how to take control of the situation.

Marcus, frustrated because his super-speed wouldn't do him much good in this small space, nonetheless made an attempt to race toward Kevin to reclaim the crystal ball, but Dale had anticipated this move and grabbed him by the arm to maneuver him back into the chair. He shifted Dominique next to Marcus and apologized as he tied them up with the remainder of the rope he had brought in from his car.

"I really didn't want to have to do this, but I don't have time to argue with you. We only have a minute or so to get everything ready," Dale explained as he tied the last knot and gave it a little tug to ensure it wasn't going to give them an opportunity to escape.

Rani and Javier had checked everywhere they could without being seen by the security guards at the end of the hallway with the exterior door. None of the offices were lit, but they had quietly tapped on each door and announced themselves with zero response from those they were seeking. Rani had even zipped through the lobby and outside to check the parking lot while Javier held the door behind Donna's desk slightly ajar for her to return to the hallways behind the reception area. They were back to the corridor where they knew their friends must be hiding. Rani whispered a plan to Javier who nodded solemnly at her.

On the count of three, she sped toward the end of the hall where there were two doors, one on each side. She could see one was labeled as a supply closet and the other stairs. She barely had time to register the options before deciding the stairwell was the most likely hiding place for three people.

She opened the door and slipped through it right as one of the security guards looked up, having sensed movement. Luckily, the wind behind him was so vicious, he assumed it was just something that got caught on a draft since he couldn't see a sign of any intruders.

As per the plan, Javier had given Rani a one-second head start before he strolled across the hallway whistling to himself. He was tall enough that from down the hall, the security guards couldn't tell that he was a child. He gave them a nod and continued on his way. The security guard nodded back and then returned his attention to the new lock he was holding in place while his coworker used a drill to install it.

Sharon jumped back in surprise as the door opened and closed almost immediately after. Joel, who had been standing just out of range of the swinging door, had the foresight to grab the handle before the latch clicked all the way shut.

"Rani!" Sharon whispered on an exhale. "Are the security guards still just outside the door?"

"Yeah," Rani confirmed. "Javier distracted them while I raced down the hall and through this door. I'm so glad I found you! We were so worried when we didn't know where you were and then we saw those guys out there."

Robby gave her a quick hug. "We're so glad you found us! What's going on? We've been trapped here while the guards fix the door. I wanted to burn this one open too, but mom said we'd already destroyed enough property."

"How did you guys get stuck in here?" Rani asked.

"It was so cool!" Robby's face lit up as he whisper-shouted an explanation. "I used my heat vision to burn the lock. But as soon as we got in the building, we heard on the guard's walkie-talkies that they were looking for us. So we ran in here to hide from the guards and then found out the door was locked after we'd already shut it. We checked other doors on the stairwell, but they're all locked and need a badge except the one on the roof, and there was no way down from there, so we came back here." He gasped for breath, slightly dizzy from his animated retelling of their adventure.

"Wow," Rani's eyes were giant as she took it all in.

Joel added, "And Robby did want to burn a hole in this lock too, but between the destruction thing and the fact that the guards were standing right outside this door by the time we got back from the roof, we've just had to sit here and wait. I already almost went to ShowBiz Pizza jail, I don't want to go to hospital jail."

Sharon had brushed off one of the steps and now sat with her elbow on her knee and her chin in her hand. She gave Joel a tired smile. "I agree. I don't think I'd be able to get you out of this one."

"Not if you were in hospital jail with me!" Joel teased.

"I'm not sure what's going on out there," Rani pointed back in the general direction of Chad's office. "The door to the X-Ray room was locked, and everyone was trying to get in when Javier and I came to find you guys. So what's the plan?"

Sharon looked at her watch and her shoulders drooped slightly. "I mean...right now it's almost 9 o'clock. Unless you guys have someone who has already overtaken Dale and regained control of the X-ray machine, I have no idea how we're going to pull this off tonight."

Rani looked crestfallen. Joel, who hadn't wanted to change back anyway, looked away. Even though he wanted to stay the way he was, he had been really excited for his friends who were miserable since the change, and he was uncomfortable witnessing Rani's depression. Robby gave Rani another awkward hug. He had wanted to finish this tonight, but honestly, he wasn't too bothered for himself. However, he did want Marcus and Rani to switch back. And he really wasn't looking forward to hearing Dominique whine for another month. But in every scenario that he had considered while they waited for the guards to leave, he immediately realized the fault and dismissed it. He turned to Rani, "I don't think there's much Joel and I can do to get back to the room in the next few minutes. But you need to save yourself. I'll hold the door while you run. Get Javier and you guys go help the rest."

Rani looked at him with a glimmer of hope and a lot of gratitude. "Are you sure?"

He gave her a lopsided smile and said, "Yeah. You go. We'll get out of here when they're done with the door and meet up with you guys."

Rani looked up the stairs and then back at Joel and Robby. "What if I go around and try to get to the second floor and let you out there?"

Robby shook his head firmly. "First of all, there's no time. Second, unless there's an elevator or something, there'd be no way for you to get to the second floor. And we just don't have time to figure all of that out." He paused and then assured her. "Seriously, go. It's okay."

Rani looked to Sharon, who nodded her agreement, and then stood by the crack in the door to bolt out as soon as Joel eased it open.

---

"Kevin, put the crystal ball in the bag," Dale said over his shoulder as he rolled the chair with the kids in it away from the machine. He didn't want them exposed to the radiation. But he made sure they weren't close enough to Chad that they could help each other. It was tricky in the small space to get everyone situated in exactly the right way.

After Kevin nestled the ball in amongst the candy, Dale took the bag and positioned it on the machine to run the scan. Then he hit the button to start the X-ray. In a few agonizing seconds, it was over.

Although he didn't say anything, Marcus had noticed a few green sparks pop underneath the bag during the X-ray, and he was sure it had worked.

Dale picked up the bag, but Dominique wasn't done with him. From where she sat tied up in the chair next to Marcus, she asked, "How exactly do you think you're going to get out of here? If Sharon or any of our team are behind that door, they aren't going to just let you walk out."

Dale paused before turning around to face her and spoke with sincerity. "Dominique, I know you think I'm the villain. But in real life, people aren't one-hundred percent good or one-hundred percent bad. I'm not Darth Vader, and you aren't Princess Leia."

Dominique bristled at this reference, but of course, Dale didn't know that she would have been Princess Leia if she'd only made a decision about her costume sooner.

Imagining what she could do to these guys if she had those powers, she suddenly had a better understanding of why Joel and Javier might not want to change back. This whole experience would have been immeasurably better if she had just chosen a costume that worked for her instead of against her. While Little Orphan Annie was scrappy during her time at the orphanage, even she had relied on Punjab to save her when the bad guy came after her. Dominique was feeling that sense of helplessness now and hoping someone was on the way to save them.

Marcus spat out, more bitter than Dale had ever heard him, "Well I hope you don't think you're Luke Skywalker or Han Solo in this situation. You might not be cutting off our hands, but you most certainly aren't the hero here."

Dale addressed both children as he continued, "I truly hope that you can change back. I'll be keeping the crystal ball with me until Kevin and I can make sure we are somewhere safe and that his leg has been repaired. Then I'll return it so you guys can try next month."

Dominique finally had to admit that Dale had covered all of his bases, and she slumped down in the chair she shared with Marcus, pulling him down with her a little as she did so. Dale and Kevin moved the filing cabinet back out of the way, then Kevin muttered an embarrassed "good luck" to the kids while father and son turned to leave the room.

As expected, when Dale opened the door, there were people standing there. Rani and Javier had made it back, and Javier's hand was raised to knock when Dale found him there. No one knew what to say for a moment, but then Rani saw a glimpse of Chad tied up and pushed past Dale and Kevin to check on him. As soon as she was in the room, she also saw Marcus and Dominique, who wept with a combination of relief and defeat when she saw her friend there to rescue her.

"Rani," Marcus tried to catch her eye as her attention shifted around the room, taking in everything. "They have the crystal ball."

Rani's head swung back in their direction so fast that her braid slapped Chad in the face.

Dale nodded to confirm. "And we're going to take it and walk out the front door."

Kevin rushed to fill in the part that she missed. "But we'll give it back to you. Probably tomorrow. You can still change back, just not right now."

"What if I try to stop you?" Rani challenged Dale.

"You could try. There's a possibility that the crystal ball gets broken in the scuffle though because I won't let it go easily since it's my insurance policy to get out of here. And then you have no chance of changing back. It would be smarter for you to let us leave."

"And we're supposed to trust that you'll actually give it back?" Sarcasm dripped from her voice as her face reflected her skepticism.

"Rani," Kevin looked wildly uncomfortable, but he felt a strong need to press on, and so he gathered his courage and did. "You saved my life. But I was already broken. I can't live like this. I need the help. But I promise, I won't betray you." At the look on her face, he hastened to add, "Not again."

After a few more moments of awkward silence, Dale took a chance and walked toward the door, ushering Kevin in front of him while Rani rushed to untie Chad, Marcus and Dominique. Javier took a deep breath, turned invisible and took advantage of the moment that it took Kevin to angle his crutches around the door for the sharp turn into the hallway.

In his invisible state, Javier snatched the pillowcase out of Dale's grasp with his left hand and extracted the crystal ball with his right. Dale briefly lost his balance when he was unexpectedly tugged forward by the pillowcase and wheeled his arms around to avoid falling. His arm collided with the crystal ball, which Javier didn't have a good grip on yet and sent it hurtling toward the ground. Rani's hands were still caught up in the rope that she was releasing from Marcus's wrists and neither of them had a chance to use their super-speed to grab it before the top of the crystal ball collided with the hard floor.

Everyone watched in horror as the base and part of the crystal ball spun on the tile toward Dominique's feet while the larger piece ricocheted off the bottom of the X-ray machine and went back toward Dale. He scooped it up, grabbed the pillowcase full of candy and ran behind Kevin, who was already almost to the lobby.

Javier dropped to his knees to pick up the piece with the moonstone base still attached and moved his hands around the floor, searching for any additional pieces that might have broken off. He tried to apologize, but Marcus cut him off by saying, "We can talk about it later, Dale took the biggest piece. We have to get it back." And they all ran out the door and down the hallway.

But by the time they got to the lobby, Dale and Kevin were gone. Nicki and Jasmine stood there looking helpless as Donna stood before them asking where their parents were and telling them that they couldn't be there without adult supervision. The animals had vanished into thin air a minute or two before and Donna suspected the girls had something to do with it, but she wasn't quite sure how or what to do about it. She was mostly relieved that she didn't have to figure out how to capture a monkey, a fox and a duck in her lobby while the security guys were busy with the back door.

---

As soon as the security guards finished up with the door repair and went to resume their rounds, Sharon, Joel and Robby made their way back to the lobby where Donna was still insisting that the girls needed a parent.

Sharon gathered all of the children and the dejected group made their way back to the parking lot, where Sharon had to explain to a shocked Anil what had just happened. The kids who had made it to Chad's room filled in details from their perspective. Eventually, Sharon took the rest of the children home and called their parents to let them know how the plan had been hijacked.

# EPILOGUE

At dawn on Monday, December 1, Dale and Kevin woke up as soon as the sun sneaked its way through the flimsy aluminum blinds in their motel room. They had slept in their costumes (neither were sure when it was okay to take them off), Kevin as The Flash and Dale as Superman. Dale had decided not to press his luck by adding accessories in order to placate his son.

Kevin moved first. He was eager to test out his foot. He carefully placed both feet on the floor and gingerly leaned forward to add weight. He didn't feel any pain, and a slow grin spread across his face. He and Dale had used tools they brought along with them to remove the cast before Kevin consumed the candy the previous night, and then wedged his leg between pillows and towels to keep it in place while he slept. He had also removed the eyepatch, hoping that both his leg and his eye would heal when he ate the candy without anything remotely resembling a pirate costume.

Dale quickly sat up from his bed and looked expectantly at him. Kevin had a look of wonder on his face as he stood and tested it gently one more time and then gave a little bounce. Finally, he flung open the door to the motel and raced around the parking lot without so much as a twinge.

Within a couple of seconds, he was back in front of his dad, who broke into a wide grin and gave his son an enormous hug. As Kevin pulled back, something caught his eye. "Hey Dad, I just noticed that your Superman shirt is on inside out. Has it been like that this whole time?"

Dale looked down in alarm. "I guess so, everything was so chaotic last night, I didn't notice. I wonder if it still worked."

Dale stepped away from the building, then took his turn bouncing on his toes before taking off like a bird in the sky and shouting with excitement that his lifelong dream of flying finally came true.

As Kevin watched his dad zoom around, the smile slowly slid off of his face. He suspected Dale was up to more than just fixing an old injury. It occurred to him that he should use this opportunity to take the piece of crystal back to Jasmine while his dad was preoccupied. Using his new super-speed, he grabbed the jagged chunk of crystal and raced to Sharon's doorstep, then rang the bell.

A few moments later, Sharon slipped around the door and out onto the porch. "What are you doing here?" she hissed at Kevin through clenched teeth.

"I wanted to return the crystal, like I promised. But I don't know where Jasmine lives and I know you'll get it to her." He had trouble meeting her gaze and his cheeks flushed a bright red as he ducked his head while he explained.

Sharon reached out and took it from him just as Robby opened the door and joined them on the porch.

"What do you want?" Robby glared at Kevin.

Sharon held out the glass shard and said, "He's bringing back the piece of crystal that Dale took. Are the other kids awake too?"

"Not that I saw," Robby replied his voice drenched in animosity as his eyes stayed on Kevin's face.

Sharon looked at Kevin and asked, "Where's your dad?"

At this, Kevin dragged his head up and spoke directly to Sharon. "He put on a costume and ate some candy last night. Superman. He's flying around right now, so I thought I'd race over here to drop this off while he's busy."

Robby looked at him skeptically before asking, "What do you mean 'race over here?'"

Kevin shuffled his feet so the previously broken one was a few inches in front of him. "I wore a Flash costume and now my leg is fixed. I should probably get back before he notices."

"Wait," Robby held out a hand. "Does this mean you're The Flash and a pirate?"

Kevin's forehead wrinkled as he considered the possibility. "I mean, my eye seems okay now. But I didn't really have other pirate-y qualities before. Not that I noticed anyway."

Robby snorted and said, "Seems to me you swiped that crystal ball without any trouble."

Kevin nodded. "That's true," he mumbled. "But that was one time. I didn't turn into a full-time thief or anything. I don't have strong urges to go live on a boat. I think it's mostly just the Flash thing. Anyway, I'll leave you guys alone. Thanks for getting that back to Jasmine." Kevin nodded his head toward the crystal that Sharon was still holding as he slowly backed off of the porch onto the sidewalk.

"Kevin," Sharon started and took a small step forward. "Why did you come here without telling Dale?"

Again, Kevin looked uncomfortable. "I don't know. I just have a weird feeling. He sometimes does stuff that I don't agree with. Like buying that crappy equipment in the first place. I didn't want him to argue with me about returning it."

Sharon nodded thoughtfully. "Okay, well be careful. He's going to find out."

Kevin gave her a sad smile. "I know. If he's up to anything, I'm determined to find out what it is. And then put a stop to it."

## QUESTIONS

How would today's technology make the adventures in RA-D8 different? What would make it easier (for example, cell phones) or potentially more difficult (like social media)?

How was the experience different for the characters who received cool powers versus for those who weren't as happy with their costume choices?

What costume would you want to live with long term?

Would you eat the candy to take on properties of a costume?

Do you think Dale is a bad guy? Was he a good dad?

Have you been in a situation where people were bullied for something they couldn't control? What did you do?

# ACKNOWLEDGMENTS

First and foremost, I have to thank my husband of 20 plus years. When I got furloughed from a job I loved, he's the one who suggested I write so I didn't drive myself (or him) crazy. He also gave me the concept for the book, so without Kris, there would be no RA-D8. On days when I didn't know how to get from point A to point B in my story, he'd take long walks with me to chat through what I was trying to accomplish and craft a plan to make it happen. This book is very much a product of his mind. And if it ever gets made into a movie or TV show, the actor who plays Kevin should give Kris a big thanks for elevating your role from a very minor character to one who is rather significant.

Second, I need to thank my kid. She helped me with so many aspects of the book, both writing and the choices I had to make in the design and publishing process. She has a remarkably clear idea of what makes an appealing cover design and spent a lot of time going through stacks of novels to tell me why each one spoke to her. There are also little bits of Riley in Nicki and Robby. She was my inspiration for writing for this age group and my reason for living on both good days and bad.

Once the writing was done, the hard part started. And that's when my friend Alicia Miller Ennis stepped in. A college roommate in a previous life, we had drifted separate ways. But when I asked if she could edit my book, she was right there, despite trying to help a remote learning kinder-gartener during the pandemic while working a full-time job. So I must thank both Henry, for sharing his mom, and Alicia for being the kind of friend who is there for you even years after you've seen each other.

I also owe a huge thank you to Paula Krause, who was my cheerleader for this crazy adventure, but she also let me borrow her Mac so I could format my book. Which turns out to be a bigger deal than a novice would think!

They say a picture is worth a thousand words, and I could easily write a thousand words about the painful journey to getting a cover design. But then I found Ian Bailon and he created something I fell in love with at first sight.

And finally, I want to thank my readers. Working in corporate America, I hadn't had time to write for fun and this was clearly something I needed even if I didn't know it. I hope enough of you love my book and share it with your friends that I can write more. My dream is to do this for a living and with your help, it might just come true!

# ABOUT THE AUTHOR

Stevie Alexander lives in North Texas with her husband (who was unanimously voted Official Husband of the Year 2020 in their household) and one kid (future YouTube star and current second degree black belt in taekwondo). They have the obligatory two pets (a dog and a cat who plays fetch more than the dog). In the life she planned for herself, Stevie was a marketing executive in the travel industry. When Covid laughed at her plans, she took her chance and fulfilled her dream of writing a book.

facebook.com/steviealexanderauthor

twitter.com/stevie_author

instagram.com/steviealexander_author